Kaden stared into her eyes and the room shrank.

"Were you the little girl in the story?" His voice was a deep caress, drawing Courtney closer.

"What?"

He swept her hair off her face. "Were you that unhappy girl?"

She didn't want to talk. Didn't want to move. She wanted him to touch her. "I...I was making up a story for the kids."

"Right." He tucked a curl back behind her ear, and a single finger stroked down her cheek. His blue eyes locked on hers as he brushed her lower lip with his thumb. "I'm so sorry."

Her breath caught in her chest.

Finally, Kaden was going to kiss her...

Dear Reader,

Ever since I started the Fitzgerald House series, I've wanted to redeem Courtney Smythe (she sure has been nasty). I wanted to figure out why she hasn't thrived like her brother, Gray. Of course, her father calling her a "pretty little ornament" hasn't helped.

When her dad cuts off her money and insists she find a job, Courtney suspects Gray caused her problems. She heads to Savannah, hoping her father will cool off. But Gray won't let her sponge off him. Courtney works for the B and B. And fails. Tries to get the attention of the hot handyman. And fails. When she becomes a nanny to the kids living at the B and B, she finally finds her calling.

As a child, Kaden Farrell's grandfather saved him from his drug-dealing parents. So when his grandfather breaks his hip working at Fitzgerald House, Kaden rushes to his side. At the B and B, his FBI drug-task-force job and his grandfather's health intersect. The dealer he's been chasing dropped her daughter off with the kid's father, who lives at the B and B. Kaden, pretending to be a handyman, cozies up to the girl's beautiful nanny. Even though Kaden's not sure he even likes Courtney, sparks between them fly.

I love hearing from readers. Contact me at www.nandixon.com and sign up for my newsletter, or visit me on Facebook at www.Facebook.com/nandixonauthor. If you'd like to see the pictures that inspire me, check out www.Pinterest.com/nandixonauthor.

Enjoy Savannah!

Nan Dixon

NAN
DIXON

Undercover with
the Heiress

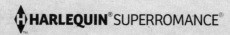
HARLEQUIN® SUPERROMANCE®

Recycling programs
for this product may
not exist in your area.

ISBN-13: 978-0-373-64040-9

Undercover with the Heiress

Copyright © 2017 by Nan Dixon

Printed in U.S.A.

Nan Dixon spent her formative years as an actress, singer, dancer and golfer. But the need to eat had her studying accounting in college. Unfortunately, being a successful financial executive didn't feed her passion to perform. When the company she worked for was purchased, Nan got the chance of a lifetime—the opportunity to pursue a writing career. She's a five-time Golden Heart® Award finalist and award-winning author, lives in the Midwest and is active in her local RWA chapter and the board of a dance company. She has five children, three sons-in-law, two granddaughters, a new grandson and one neurotic cat.

Books by Nan Dixon

HARLEQUIN SUPERROMANCE

Fitzgerald House

Southern Comforts
A Savannah Christmas Wish
Through a Magnolia Filter
The Other Twin

Visit the Author Profile page at Harlequin.com.

To Mom and Dad always.

To my fabulous family. Thank you for your love and support. I'm dedicating this one to the women: Meghan, Allison and Anne. I couldn't be prouder.

I must thank my Harlequin team: Megan Long, Victoria Curran, Piya Campana, Deirdre McCluskey and the wonderful group who bring my books to my readers. And of course, my marvelous agent, Laura Bradford.

My critique group challenges me to dig deeper. Thank you Ann Hinnenkamp, Leanne Farella, Neroli Lacey and Kathryn Kohorst. And my Golden Heart® sisters keep me sane—Dreamweavers, Lucky 13s, Starcatchers and the Unsinkables. And my writing community—MFW, you're the best.

Of course I can't forget the group that started it all: my sisters. Mo, Sue and Trish.

CHAPTER ONE

May

"HOW MANY BODIES?" Kaden ducked under the yellow police tape and climbed the rotting porch steps.

"Three." The photographer pointed at the man by his feet. "One here. Two inside."

Kaden flashed his credentials at the uniform guarding the door. Plywood covered the cabin's windows. The siding might have been white once. Now it peeled off termite-infested wood. Cement blocks propped up a corner of the wraparound porch. The place would probably blow over in the next tropical storm to hit the coast of Georgia.

Local deputies, DEA and FBI sifted through the crime scene. He took a deep breath and gagged on the stench. Covering his mouth with his sleeve, he headed inside.

Plastic bags lay scattered on the floor. Drug residue covered tables lining a wall. An empty garbage can was tipped on its side. Apparently, the dealers had left in a hurry. If they were lucky, they might find prints.

The medical examiner knelt next to a second body.

Six-one or six-two. Male. Caucasian. Must run 220.

"Hey, O'Malley." Kaden stared at the dried blood on the floor. "Do you have a cause of death?"

"GSW. All three bodies." The medical examiner glanced up. "How are you, Farrell?"

"Frustrated we can't shut this ring down."

The FBI had been chasing Heather Bole and Thaddeus Magnussen for months trying to stem the flow of drugs coming through Georgia and Florida.

He nodded at the vic's bloated face. "At least Magnussen's no longer terrorizing the streets. Don't suppose we got lucky and Heather Bole is here somewhere?"

"Not here. We'll check the blood type and see if there's more than our victims." She shifted. "Need to show you something."

O'Malley rolled the body onto his side, using her head to point. "Check out the streaks under the body."

"Is that blood?" Kaden backed up to get the full picture. "It looks like something was dragged out from under him as he bled out. Did he fall on something?"

She shrugged. "Maybe a someone. We found this beneath the body."

She held up an evidence bag. It contained a bloodstained sneaker. Pink. Small. No laces. Fluff filled the shoe's ratty Velcro.

"Damn it. A kid was here." He swallowed.

"Yeah." O'Malley waved over her assistant. "This one's ready for the lab."

Kaden unclenched his teeth. A kid. A little girl by the look of the shoe. He would check the file, but he thought Heather had a daughter who was young. Three? Four? The task force had gotten that intel but hadn't been able to get the kid to safety.

His granddad had rescued him. Now, getting children away from their criminal, drug dealing parents was his life's mission. He would save the kid and put Heather Bole behind bars.

July

"ANOTHER DEAD END." Kaden slammed down the conference room phone in the Atlanta FBI office. "Two months and every time someone spots Heather Bole, she vanishes."

The partial print at the triple-murder site had a 75 percent chance of being Bole's. It was enough to bring her in for questioning. If they found her.

"We're hearing rumors Bole has partnered with Hector Salvez." His boss rubbed his short dark hair. "Hector's a hothead. That might make Heather easier to find."

Roger leaned back in his chair and it let out a loud screech.

The noise crawled down Kaden's spine. "Not soon enough."

"Is this about the daughter? Are you worried she's in danger?" Roger asked.

"Kids shouldn't grow up in that environment." Kaden rolled his neck and the vertebrae clicked.

Saving kids from the drug life was why he'd joined the FBI, why he was on the task force. If he could rid this part of the world of drugs and dealers, he'd be content. "Heather is moving…a lot. Could be Magnussen's brother is seeking revenge."

"Maybe." Roger's chair squealed again. "Maybe they'll all kill each other and make our lives easier."

"DEA has a witness that swears Bole had her kid with her before the shootings." Kaden tugged on his tie. "She and Rasmussen ran together for five years. Now what's Bole up to?"

"Taking over?" Roger held up the picture of the blood streaks. "If Heather shot him, it was pretty damn cold to shoot her partner with her kid in the room."

"Five years ago she was a two-bit dealer in Atlanta. Then she moved to rural Georgia and started cooking meth." Kaden tossed his empty coffee cup into the trash. "*Breaking Bad* has made people think cookin' is easy money."

Roger shook his head. "We'll catch her eventually."

Kaden nodded. But this case involved a kid. For weeks he'd worked the streets, talking to as many of Heather's associates as possible. The other task force members had worked their own connections.

Nada. Unless Bole was traveling on a fake ID, she had to be in the area.

Or she'd been dumped at sea. Always a possibility on the coast. He wasn't worried about Heather, but the kid, Isabella, didn't deserve this.

Roger tapped the table. "I need updates on your other cases."

Kaden nodded and they discussed his active cases.

As they were wrapping up, Kaden's cell rang. He peered at the unknown number.

"Go ahead," Roger said.

"Kaden Farrell," he answered.

"Hi, Kaden. This is Abby Fitzgerald. Your grandfather works for my family's B and B."

His heart gave a loud thump. "Is everything all right?"

"Nigel fell off a ladder. We're at Memorial Health Center in Savannah."

"Is he all right?" He clenched his phone. His grandfather was his only family.

"He's getting X-rays right now." Her soft drawl did nothing to soothe the panic racing through his chest. "They suspect he broke his hip."

Crap. Broken hip? "I'll be right down. What hospital again?"

She repeated the name while he scribbled.

"He didn't lose consciousness," she said. "But I thought you would want to know."

"Thank you. I'm leaving right now." He hung up and filled in Roger.

"Go." Roger waved him away. "I'll let you know if we hear anything new."

Kaden rushed to his apartment. He grabbed his go bag, threw in his laptop and Dopp kit, and headed out of Atlanta.

Traffic on I-75 was bumper-to-bumper. Even the left-hand lane, void of trucks, barely moved at the speed limit. He longed to go hot and let the sirens get him to his grandfather.

Nigel had saved him. Pulled him away from his useless parents and shown him he could have a normal life. A life that didn't require moving all the time and keeping an eye out for cops or DEA agents.

The miles crawled by. He merged onto I-16, hoping traffic would ease. No luck. Container trucks filled the right-hand lane, heading to the port of Savannah. He hit the radio and tuned into CNN, then the BBC, trying to knock out the voices in his head that were warning him he might lose his last family member. Even deep breaths didn't ease the tightness in his chest.

Clutching the steering wheel, he exited on the 516. A broken hip at his grandfather's age could be deadly. When he got to Waters Avenue and then Lexington, he exhaled. Finally.

He scouted the full ER parking deck. His fingers drummed the steering wheel. On the second pass, a car backed out and he grabbed the spot.

Dashing to the ER receptionist desk, he said, "I'm looking for Nigel Ganders."

The young man searched. "He was just admitted."

Kaden followed the directions to the correct floor, stopping at the nursing station to verify his grandfather's room number. His heart pounded as he pushed open the door. And found a roomful of strangers.

"Kaden?" Granddad waved a finger at the three redheaded women in the room. "Who called my grandson for something this piddling?"

"I did." One of the women shook her finger back in Granddad's face. "He's your emergency contact. Of course I called him."

Granddad stared at Kaden. Then he touched his heart.

Tears threatened to spill from Kaden's eyes. It had always been their signal. When Kaden had been playing basketball or giving a speech, it had been that small gesture that let him know Granddad loved and was proud of him.

The woman with a ponytail walked over, holding out her hand. "Hi, I'm Abby Fitzgerald. I called."

"Nice to meet you." Kaden's response was automatic, but he stared at his grandfather. Nigel's gray eyes were bright and his posture straight. His full head of white hair was as tidy as if he was heading to church instead of lying injured in a hospital bed.

Granddad made introductions. The other two women were also Fitzgeralds; Bess, long hair, and Dolley, short curly hair. He'd heard enough about the sisters from his granddad that Kaden said, "I almost feel like I know you."

"Good. You'll be staying in Savannah, right?" Abby asked.

"Yes." No question. Kaden would be here for his grandfather.

"Wonderful." Abby stepped out of his way, letting him move next to the bed. "You'll be our guest at Fitzgerald House. No charge."

Dolley grinned at him. "I've put a hold on a Carleton House room."

"That's not necessary." Kaden looked at Granddad.

His grandfather shrugged. "No use protesting. They always get their way."

"He's right." Abby smiled and patted Kaden's arm. "At the B and B, you're closer to the hospital than at Nigel's house out on Tybee Island."

"Umm, sure." Kaden would have slept at the hospital.

"Good. Just head over when you're ready. Here's the address." Dolley handed him a business card and then frowned. "I don't think Nigel's ever said what you do up in Atlanta."

He hesitated. "I followed in my grandfather's footsteps."

"Construction?" Bess asked.

"Yes," he lied. Few people knew he worked for the FBI and fewer knew about the drug task force. It was necessary to keep everyone and their families safe.

After exchanging phone numbers, Abby kissed Granddad's cheek. "I'm heading back to Fitzgerald House. Call if you need anything."

Dolley and Bess also kissed his granddad. "You take care of yourself," Bess whispered loud enough for Kaden to hear.

Women loved his granddad. But not as much as Kaden did.

Once they were alone, his grandfather complained, "You didn't need to drive down from Atlanta."

"Of course I did." Kaden wrapped his arms around Granddad's shoulders. His Green Irish Tweed aftershave cut through the bite of hospital bleach burning his nose. He gulped deep breaths to capture the sandalwood scent. "What did the doctors say?"

"I fractured my hip."

"How?" Kaden took the chair, but reached for his hand.

"Painting." He grimaced, his thick white eyebrows forming a line. "I just wanted that last little bit and stretched too far."

"You know better than that." Kaden squeezed his hand. "You weren't hopping the ladder along the outside of the wall like you did the first year I lived with you, were you?"

"I gave that up twenty years ago." Granddad closed his eyes. "You shouldn't have come."

"I'm here for you." Kaden's heart pounded a little harder as lines of pain etched his grandfather's face. "Did they schedule your surgery yet?"

"They're working on it." His grandfather gave him his infamous no-nonsense look. "I don't want to pull you away from your job."

His work was important, but some days it felt like he was holding up an umbrella to battle a tsunami. Drugs flooded the southeast states and innocents were getting hurt.

"I'm not leaving you alone to deal with this." Nigel had saved him. "I'm right where I belong."

"'RIKKI-TIKKI HAD A right to be proud of himself—but he did not grow too proud, and he kept the garden as a mongoose should keep it, with tooth and jump and spring and bite, till never a cobra dared show its head inside the walls.'" Courtney closed the book and smiled at the circle of children at her feet.

"Read another," Jamison called in his strong Southie accent. "With more bad cobras!"

"I can't." Courtney shook her head. "Our time is up."

Actually, she'd run over the library's reading

hour. But she'd wanted to finish *The Jungle Book* story. "I'll see you next week."

As she pushed up from her small chair, Jamison wrapped his arms around her knees. "Thank you, Miss Courtney."

"You're welcome." She hugged the little boy. "Thank you for paying attention."

Two months ago, Jamison hadn't been able to sit still for more than five minutes. Now he sat for the entire story hour. She nodded as his mother took his hand. He'd learned she wouldn't read if he was talking or running around.

Grandmothers, sitters and older siblings gathered up the rest of the children.

"Your reading group keeps growing." Marlene, the librarian who organized the volunteers, took the book from Courtney.

"It's fun." And her little secret. No one knew about her weekly visits to this Southside Boston library.

Even though the book's language had been formal, the kids had been great. How wonderful it would be to put together words to ignite the imaginations of children. Of course, today's books couldn't be as lyrical as Kipling's writings, but oh, to be able to read something that she wrote to children. How amazing.

Not that it would happen. On her drive home, she rubbed the wrinkles in her forehead. Being her parents' pretty little ornament took most of her day.

To maintain her image, it took hours of shopping, salons and working out.

As she approached the gates of the family mansion, a dark shape darted from the bushes. She jerked the steering wheel. Metal scraped stone. She slammed on her brakes and her body jammed against her seat belt. "No!"

She threw the convertible into Park, jumped out and rounded the hood. Had she hit whatever had run in front of the car? She peered under the car, but didn't find an injured animal.

Damn. Her front bumper was toast. Not again. Father would go ballistic.

She glared. They needed to expand the front gate. This was the third time she'd turned a *teeny* bit too tight and wrecked her pretty car.

Driving to the portico, she stomped up the entry stairs. Marcus had the door open before she hit the top step.

"Did you have a nice afternoon of shopping?" He took the bags from her.

She always said she was going shopping, which she did. It just wasn't the entire truth. Her parents wouldn't see the value of her spending time in a South Boston library.

She shook her head, curls whipping across her face. "I bumped the gate."

One white eyebrow shot up. "Again?"

"An animal jumped out from the bushes."

"Oh, Miss. Did you hit it?"

"No." She laid her hand on his arm. "Could you…?"

"I'll call the repair shop." He tipped his head. "Your father would like to speak with you."

She frowned, then forced her face to relax. She didn't want a permanent furrow between her eyebrows, but it was hard. Nothing was right in her world. It had been off-kilter for months. "Where is he?"

"In his study." Marcus headed up the left stairway with her packages.

Courtney's heels clicked on the black-and-white foyer tiles. She longed to kick off her shoes, but she wasn't sure what Father wanted. Had she done anything that might have irritated him lately? Last month it had been how late she was coming home, as if that mattered now that she was twenty-six. The month before he'd lectured her for a half hour about gossiping at the dinner table. And in February it had been the way she treated her new sister-in-law.

I can't help that I'm not my perfect brother.

Outside Father's study, she straightened her shoulders and smoothed the skirt of the red Versace sheath she'd worn to lunch with Gwen. Her eyes didn't pop as much when she wore red. Now she wished she'd bought the dress in green, too.

She'd buy the green dress tomorrow. Better yet, she'd have them deliver it to the house.

Staring into the hallway mirror, she forced a smile onto her face and arranged her black curls so they cascaded over one shoulder. She was her father's princess, even though he hadn't called her that in years. The blasted furrow formed between her eyebrows again. She pressed on the hideous lines and took a deep breath. Opening the door, she glided into the room.

Father didn't look up. He pointed to a guest chair and kept typing.

She stood next to the chair. Her dress looked so much better when she stood. She examined her manicure and waited.

Still not looking up, her father ordered, "Sit."

Courtney gritted her teeth, but obeyed, moving around the chair. She slipped into her seat just as she'd been taught in the finishing classes she'd been forced to attend during high school.

Instead of crossing her ankles, she rebelled against the voice in her head and crossed her legs. By crossing her legs, she could admire the red soles of her Louboutin heels. They were a perfect match with her dress. She sat with her back ruler-straight, remembering the way the instructor had made her balance a book on her head.

Wasn't she her father's perfect daughter, dressed to the height of fashion? She folded her hands in her lap, but what she really wanted to do was thread her fingers through her pearl necklace. It had been a gift for her sixteenth birthday from her father, but Mother had probably signed his name to the card.

She could wait him out. She didn't have anything else to do.

He looked up. Inhaled and exhaled. Twice.

Uh-oh. What had she done? He couldn't already know about her car. She chewed her thumbnail, then quickly dropped her hand to her lap and twisted her fingers together.

His gray eyes narrowed and he held up an envelope. "Do you know what this is?"

Was he kidding? "An envelope?"

"Your credit card bill."

She nodded, feeling her eyebrows coming together again. "Okay."

"No. Not okay." He pulled out the wad of paper. "Five thousand dollars at a shoe store?"

Shoes? She tapped her lip with her fingernail, longing to chew on it again, but she wasn't fifteen anymore. "There was a sale."

"So you spent five thousand dollars?" He spread out the pages, facing her. "We talked about this two months ago."

"About what?" Whoops. She'd forgotten about that lecture. Paying bills wasn't her responsibility. It was her father's.

"About wasting money. About your shopping excesses." He pushed back a black curl that slipped across his forehead.

She'd inherited her father's hair, but she hoped never to see the white that peppered his. He might look distinguished, but women had to hide any sign of aging.

"It was an incredible sale." She pointed to her shoes. "No one else I know owns this pair." Or most of the shoes she'd picked up that day.

His face turned red. "Because they aren't spend-thrifts."

"You always tell me to look my best." It was all he'd ever expected.

"You have a mountain of clothes." He pointed at the bill. "Two mountains of clothes based on the money you've spent. You're done."

"Done?" What was he talking about?

"I want your credit cards."

"What for?" She couldn't catch her breath.

"As of today, the endless spending stops."

"But…"

He held out his hand and she dug into her Furla wallet. He stared at each card as she handed it to him. Pulling out scissors, he said, "Cut them up."

"But what will I do?" If she couldn't charge meals, drinks or clothes, what else was there?

"Get a job. Make your own money." Her father threw up his hands. "Marry one of those worthless boys you hang around with and spend *their* money."

He'd never been this angry. Ever. She swallowed and took the scissors and the first card. She cut it in half. Then half again. And kept going. The handle of the scissors imprinted on the base of her thumb.

It hurt, but she couldn't complain while her father glared at her.

"You now have a five-hundred-dollar credit limit on this card." He held it out. "I expect that to be used for gas and parking to get you to job interviews."

This couldn't be happening. She leaned over the divide of his desk, touching his hand. Then she smiled, the smile that used to get her father's attention. "Daddy, just last week you told me you liked the way I dressed."

"Because that's all you're good at doing. Looking pretty." He spit the words out and flipped her hand away.

She waved at her dress and shoes. "It costs money to look like this. Ask Mother."

"You should have enough clothes to do that for years to come." He stood, leaning on his fists. "I mean it. It's time you got a job."

Her spine slumped against the back of the chair. The imaginary book balancing on her head tumbled to the floor. The furrow between her eyebrows dug deep. "A job?"

"A job."

Her heart hammered in her chest. "I guess I could be a—a personal shopper."

He scowled. "You're a Smythe. I expect you to get a *worthwhile* job."

"Of course, Daddy." With her spine as straight as a ruler, she left the room.

Worthwhile job? She swallowed back tears. She was qualified to do…absolutely nothing.

COURTNEY SHOVED THE throw pillows covering her bed to the floor.

How could she get a job? Her father hadn't let her go to the college of her choice. She'd been accepted at Yale, Gray and Father's alma mater. But dear old dad had forced her to attend Mount Holyoke, her mother's college.

Daddy saved all his pride for Gray. Her brother had been on the dean's list his entire college career. The first semester of her freshman year, she'd worked hard and made the dean's list, too, hoping her father would relent and she could transfer. But he hadn't been impressed. It wasn't Yale, right? In rebellion, she'd gotten an English degree with an emphasis in Renaissance literature, and hadn't paid attention to her grades. She'd gotten to read and that was fun. Would someone pay her to recite Shakespeare soliloquies?

She flopped to the center of her canopy bed, not caring that her shoes were on her white comforter.

A job.

She'd had one job during high school. When her aunt and uncle had gone to Europe for a month, she'd taken care of her two young cousins. Their cook had still been in residence, but she'd been responsible for the children. How would Nanny look on a résumé? Two consecutive summers of working for a few weeks should wow a perspective employer.

U won't believe what happened, she texted Gwen.

No reply. Right, Gwen was getting a facial.

She touched her cheek. How would she pay for next week's facial?

She'd talk to Mother. Her mother would calm Father down. She couldn't live on five hundred dollars a month. Who did that to their only daughter?

Courtney hadn't even known there was such a thing as a credit limit. She rubbed her forehead. Although last January, Laura had complained she had to watch her spending. Courtney and Gwen had quietly stopped hanging around with her. Since she and Gwen didn't invite Laura anywhere, her entire posse excluded her.

She sat up with a jerk. Would that happen to her? Gwen's text ringtone, "My Best Friend," sounded. What happened?

She couldn't tell Gwen. She tapped her nail against her lower lip. I hit the driveway pillar again.

Again?

Yes ☹ She should be adding tears.

Club 2nite?

Her heart pounded. What was she going to do? Can't. Family dinner.

K. 2morrow?

I'll let you know. She would avoid everyone until this crisis had passed. Mother would fix everything.

She stripped off her sheath and stepped into her closet to hang it with the rest of her red dresses. This was her haven, her beautiful clothes. Her armor.

She placed her heels in their spot next to the rest of the pairs that had caused this firestorm. She stroked her gorgeous new Manolo Blahnik boots. Okay, they hadn't been on sale. Actually none of the shoes had been on sale, but it seemed like a reasonable excuse when she'd blurted it out.

Her fingers tapped her bare thigh. What could she wear that would make her look fragile and innocent? She twirled in a slow circle. Audrey Hepburn. White sleeveless blouse. Skinny black capris and black ballerina flats. She'd pull her hair up. Emphasize her eyes. She wasn't as thin as the actress, but she was willowy. Who could punish Audrey Hepburn?

Maybe she should take up acting. She'd done that all her life.

Her hand shook a little as she added eyeliner and more mascara. Then she pulled her mass of black curls into a French twist.

She checked her appearance one more time before slipping on her shoes. The look worked.

Straightening her shoulders so an imaginary

book lay flat on her head, she forced her feet into *the glide*. It was her term for the walk she'd learned in her finishing classes. Like a ballerina, she floated down the hallway to her mother's sitting area.

Her mother worked at her desk, the tip of her Montblanc pen tapping her lip.

"Mother?"

"Courtney, what do you think about a fire-and-ice theme for the ballet foundation's benefit?" Mother asked.

"In August?"

Mother nodded, her blond hair swaying.

When Courtney was a child she'd wanted her mother's straight blond hair instead of her father's curly black hair. Now she didn't know what she wanted. Her life no longer fit. "I don't think fire-and-ice will work. I assume you would want ice sculptures and since you're using the terraces, melting would be a problem."

"I agree with you. But Dorothy *loves* it." Mother set down her pen. "Maybe you want to join the committee and give us fresh ideas?"

Would it get her out of finding a job? "Maybe."

Mother finally looked up. "That outfit looks good on you. Is it new?"

"The pants." And shoes. Part of the infamous shoe purchases. She stroked the ballerina sculpture that graced her mother's desk. "Have you talked to Father?"

"This morning." She eased back in her chair. "Why?"

"He's upset." She moved to the coffee table and picked up the book her mother was reading. Some thriller. Not her style.

"About?"

"The shoes I bought last month." She pointed to her feet. "But these are adorable."

Mother stood. "He's upset about a pair of shoes? That's strange."

"I bought more than one pair." She turned, the words rushing out. "I showed you everything the day I bought them. You didn't complain."

Her blue eyes narrowed. "Did he put you on a budget?"

"Budget? He made me cut up my credit cards." She ran and took her mother's hands. "You have to help me. He said I have to find a job."

"A job?" Mother shook her head. "He's been listening to Gray."

"Can you help? I—I can't work." She didn't know how. "All my friends will abandon me. How will I hold my head up? Without credit cards I'll be stuck in the house."

"I'll talk to him at dinner. We'll work this out." Mother wrapped an arm around her shoulder. "Let's go down and pour him his Jameson. Lord knows why he developed a taste for it. It's Gray's wife's fault. But maybe it will mellow him out."

Was it the darn Fitzgeralds putting this stupid

job notion in her father's head? It would be just like his brother's wife and her sisters to be envious of her life and whisper things to Gray. What did men see in them, anyway? Gray had given up a relationship with her best friend, Gwen, for the woman he'd married last February. Courtney had suffered through being a part of the wedding party. She and Gwen had envisioned a *totally* different wedding. Classy. It wasn't fair.

Courtney followed her mother to the library. Just inhaling had the tension in her shoulders easing. Two stories of books soothed her. Heading to the small bar, she added ice to a tumbler and poured Jameson from a Waterford decanter. She'd always liked watching Mother prepare Father's before-dinner drink. Once she'd turned ten, serving her father's drink had become Courtney's job, but he'd never noticed.

"What would you like?" Courtney asked.

"Wine, please. Marcus should have decanted a shiraz."

The correct stemware was set on a salver. She poured two glasses to the perfect center of the bell, then moved to her mother's chair and handed her the wine.

Courtney swirled her glass, tipped and watched the legs. Then inhaled. Taking a small sip, she let the wine linger in her mouth. Chocolate. Peppers. She frowned. "Are you catching blackberry?"

Her mother repeated the wine tasting steps. "I am. You have a great palate."

Maybe Courtney could become a sommelier. Select wine for her friends as they dined. She shuddered. That was not going to happen. Mother needed to fix this.

Father entered the room, swiped the tumbler off the bar and brought it over to the sitting area. "Thank you, Olivia. It's been a long day."

"Thank your daughter. She prepared it for you."

He nodded, not even looking at Courtney.

She started to open her mouth.

Mother shook her head.

Biding her time wasn't her strength, but Mother had married the man. She should know how to get him to do her bidding.

"How was your day?" Mother asked Father.

"Market tanked. One of the companies I was looking at acquiring found an angel to finance them." He took a deep swallow of his whiskey. His glance shot over to Courtney. "The only good thing that happened was Gray cleared inspections on his Back Bay project. They should get the certificate of occupancy soon."

Her brother scored another success. Rah. Family dinners always made her feel invisible. Gray was the only child her father ever talked about. *Gray this, Gray that. Gray. Gray. Boring Gray.* Why couldn't her father recognize that she added color to the Smythe family?

Courtney asked, "Is he back in Boston?"

"No. He's bidding on property near Savannah." Father set his glass on the silver coaster on the coffee table. "He's adding a Savannah office, too. Not just working out of Boston."

And the perfection that was Gray continued. She slipped deeper into her chair, wanting to blend into the fabric.

Marcus entered. "May I serve dinner?"

Mother looked to Father, who nodded.

"Would you like another drink?" Courtney asked him.

He thrust the glass at her. She plucked ice cubes from the bucket and splashed another shot in the tumbler.

Father took the glass, then headed to the dining room.

Mother whispered to him. *Please let her make a dent in his stubbornness.*

Father sank into the head chair. Mother sat to his right and Courtney to his left. If Gray was here, he would have this seat. She'd be forced farther down the table. Who said there wasn't still a hierarchy, like in the Regency romance novels she loved to read?

She was nothing.

They pulled cloches off their plates. Her stomach twisted. How could she eat dinner without a solution to the chaos her life had become?

"Can I ask why you took Courtney's credit cards away?" Mother asked.

Thank goodness. Courtney cut a small piece of lamb chop. Mother would fix this.

Father pointed his loaded fork at Courtney. "I'm done supporting her shopping habit. It's time she get a job."

"You never asked her to work before." Mother didn't look at her. "Why now?"

"In the first six months of this year, your dear daughter has spent a hundred thousand dollars on travel, clothes, shoes and parties. Families live on that." He slammed down his silverware. "She needs to discover what it's like to earn a living."

The lamb she'd swallowed formed a lump in her throat. Coughing, she grabbed her wine and swallowed. "I'll—I'll do better. Put me on a budget. Please, Daddy."

"If you don't want to work, then have one of those boys who fawn around your skirts marry you and take on your useless habits."

Useless. Tears burned her eyes.

"That's uncalled for," Mother hissed. Her head snapped back and forth. She was probably worried the servants would overhear the argument.

"I've had it." He emptied his whiskey and pointed at Courtney. "Gray is right. You need to stand on your own feet."

Of course. Mr. Perfect. He'd caused this mess.

If Gray had been the impetus, then he should

be the solution. In a soft voice she asked, "Gray is opening an office in Savannah?"

"Yes." Father sighed.

"Maybe he'll have a job for me." She'd pretend to go to Savannah for work. At least until her father calmed down.

Her father's gray eyes held hers for almost too long. "You plan on becoming a carpenter?"

She blinked. "He'll need help decorating or answering phones or…" What else did people do in offices?

He snorted. "Good luck."

"Why, thank you, Daddy." Did she hit the last word too hard?

She could head to Savannah for a week or two. Time to escape Boston and take a vacation. "Will you up my credit card limit so I can drive to Gray's and not have to sleep in my car?"

"Of course he will." Mother glared at her husband.

Good. Mother could make this problem go away. Courtney would take a road trip.

CHAPTER TWO

"ARE YOU SURE this is all you need?" Kaden arranged a picture of the grandmother he'd never met on his grandfather's nursing home dresser.

"I just want my own PJs, robe, clothes and a picture of my wife," Nigel sighed. "But I'd rather be home."

"Not yet." Kaden's chest tightened. He'd just checked his granddad into a highly-rated, long-term rehabilitation center. Even though his grandfather had come through the surgery like a champ, he needed care and physical therapy. Now to get Granddad to accept that he needed to stay here. "How does that look?"

"Fine," he grumbled. "This darn hip made me miss Bess and Daniel's wedding. The Fitzgeralds throw the best parties."

They'd talked about this thirty minutes ago. Granddad's pain meds messed with his memory. Kaden said, "There will be other weddings."

"I'd like to see my grandson married."

"Not on the horizon." Kaden avoided his grandfather's eyes. "Bureau keeps me too busy."

"I can't have you hovering by my bedside for weeks." Nigel shook his head. "Head back to Atlanta."

"We've had this conversation." Kaden patted his

shoulder. Bones protruded that hadn't been there before. "I'm taking a well-earned vacation."

"That's ridiculous. You'll go crazy sitting around."

"I picked up something to while away the hours between your torture sessions." Kaden dug in the bag, grinning. "I mean your physical therapy sessions."

He set a chessboard on a rolling table. Aligning the pieces, he took a white and black pawn and mixed them behind his back. He held out his closed hands. "Your choice."

Granddad tapped one. White.

"You open." Kaden set down the pawns. "How many hours do you think we've played chess?"

"At first you couldn't sit for more than fifteen minutes. What a squirmy seven-year-old you were." His grandfather advanced his pawn. "But hundreds of hours, I guess. Maybe thousands?"

Kaden answered by advancing his own pawn and the game was on. The only sound was the felt of the pieces on the cardboard and the muffled echoes of voices in the hallway.

"When you were young, you never looked ahead more than one move." Granddad moved his knight, threatening Kaden's bishop.

Kaden could sacrifice the piece for his longer strategy. He moved his queen.

A big smile broke over his grandfather's face. He pointed a long elegant finger at Kaden's side of the board. "You're getting trickier."

"I learned from the best." Kaden swallowed

back emotions bubbling up into his throat. He'd learned *everything* from this man. His grandfather had shown him how to live with honor. He'd never learned that from his worthless parents. "Why did my mother turn out so…bad?"

Granddad sank into the pillows, pushing back his thick white hair. "You've never asked me that question."

"Because I was so relieved to be saved from that…life." Kaden got out of the chair and walked to the window that overlooked a small garden. "I was afraid you would send me back to them."

"Never." Granddad's voice was low. "When your grandmother died, I was…lost. Your mother was thirteen. She needed me and I wasn't there."

"She knew right from wrong. She knew drugs were bad."

"I should have helped her." His grandfather inhaled. "I didn't push through my grief. By the time she was eighteen and pregnant with you, she wouldn't listen to anything I said."

"But you tried." He remembered that much. Whenever Granddad called, his mother would throw the phone, or pots, or whatever was at hand.

"Too late. If I'd done more, maybe Kaleb would still be alive. I should have saved both of you." Sadness filled his grandfather's intense blue eyes. Eyes that had barely faded over the years.

"It wasn't your fault," Kaden choked out. He was responsible for his brother's death, not Nigel.

"You were seven." Granddad shook his head. "Thank God your mother called me, even though all she wanted was bail. At least I rescued you from that Florida hovel."

"You made me the man I am today." Kaden would have said more, but his phone buzzed in his pocket.

Checking the caller ID, he said, "It's my boss."

"Go ahead." Granddad closed his eyes, looking twenty years older. "I need to rest."

Kaden's heart took another hit. Walking to the opposite corner of the room, he answered, "Farrell."

"Heather Bole's kid was dropped off in Savannah." Roger's words were clipped.

"She's here?" He clenched the phone. "In Savannah?"

"She was. Back in May." Papers shifted on Roger's side of the conversation. "The father is filing for full custody and wants to find Bole. He contacted the Savannah police a couple of weeks ago."

"Is this guy involved with one of the gangs?"

"Nothing we can find," Roger said. "The detective said this Forester guy was suspected of dealing in high school, but either he's kept a low profile or he's out of the life. Savannah cop thinks he's clean, but I'd rather you make your own assessment."

Kaden straightened. "This might be the break we need."

"I know you're helping your grandfather, but

could you talk to the dad? I want the interview to come from my team. From you."

And Kaden knew why. Roger's ex-wife ran the FBI office in Savannah, Roger the Atlanta office. The Bureau was hard on marriages. Kaden had never had any problems with Margaret, Roger's ex, but Roger carried a grudge.

He glanced at his sleeping grandfather. He could take an hour to talk to this man. "Sure."

Roger rattled off the Savannah detective's contact information. Kaden moved into the hall. When the man answered, he explained why he was calling.

"The father's name is Nathan Forester." Detective Gillespie gave Kaden a quick recap and Forester's phone number.

Kaden peeked into his grandfather's room, but he hadn't moved. One more call.

"Forester," the man answered. A saw squealed in the background.

Kaden introduced himself. "I'd like to talk to you about Heather Bole."

"Do you know where she is?" The background noise faded.

"No. But we're looking for her, too. I'd like to ask you a few questions. When would be convenient?"

They set up a time to meet and Forester gave him an address. "I'm in the carriage house in the back. Second floor. If you have trouble finding the apartment, just call or text."

After hanging up, Kaden stared at the address. Why was it so familiar?

He searched the location and jerked when it came up. Couldn't be. He was heading to Fitzgerald House.

"COURTNEY?" GRAY BLOCKED the doorway, not letting her inside. "What are you doing here?"

"Surprise!" Courtney faked a smile. "I'm here to visit you."

"What?" Gray crossed his arms. "You never wanted to before."

Why wasn't he inviting her into his house? She forced a smile. "I'm here now."

"Here? Staying at Fitzgerald House?" Gray's words were as much a barricade as his body.

"I was hoping I could stay with you. With my family." Courtney didn't want to *beg*.

He hesitated, finally pulling her into a hug. His shirt was unbuttoned and his hair was damp. "No one told me you were coming to Savannah."

"That's why it's called a surprise." She poked him in the belly. "I haven't seen you in a while."

"I was in Boston two weeks ago." Gray frowned. "You were too busy to have dinner with me."

"I'm making up for it now." She went for perky, but her voice wobbled.

What if Gray wouldn't let her stay in his carriage house? Last night, she'd splurged on a nice Charleston hotel. She wouldn't have enough money on her credit card to pay for another hotel. Being short of money sucked.

"You want to stay here?" Cynicism filled his voice. "With Abby and I?"

"I want to spend time with you." She wrapped an arm around her brother's waist, hoping she didn't sound desperate. She hated the panic that had crept into her voice over the last few days. "I thought it would be…fun."

"Here? You want to stay here?" Gray stepped out of the doorway and led her inside—*finally*.

Abby, his wife, came down the central stairs, also looking like she'd just hopped out of the shower. Her strawberry-blond hair was wet and pulled back in a high ponytail. Did she not know that style was so nineties? Her green eyes glowed. "Courtney?"

Oh. *Oh*. She swallowed. Gray and Abby had been…oh.

Courtney hurried over and gave her sister-in-law air kisses. "Hi, Abby."

Gray crossed his arms. "She's here for a surprise visit."

"That's wonderful." Abby gave her a hug. "It's been months since you were in Savannah. Let me get our guest room ready."

Abby headed down the main floor hallway.

Courtney tipped her head at her brother. "At

least your wife is more welcoming than my own brother."

"What do you want?" Gray asked.

"To visit." She wouldn't let terror fill her voice.

"Why?" He stared like he could peer into her brain and dig out her reason.

"Boston got…boring." She wasn't discussing her problems. Gray would be sanctimonious about her issues with Father. Holding out her keys, she asked, "Could you get my luggage?"

His blue gaze locked on hers.

She knew better than to look away. Instead, she smiled.

Gray snapped up the keys and headed to the door.

Okay, maybe her relationship with her brother hadn't been exactly cordial since he'd broken up with Gwen. And maybe her bringing Gwen to Savannah and trying to get them back together hadn't been well thought-out. But he was her *brother*.

Gray had gotten her into this mess. She shook back her hair and headed to the great room, sliding into a comfy leather chair. She would hide in Savannah until Father reinstated her cash flow.

Her call with Mother last night hadn't given her any new hope. Courtney spun her gold bracelet around her wrist. She liked the way it made her hand look so petite.

How much could she sell it for?

"Little help here?" Gray called from the doorway.

She waited for Abby to come out of the guest bedroom. Nothing.

"Courtney, grab your bags," he grumbled.

She pushed off the sofa. "You need a Marcus."

"No, we don't. Get used to it. And there's no maids to make beds or clean the house." He shoved her makeup case into her hands. "You have luggage for a month. What's going on?"

"I—I didn't know what kind of weather to expect."

"It's summer in Savannah." Gray drew together his black eyebrows. "Hot and hotter."

"You'll get wrinkles if you keep frowning like that." She felt her own ridges forming on her forehead. Shoot.

While Gray went back to her car, she grabbed a suitcase and tugged it to the bedroom.

Abby smoothed out a pale yellow comforter. Better Abby than her. The Fitzgerald family had been making beds and running their B and B most of their lives.

"This is nice." Gray and Abby's home had that old carriage-house feel with aged wood floors and beams, but the guestroom was light and bright. Unlike in the bed-and-breakfast, antiques wouldn't surround her here. "It doesn't feel two hundred years old."

Abby fluffed the green and pink throw pillows.

"As much as I love Fitzgerald House, I wanted something different in my home."

"Thank you for letting me stay." Courtney needed Abby on her side if she was going to hide out in Savannah. "I probably should have called, but it sounded like fun to surprise Gray."

"Well, you're here now." Abby straightened. "We'll eat dinner in the main house around seven. You can tidy up or rest until then. I have to prep for the wine tasting."

Gray pulled two more suitcases into the bedroom. Abby's eyes flared open and she stared at Courtney for a long moment. With a shake of her head, Abby brushed a kiss on Gray's cheek. "I'll see you at Fitzgerald House."

"Thank you, big brother." God, she needed Gray and Abby to stop looking at her like she had two heads. "I'd better call Mother. The drive down here was fun, but you know how she worries." She kept her voice super cheery. "Any message you want to pass on to Mother or Father?"

"Just say hello." Gray followed his wife out the door.

Excellent. Maybe Gray wouldn't talk to the parental units for a couple of days. She needed time for this problem to blow over.

Mother answered.

"I'm in Savannah." Courtney settled back against the pillows on the bed. "Gray and Abby say hello."

"I'm so relieved. That was a long drive by your-self."

"It was…fun." She couldn't remember the last time she'd been alone for three days. If she'd had full access to money, it might have been even better. Unfortunately, each time she used her credit card she'd worried she'd run out of credit. Who could live that way? Mother had tucked cash in her purse, but Courtney might need that later. "Have you softened Daddy up?"

"I'm trying, honey. But he's intractable." Her mother sighed. "Maybe by taking a job with Gray, it'll show your father that you're changing."

"Sure. Right." Her chest ached. Was she losing her mother's support? "Please keep working on him."

"I will, dear."

They talked for a few minutes, but Courtney's brain wasn't functioning. Mother had to succeed. She didn't want to stay in Savannah. She wanted to go home.

KADEN PARKED BEHIND the B and B. Two carriage houses existed on the combined property. One was under construction, while the other looked like a home.

He found Forester's number in his call log and texted him. I'm in the Fitzgerald House parking lot, where should we meet?

The reply came back: Coming down.

Kaden leaned against a shed near the parking lot, giving him a view of the entire courtyard. It stretched a full block from Fitzgerald to Carleton House. When the sisters had added the second mansion to the B and B, Granddad had been mighty proud.

After Nigel had turned sixty, he'd sold his construction business. Then he'd gotten bored with retirement. Now he worked as handyman and sometimes chauffeur for the sisters. Maybe after he recovered, he should actually retire.

A door on the second floor of the nearest carriage house banged open and a small boy dashed out.

The kid ran down the stairs, his shoelaces flapping. He could take a header and crack his skull open.

Kaden's heart rate picked up and he hurried to the steps. Could he catch the kid if he fell?

"Josh!" a deep voice called from the top of the steps. "Slow down."

"Miss Abby's saving a treat for me," the kid yelled.

"You won't be eating anything if we end up at the ER." A man came down the steps with a little girl on his shoulders.

When the boy was safely on the stone walkway, Kaden released the breath he'd been holding.

The man hadn't noticed him yet. But the girl stared holes in him. She had fluffy blond hair.

Heather's kid? She looked younger than he thought a four-year-old should be, but what did he know?

When the man and child reached the bottom of the steps, Kaden stepped closer. "Forester?"

"Agent Farrell?"

Kaden nodded. He glanced around. Luckily, the courtyard was empty. "Just Kaden, please."

Forester swung the little girl off his shoulders. "Issy, go join Josh in the kitchen."

Issy. Short for Isabella. Heather's kid.

The little girl bit her lip, staring at Kaden.

Did she guess she wasn't safe around him? Somehow kids saw right through him. He forced a smile. She backed closer to her dad and clung to his leg.

"Hang on. Let me take Issy inside." Forester pointed to the door the boy had run through.

Kaden moved to a small ironwork table next to a fountain. If guests tried to eavesdrop on their conversation, the splashing water would muffle their voices.

Forester didn't take long. He returned and held out a hand. "I'm Nathan."

Kaden had reviewed Nathan Forester's profile. He was part owner in a family construction company. That explained the sound of the saw in the background when Kaden had called this afternoon.

Nathan took a seat and stretched out his legs. He didn't say anything, just waited. The guy's eyes were clear. He didn't look like he was a user, but the smartest dealers didn't use their own product.

Kaden opened his phone to a picture of Bole. "Do you know this woman?"

"It's Heather. Heather Bole. I met her when I worked in Atlanta. We dated about five years ago. Not for long. Then she took off with some guy." He glanced over at the kitchen door. "Just before summer, she walked into my work site and dropped off Issy. Isabella. Said she's my daughter. Which I didn't doubt for a minute."

"This was May?" Kaden leaned forward. The timing fit.

"Yeah."

"You didn't know about your daughter before?" Kaden asked.

"Her mother never told me." Nathan ran his fingers through his hair, his lips forming a straight line. "After Heather dropped her off, Issy barely spoke."

Didn't speak? "Did Heather say where she was heading?"

"She said she'd gotten a DUI and was ordered into treatment, but I couldn't find her anywhere."

"Was Heather with anyone?" Kaden pulled up a picture of Hector Salvez. "Maybe this guy?"

"There wasn't anyone with her or in the truck when I chased her down the street." He closed his eyes. "What mother doesn't tell the father of her child about their daughter and then dumps her with a birth certificate and barely any clothes?"

Kaden's nostrils flared. One just like his own

mother. "Did she say where she'd been? What she'd been doing?"

"No." Nathan opened his phone and scrolled to a photo, tipping it so Kaden could see the screen. "Issy keeps drawing this picture. Do you know anything about that?"

The paper had stick figures on it. A small yellow-haired person was squashed under a bigger stick figure with black hair and a beard. Red slashes covered the bigger stick figure.

Kaden swore. "She *was* there. Poor kid."

"You know what this is? Where this is?" Nathan's fists pressed against the table.

"Border of Georgia and Florida," Kaden said. "It's a drug house. There was a shooting. Three dead."

Nathan pushed away from the table and paced to the fountain and back. Leaning his fists on the table, he growled, "And Issy was there? In a house filled with drugs and guns?"

Kaden took in the fire in the man's eyes. The tension in his body.

"Based on the blood smears, we suspect someone about the size of your daughter was at the scene."

"Oh, God." Nathan collapsed into the chair, clasping at his neck. "I… Could you talk to her therapist? Maybe this new information will help. I want Issy to feel safe. Be safe."

"Sure." Kaden wasn't sure what more he could

tell a therapist, but Nathan was suffering. He was so upset it made him think the guy was clean. "Do you have any idea where Heather might be?"

"I've racked my brain for months, trying to recall everything she ever said." Nathan blew out a big breath. "I think she grew up in Alabama."

"Mobile."

"If Heather's involved in drugs I will never let her touch Issy again. I want full custody."

"I understand." Kaden stared the man in the eye. "But you have a track record with drugs and dealing, don't you?"

"In high school, small-time. I was a screwup." Nathan gripped the table. "But I'm not anymore. Haven't been for a decade. Run me."

"Already did. We haven't found anything to indicate you're still involved."

Forester backed off, his shoulders easing. "You won't find anything. I have a daughter. My fiancée has a son. I'm not screwing up anything with her or the kids. They're everything to me."

Kaden was starting to like the guy. He handed him a business card. "If you hear from Heather, let me know."

"I will."

The kitchen door creaked open and Abby walked over to the table. "Nathan, we're ready to eat."

"Are we done?" Nathan asked him.

"Yes."

"Kaden?" Abby asked. "I didn't know you and Nathan knew each other."

"Hi, Abby." Kaden stood. "We just met."

Nathan's eyebrows shot up. Then he gave a short nod.

"Is Nigel settled at the rehab center?" she asked.

"Yes." Kaden grimaced. "He already wants to go home."

She patted his shoulder. "He's right where he needs to be."

Nathan stood, too. "You know Nigel?"

"He's my grandfather." Pride filled Kaden's voice.

"Wonderful man," Nathan said. "Sorry he fell."

"Thanks."

"Kaden?" Abby asked. "Have you had dinner?"

He didn't remember having lunch. "No."

"Then join us," Abby said.

"I…" Kaden couldn't think of the last time he'd sat down to a meal that hadn't been with his grand-dad or other agents. Usually he ate takeout or a nuked dinner alone. "That would be nice."

"I'll hold dinner for you then." Abby pointed at a door. "Come into the kitchen when you're ready."

Once Abby left, Kaden touched Nathan's arm. "I need to keep the fact that I'm with the FBI between us. I'm only in Savannah because of my grandfather."

Nathan raised his eyebrows. "Are you undercover?"

"My…cover is on a need-to-know basis." Like all task force members.

"Sure." Nathan nodded.

"Thanks," Kaden said.

It wasn't only the task force policy of secrecy. His job was on the line. Roger had fired a loose-lipped co-worker two months ago.

And if Roger's ex-wife got wind he was talking to people in her jurisdiction, it would add fuel to their personal war. He'd hate to be caught in their crossfire. Secrecy was the best policy.

COURTNEY KICKED A suitcase out of the way. She missed having maids to clean and iron her clothes. Sure, she packed and unpacked her own bag when traveling, but for this trip, she'd taken more clothes than normal. Help would be nice.

If she complained, Gray would roll his eyes. Why had she painted herself in this corner? She needed her brother's help, but Gray was suspicious of everything she did.

If she could hide for a week or two, Father would calm down. Mother promised. But waiting meant getting through tonight's dinner and being around Gray and the *love of his life*. Gag much?

Her brother tapped on the door. "You ready to walk over for dinner?"

She pushed off the bed. "I guess."

He peered at her luggage spread through the room. "You didn't unpack."

"I…freshened up after the drive." She brushed a curl off her cheek. She'd been reading and lost track of time. "I'll work on it tonight."

"How long are you staying?" he asked as they headed into the courtyard.

She clenched her hands into fists so she didn't gnaw on her thumbnail. "A couple of weeks?"

"Weeks? Did your clique dethrone you as queen?" He slapped a hand on his chest. "How will they know who to snub and what club is hot? How will they decide what party to attend without your…wisdom?"

She shivered. Gwen would take over. Her friend would love that. "You don't have a high opinion of my life."

"Nope." He was so…blunt.

They passed a stone sculpture of the three Fitzgerald sisters set into a crumbling wall surrounded by flowers. "I suppose you think I should be more like the Fitzgeralds. Setting my hooks into men who can finance their B and B."

Gray grabbed her arm and spun her to face him. "What?"

"Ouch." She tugged and he released her. "Abby set her hooks in you and you bought her a mansion. Bess just married a contractor. You don't think she has to pay full cost for the work they do at the B and B, do you? And what about Dolley? She made a play for that photographer. Now her photos are published."

"How can you think that? The Fitzgeralds are the hardest-working family I know," Gray spat out. "I admire what they've done. You should emulate, not scorn, them. None of the trust-fund babies you run with could survive what they've survived."

"But—but Abby married you and you bought her all this." She waved her arms around the B and B.

"Because I love her." Gray raised his hands. "I want to help her make her dreams come true. But she's the one with the ideas and work ethic."

"But…" The Fitzgeralds couldn't be so…so virtuous.

"I'll warn you once." Gray's blue gaze froze her in place. "If you're nasty or mean to Abby, or her sisters, or their husbands or fiancés, hell, to any B and B staff, you're gone."

Her stomach flopped. *Gone?* Where could she go? She couldn't *afford* anything. "You'd choose them over me? Your own sister?"

"Absolutely." He crossed his arms, his face as hard as the driveway pillars at home. "Are we clear?"

"Yes." Her voice shook. Why was this happening? Why couldn't her life go back to normal? "But…"

"No. No *buts*." He exhaled. "Sometimes I wish we'd grown up poor. Then maybe you would have used the brain I know you have."

He was as relentless as a boxer in the ring, but she wouldn't let him see how much he'd hurt her.

She'd had plenty of practice with their father. "I'm *glad* we aren't poor."

He set his hand on her back and directed her toward Fitzgerald House. "I want you to *do* something with your life."

"That's easy for you to say, you went to Yale." Bitterness bled through her words.

"Your education was good." He squeezed her shoulders. "There had to be a reason you chose literature as your major."

"I love literature." In addition, she could run her sorority without worrying she would fail a course. Would sorority president look good on a résumé?

"I endured English classes," he said. "Too much reading."

"That was the best part of my degree program." She loved escaping into someone else's life. It was more fun than her own. Changing the subject, she asked, "Do you always eat at the B and B?"

Gray shrugged. "On the nights Abby runs the wine tastings."

"But there are all those…strangers at the B and B."

"You mean like when you eat in a restaurant?"

"Oh."

Courtney followed him through the garden's winding paths. Lush green plants cascaded over rocks. Palm trees of all sizes shadowed beds filled with red, yellow and pink flowers. She barely recognized any of the plants. She was as out of place here as a palm tree would be on the banks of the Charles.

She wanted to go home. Wanted to have some-one else deal with money and cars and let her deal with managing her friends.

Gray held the screen door. The scents as they walked into the large kitchen were amazing. Lemon, basil, licorice? And fish.

Gray hurried to his wife like he hadn't seen her in weeks. A mob of people filled the room.

She straightened. She'd thought it would only be Abby, Gray and herself. Instead, Abby's family was here. The three sisters were connected at the hips. Now it wouldn't be a quick meal. She'd have to chat with people who thought she was a bitch.

She shook back her curls. What did it matter? She'd be back in Boston and away from here soon enough.

Dolley, the youngest sister, said something and Liam, the documentary maker she'd latched on to, laughed along with the rest of the adults. Every-one but her.

What would it be like to laugh freely and not care if the laugh lines became permanently en-graved on your face?

They were talking about Bess and Daniel's hon-eymoon. Courtney hesitated next to the kitchen sitting area.

The boy who'd been in Abby's wedding sat next to a little girl. What was his name? "Jason?"

He looked up from scribbling in a sketch book. "I'm Joshua. Josh."

"Hi, Joshua Josh." She sat across from the kids. "What are you coloring?"

He raised his eyebrows. "I'm drawing."

She could see ears and the body of a dog forming under the pencil strokes. "Is that your dog?"

"It's Carly, my uncle's dog. But Papa says we get a dog as soon as our house is ready."

"You're very talented." She looked over at the tiny blond-haired girl. "What are you working on?"

She held up a coloring book.

"Issy doesn't talk much. 'Cuz of stuff," Josh said. "She always colors *princesses*."

"I see that." Pink exploded over the page. "Very pretty."

Issy pointed to the page she wasn't coloring.

"You want me to color with you?" Courtney asked.

Issy's brown eyes brightened.

"Thank you." She knelt on the opposite side of the coffee table and picked a purple crayon from the pack. "Do you know your colors?"

The little girl nodded.

Courtney held up the crayon in her hand.

"Purple," the little girl sang.

"Right." Two princesses were on the page. "Which dress should be purple?"

Issy tapped one.

As they worked, Courtney asked her to name the colors each time she changed crayons.

A blond woman came to the sitting area. "Hi, Courtney, can I get you something to drink?"

Courtney looked up. Everyone in the kitchen had wine or beer. "Umm, a glass of wine? Whatever everyone is drinking."

"We're having prosecco." The woman smiled. "I'm Cheryl."

"Cheryl. Thanks." She pushed the crayons back to Issy.

Gray would expect her to socialize with the adults, people who despised her. She'd rather play with the kids, but she stood. "Thanks for letting me color."

The kitchen door opened again. This time it was a stranger. The man's dark brown hair was short. She'd never been enamored with the clipped look, but it made his steel-blue eyes stand out.

She arranged her hair so it draped over her shoulder.

"Am I in the right place?" the stranger asked.

"You are. Kaden, come in." Abby took his hand and pulled him into the center of the kitchen. "I was afraid you'd changed your mind about dinner."

The hottie shook his head. "No, just my clothes."

He wasn't dressed in jeans or shorts like the other men. He wore nice Dockers and a polo. Not the best quality, but not the worst, either.

Cheryl handed Courtney her prosecco. Turning

to the stranger—Kaden—Cheryl asked, "How is Nigel doing?"

Nigel. The name rang a bell. Was that the old guy who worked for the B and B?

"Complaining he wants to go home."

"Oh, dear." Cheryl bit her lip. "He can't. He needs physical therapy, right?"

Kaden nodded.

Courtney wished she'd worn one of the sundresses still packed in her bags, but her white top and coral capri pants were dressier than any other woman's outfit in the room. She moved toward the cluster of people standing near the table, swaying her hips a little.

"Hi, Courtney." Dolley nodded in her direction, no smile on her face.

"Courtney," Bess said. "I didn't know you were here."

The two Fitzgerald sisters looked at her, waiting for an explanation. Courtney wouldn't let her teeth grind. "I surprised Gray."

"Oh." Bess shoved her long red ponytail over her shoulder. Didn't the Fitzgeralds realize men preferred women's hair to be cascading around their breasts? It fueled their imaginations.

Liam wrapped his arm around Dolley's waist. One of the twin brothers set a hand on Bess's shoulder.

"Daniel, you remember Gray's sister?" Bess asked.

He nodded, drinking his beer.

"Good to see you again, Daniel," Courtney lied. Twin One identified.

Everyone stared at her. Were they waiting for her to speak? Or was it her clothes? Could she help it if she was beautiful? Sure, the Fitzgerald women had their...charm. But she'd been taught to highlight her assets.

"People, meet Kaden." Abby introduced him to everyone, even Cheryl—an employee—and Nathan, Twin Two, who was apparently engaged to Cheryl and father of Issy.

When Abby introduced her, Courtney set her hand in Kaden's, letting her fingers linger. "Lovely to meet you."

His eyebrows arched a fraction. "Nice to meet you."

Oh, my. Her belly did a lovely slow roll. He was a good-looking man.

Kaden turned and said something to Daniel.

She let her hand slip to her side. Her breath hitched on a bubble of panic. Men didn't turn away from her.

Everyone talked in groups, excluding her. They talked in shorthand. She couldn't keep up. Courtney rolled her shoulders. Who cared? These people weren't part of her world.

"Let's eat," Abby said.

Cheryl and Abby laughed and talked as they brought platters and bowls to the table. Everyone was part of a conversation. Everyone but her. Even Kaden slipped into the flow.

She waited until someone told her where to sit, then glided into the chair next to Josh. Since she sat directly across from Kaden, maybe she could figure out why he hadn't flirted with her.

She waited through grace, then passed dishes, asking Josh, "Can I serve you?"

He nodded and pointed to a large piece of fish on the platter. "I caught a big fish on the Fourth of July."

"You did?"

"Yeah. A red fish. My mom cooked it." He added quinoa salad to his plate and passed the bowl to her. "It was the biggest fish of the day."

"That must have been fun," she said. "I've never fished before."

His brown eyes went big and his mouth dropped open. "Mr. Gray, why hasn't your sister ever fished?"

Gray glanced over. "My sister doesn't fish."

"That's just wrong," Josh insisted.

Gray winked at him. "She might mess up her hair or clothes."

Everyone laughed. *At her.*

Heat spread across Courtney's face. "Father never took me fishing," she explained.

There'd been so many boundaries in her life. Fishing was something only Gray and dear old Dad had done. It was not one of the restrictions she'd wanted to breach.

"I can teach you." The kid looked from under his long blond eyelashes up at Daniel. "If we can take Uncle Daniel's boat out."

"Josh," Cheryl admonished.

"I guess we could fish from shore somewhere." The boy shot an innocent look at Courtney. "Do you wanna go tomorrow?"

This time she laughed with everyone. "I don't think so."

She joked with Josh and ate a fabulous dinner because, of course, her brother had married someone who was not only a businesswoman, but also an incredible chef. What sister wouldn't be miffed that her sister-in-law overshadowed her in everything? Except beauty.

She glanced across the table. Kaden wasn't even trying to attract her attention. Her stomach churned around the small bites of food she'd been able to swallow. She couldn't take his indifference any longer. "Did you grow up in Savannah?"

Kaden looked up from his plate. "What?"

"Did you grow up here?"

"I spent most of my childhood down on Tybee."

Josh leaned over the table. "I bet you fished down there."

"My grandfather and I fished." A smile broke across Kaden's face, a dimple appearing on his cheek. My, my. He was handsome. "We'd take his boat into the intercoastal waters."

"I don't know what that is, but can you take me fishing?" Josh asked Kaden.

"As much fun as that sounds, I'm here to take care of my grandfather."

"What happened to Nigel?" Courtney could almost pull up an image of a dapper older man with thick white hair.

Kaden's smile slipped away. "He broke his hip."

"Oh." That didn't sound good. "Is he okay?"

"He came through surgery well." Kaden shook his head. "Now he needs physical therapy and time to heal."

She nodded, not really understanding what healing from a broken hip entailed. "How is he handling being hospitalized?"

"He's not in the hospital anymore. He's in a rehabilitation center."

"Oh." She was so out of her depth.

"I like Nigel." Josh bounced a little in his chair. "He let me help paint the walls."

"Yeah. He's a good guy." Kaden's face softened.

"I know Nigel told us you live in Atlanta, but what do you do there?" Gray asked.

Kaden blinked. "I followed his example."

"Construction?" Gray waved his hand around the table. "We'll have to talk."

"So how long are you staying?" Dolley called down the table.

Courtney waited for Kaden to answer.

"Courtney?" Dolley asked.

"Oh, me?" She shook her head. "I'm not sure. A couple of weeks?"

"You're not sure? Oh, right. You don't have a job to go back to," Dolley said snippily.

"No, I don't. I miss my brother. I saw him a lot more when he lived in Boston." Courtney hoped she sounded convincing. "If the mountain won't come to Mohammad…"

The three Fitzgerald sisters' reddish-blond eyebrows went up at the same time. Dolley said under her breath, "Well, bless your heart."

"We're glad you're here," Abby choked out, glancing at Dolley.

"Thank you." She knew what Dolley meant. The bitch. They didn't want her here. Well, news flash, she didn't want to be here, either.

Everyone returned to their conversations, excluding her again. She didn't care about remodeling or houses or Abby's restaurant. Even Josh focused on Kaden and fishing.

Would dinner never end? *Please, Mother; I want to come home. Convince Father to let me out of purgatory.*

CHAPTER THREE

COURTNEY'S FLASHING BLUE eyes haunted Kaden as he headed up the Carleton House stairs to his room. She was a beautiful woman, but she knew it. Her moves were choreographed down to each flip of her hair. Was there anything interesting behind her stunning jewel-like eyes?

Kaden tugged off his shirt and threw it into the closet, then patted his full stomach. He couldn't remember eating a better meal. No wonder his granddad raved about Abby's cooking and hospitality. The Fitzgeralds were great. They'd invited him, a stranger, to a family dinner.

The sisters and their partners had all visited his granddad. Every day someone brought him food, flowers or company.

How did Courtney fit in? It was obvious she and Gray were related, but she had that uppity Boston accent he'd heard only when training at Quantico.

He slid open his phone and called Roger, updating him on his conversation with Nathan.

"So Forester hasn't seen Bole since she left her kid two months ago?" Roger asked. "That's hard to believe."

"I believe it. The woman let her daughter come to a gun battle."

"But two months without seeing her kid." Roger

rattled the ice in his glass, probably bourbon at this time of night.

"We never thought she was a devoted mother." Kaden pulled a water bottle from the fridge in his suite.

"What if you stayed near the B and B? Heather has to come back sometime. If you're there, you could grab her."

"I'm here for my granddad."

"I thought he was doing well," Roger said.

"He is, but broken hips are dangerous."

"I've met your grandfather. He doesn't act like a seventy-five-year-old."

"He stills needs to heal." Kaden opened the French doors and stood on the balcony, staring down at the courtyard. The scent of flowers and growing plants filled the humid night. If he could smell the ocean, he'd be home.

"You have plenty of vacation available, but both you and Heather's kid are staying at the B and B." Roger exhaled. "Maybe you can do both."

"What about Margaret?" Kaden asked.

"This is our case. My ex doesn't need to know you're there until we make an arrest."

Kaden took a deep breath. It *was* their case. He wanted to keep Issy safe. Not by being her bodyguard, but by locking up her mother. "You know I don't…work well with kids."

Silence filled the line. "Losing the Malcolm twins wasn't your fault. It was a kidnapping."

Kaden closed his eyes, but it didn't stop the bloody crime scene photos of the little boys from filling his head. If he'd made the money drop sooner, linked the gardener faster, maybe the twins would still be alive. "I don't want to be responsible for a child's life."

"Then think about this assignment as finding the mother. It's Bole we want."

Bole. Did his need to get her off the street outweigh his fear that children got hurt under his watch?

"This keeps you on the team," Roger said.

He gripped the railing. "Is that a threat?"

"I need all the man power I can muster to clear drugs off the street." Roger didn't expand on his threat.

Kaden punched the pillar. He was not getting booted from the task force. No way.

"I'll talk to my grandfather."

COURTNEY TOOK ANOTHER SIP, but her prosecco had gone flat. "Mother, you have to get Father to relent."

"Courtney, he just discovered your car was repaired before you left for Savannah."

"It's those stupid gates." She headed deeper into the garden. "Can't you suggest he have them moved farther apart?"

"No one else has trouble with the gates." Her mother's voice was more stern than normal.

Courtney scuffed her toes along the stone walk.

"That doesn't mean they're not a problem. But this time I swerved for an animal."

"Courtney." There was a scolding tone in her mother's voice.

"It's the truth. An animal jumped out and I swerved."

"Of course." Her mother sighed. "I think you should stick with your plan and work for your brother. Your father isn't budging."

"Tell Daddy I'm sorry about the car. I'll watch for animals and be more careful turning the corner." But she wasn't going to commit to working for her brother. By escaping to Savannah, she was buying herself time. That was it. "I'll call tomorrow. Please work on Daddy."

"It's best if I let the issue rest. Besides, he's traveling for the next few days."

"A few days? But I want to come home." What was she supposed to do in the meantime? "He's not coming to Savannah, is he?"

"He's heading to Toronto and then Montreal."

"Good." She didn't want Father and Gray comparing notes. "I'll talk to you later."

"Think about the direction of your life. Think about what makes you happy," Mother said, before saying goodbye.

Happy? The direction of her life? Ever since Father had practically ignored her getting on the high-school honor roll, her life had been circular. She'd worked so hard to make straight As. Dear old Dad had dismissed her accomplishments. Even when she'd set out to prove she was as smart as her brother, he'd scoffed at *her* dean's list accomplishment and then crowed about Gray's summa cum laude.

She tugged on her curls. The only praise he'd ever given her had been for her looks. Right after college she'd tried modeling, but the agency had suggested she lose ten pounds. Not going to happen.

She sank onto a bench. Laughter floated from a Fitzgerald House balcony. The fountain splashed. A cricket chirped near Carleton House and something scurried through the bushes.

Shouldn't these sounds be soothing? Instead, they highlighted how alone she was. Mother wanted her to find direction? She didn't want to think that deeply. She just wanted to go home.

What made her happy? Coloring with the kids had made her happy. Chatting with Josh at dinner had made her happy. Did that mean she wanted to be a mother?

She shook her head. At twenty-six she was too young to think about having children. And the idea of marriage… She rolled her shoulders, but couldn't get rid of the itch at the base of her neck.

There wasn't a man she'd dated longer than a month or two. No one held her attention. Most groveled too much, or were more interested in getting close to her father or Gray. Some only wanted her as arm candy.

She tapped her nail against the bench. But not Kaden Farrell. He'd barely glanced at her all through dinner. That never happened.

Kaden's dimple had only appeared when he'd talked about fishing and his grandfather. She shuddered at the thought of slimy fish making someone happy.

Mother wanted her to find her direction? If she had to hide in Savannah, she would get Mr. Kaden Farrell to look in her direction and ask her out. That shouldn't be so hard.

KADEN HANDED HIS granddad a towel.

"Thanks." Granddad wiped his upper lip. "Wouldn't want the ladies to see me sweat from my physical therapy."

"You already have a fan club?"

"There are some lovely ladies here." His grandfather settled into the wheelchair. "But I told you, you don't have to spend all day with me. Head back to Atlanta. I don't want to pull you away from your work."

"I want to be here." Kaden had so much to live up to. Granddad always put other people's needs first. He pushed the wheelchair into the sunroom. "Want something to drink?"

"Water, please. My therapist might be lovely, but she's a dictator."

Kaden laughed and headed to the coffeepot. He poured a mug for himself and then a glass of water.

"Thanks." His grandfather took a long drink. "What's on your mind?"

"How do you do that?" Kaden asked.

Granddad pointed between Kaden's eyebrows. "Whenever you want to discuss something, or something's weighing on you, you get this crease between your eyebrows. I wouldn't suggest you ever try gambling. It's a big tell."

"I'll remember not to play poker with you." He pulled up a chair so they sat facing each other.

"What's bothering you?"

"You know Issy from the B and B?" Kaden asked.

"Sweet thing. Nathan's daughter. Little girl doesn't say much. Mother just up and dropped her off." Nigel shook his head. "Never told Nathan about her."

"She's...connected with one of my cases."

"Issy?"

"No. The mother."

Understanding broke across his granddad's face. "The mother's in the drug world?"

Kaden nodded. "We're pretty sure Issy witnessed a murder right before the mother dropped her off with Forester."

"Poor kid." Granddad closed his eyes. "Thank goodness Nathan has her now."

Kaden took a deep breath. "My boss thinks the mother will come back for Issy."

"You can't let that happen. You know what her life must have been like." Granddad's fingers squeezed around his wrist. "Will the Bureau protect her?"

"They asked me to do that."

"Perfect." Granddad clapped his hands. "That's better than watching my PT."

"I'm supporting you."

"And I appreciate that, but you can't watch me 24/7." Granddad snapped his fingers. "You know what you could do?"

Kaden frowned. "What?"

"Take over my B and B duties. You've got the skills. You could help the sisters and stay close to Issy."

Take over Granddad's work? "But I'm here for you."

"Haven't you been telling me I'm right where I belong? You're twiddling your thumbs when you could be working to make sure that little girl is safe." Nigel slapped the arm of the wheelchair. "Put that mother away and get those drugs off the street."

Kaden swallowed. "You're the only family I have left."

"I know and I'm so sorry." Granddad caught his hand and held on. "I should have worked harder to find you and your brother. I will always regret that. I was so mad at your mother for being weak."

Kaden was still mad at his parents for being drug addicts. After his grandfather had taken him in, they'd both died of overdoses.

"You have a chance to make sure this little girl doesn't go through what you went through." Granddad's slate-blue eyes were filled with regret. "You can make a difference. Make up for my screwup."

"You didn't screw up. My parents did." And so had he. He hadn't kept his brother safe. Could he keep Issy safe or would he make the same mistake? "I'd have to work undercover."

"I've never told anyone what you do—just like you asked."

"The secrecy policy is for the safety of our families. I would never forgive myself if someone hurt you because of me." Kaden rubbed the back of his neck. "The Fitzgeralds think I followed in your footsteps for work."

"Construction?"

"That's what they assumed." Kaden squeezed his grandfather's hand. "Saving people is what I meant."

"It's important that you do this." Smiling, Granddad touched his heart.

Love warmed his soul. "I love you, too."

"If you have the possibility of getting one more drug ring out of commission," Granddad said, "that's more important than pushing my wheelchair around this rehab center."

"I'll…think about it." But with Granddad's support, Kaden already knew the answer. He was going to keep his eye on Isabella Forester.

"You want to pick up Nigel's duties while he's healing?" Abby pushed the plate of cookies and bars closer to him and topped off his coffee.

"It was my grandfather's suggestion." Kaden picked up a tiny filled cookie. "He's worried about the B and B."

"Nigel is so thoughtful."

"I think so."

"Okay." Abby tapped the table. "You could move into the apartment next to Cheryl and Nathan."

"Where's that?"

She pointed across the courtyard. "The second story of the carriage house."

"But I thought a restaurant was going in there?" He took a bite and raspberries, cream and sugar filled his mouth. He moaned and took another cookie.

"The restaurant takes up about half of the building." She pushed her ponytail off her shoulder. "If it really takes off, we'll expand to the remainder of the first floor. But right now there's an empty apartment."

"That would be great."

"There are two bedrooms, but no washer and

dryer." Abby grinned. "And one bedroom has this incredible princess-and-castle mural. You should like that."

"Right." He couldn't help smiling. Abby was the kind of woman who made a man relax. Unlike her sister-in-law, Courtney. "Let me show you the apartment." Abby pulled a key from a rack.

He followed her across the courtyard and past a set of stairs. "When does the restaurant open?"

"Nathan has promised I'll be able to have a guest week right after Labor Day." She unlocked a side door. "I'll open the week after that."

They headed up wooden steps that creaked and moaned. "Good security."

"What?" She frowned.

"Creaking stairs. Hard to sneak up on anyone." She laughed, but he wasn't kidding.

Abby unlocked the door and flipped on the light. "There's furniture, too."

The apartment was clean and included a reasonable-size living room and a small kitchen, including a table. The first bedroom was indeed fit for a princess. The mural was a work of art. A castle filled one corner of the wall. Princesses in bright gowns danced on a hill with bunnies and ponies.

"You can sleep in here." Her eyes twinkled.

Kaden just shook his head. "Let's see the other room."

The bed in there was large.

"This should work. Thank you."

Abby handed him a key. "I should let Nathan know I won't need his crew to fill in at the B and B."

"I can do that." It gave Kaden a chance to tell Nathan his real purpose.

Abby headed back to Fitzgerald House and Kaden went down to the restaurant and found Nathan.

"Any place we can talk in private?" Kaden asked.

"Sure." Frowning, Nathan led him to a room behind the bar. "What's up? Is there news on Heather?"

"No, but since I'm here, my superior wants me to keep an eye on Issy. We think Bole will come back for her daughter."

Nathan paced the long narrow room. "I won't let her near Issy."

"Understood. But if the only access to Isabella is here, I want to be around to catch Bole." And put the evil woman away. "That's why I'm taking over my grandfather's duties at the B and B."

"Good, good. I want her safe." Nathan tugged off his cap and ran a hand through his hair. "Issy's just coming out of her shell. I don't want that bitch anywhere near her. What do you need from me?"

"Her schedule." Kaden nodded. "I'd like to talk to the person in charge of her day care and any other place she goes each day."

"Of course." Nathan's voice cracked.

"I'll be undercover. No one can know I'm with the FBI."

Nathan winced. "I can't keep this from Cheryl."

Kaden tapped his fingers against his thigh. "Will she keep this secret?"

"She can. She will," Nathan vowed.

"Fine. I should spend more time with Issy." He didn't let Nathan see the shiver that ran down his back. "Maybe tonight?"

"Let's have dinner again," Nathan suggested. "That way she'll know you're a good guy."

"Okay." This better not be a mistake. He didn't want Issy hurt. Not on his watch.

"COURTNEY?" GRAY CALLED. "Let's go."

"Almost ready." She rubbed lotion on her pink skin. She'd sat in the garden reading, not noticing the time. Apparently, she'd stayed past her sunscreen expiration. She cringed at the idea of getting wrinkles or dry flaky sun-toughened skin. Mother would have scolded her soundly.

She'd gotten about half of her clothes unpacked, including the sundress she wore today, and then started reading and that was that. The book was wicked good.

Don't use that expression. It is not how we talk.

Well, she wasn't *wicked smart* like Gray.

She dressed and headed down the hall. Time to face her brother.

Gray waited in the entry, wearing a slate-blue

polo shirt and shorts with enough pockets in them to go wilderness hiking. He stood with his legs spread, his arms crossed and a scowl on his face.

She blurted out, "You look like Father."

"Thank you." He raised one black eyebrow over his blue eyes, eyes that were the same color as the ones she saw in the mirror every day. It wasn't fair. She couldn't achieve her brother's lush eyelashes without careful layers of mascara.

As they moved through the courtyard, Gray waved at two couples sitting at a small table.

"Do you know them?"

"They're guests."

But customer service was Abby's job. She frowned, then blurted out, "You're…different here."

"What do you mean?"

She pushed out a breath. "When you and Gwen were dating, she always complained you never made time to do the things she wanted to do."

"Gwen didn't acknowledge I worked for a living." He snorted. "I couldn't be at her beck and call for parties and outings."

It still irritated Courtney that he'd thrown over her best friend for a gold-digging Fitzgerald sister. She and Gwen had grown up together. They were best—

Courtney blinked. She hadn't spoken to Gwen since leaving Boston. Shouldn't her best friend have checked in? Told her how devastated she was without her?

What were her friends doing? She hadn't checked social media, not wanting to know life continued while she hid in Georgia.

She and Gray stepped into Fitzgerald House. The kitchen bustled and the smells were amazing. It reminded Courtney of her favorite Mexican restaurant over in Back Bay. Salad plates lined every surface and Cheryl, Abby and someone she didn't recognize worked side by side.

"Hey, handsome," Abby called out.

"How's the event going?" Gray asked.

"They loved the appetizers. Salad course is going up now." Abby tipped her head and Gray bent and dropped a kiss on her lips.

"We'll head into the library." Gray brushed hair off Abby's cheek. "We could eat someplace else."

"Give me a half hour or so." Abby nodded at Cheryl. "Nathan and the kids are coming. And Kaden will be here, too."

Kaden. The handyman's hot grandson. Courtney straightened her shoulders. Time to get her flirt on.

"Come on, brat." Gray moved to the swinging door. "We need to talk about why you're *really* here in Savannah."

Uh-oh. She didn't let the irritation in Gray's voice alter her small smile.

In the library she stalled, perusing the offerings. Peeking at Gray's stony expression, all she wanted was a drink and a place to hide. Preferably in Boston.

She put an enchilada on her plate and added a stuffed pepper, chips and salsa. When she spotted a pitcher of margaritas, she poured a glass. Hard alcohol might get her through Gray's inquisition.

"Front parlor." He didn't wait for her response, just led the way, carrying his own plate, and took an armchair. She sat on the edge of a small sofa, across the coffee table from him.

"This smells so good." She took a chip and ran it through the salsa. "Num. Your wife is so talented."

"Don't suck up. I know your tricks." His gaze was glacial. "When were you going to ask me about a job?"

Never. She sampled her drink and let the sweet taste slide down. Darn it, Abby even made great mixed drinks. "A job?"

He leaned across the table. "I talked to Father."

"Oh." She needed to regroup. "Mother's working on him. He'll relent."

"I don't think so." He sipped his drink. "Father wanted to know how you were working out."

"Just fine. It was a long drive, but I'm recovering." She looked at her brother over the rim of the glass.

"He wanted to know how you were settling into my new office." He pointed at her with a stuffed jalapeño. "Stop playing stupid. You know what I'm talking about."

She shoved her plate out of the way and stood. She paced to the doorway and back. Maybe she'd taken the wrong tack. Maybe Gray could help her out of this mess. "He was mad because of some shoes. *Shoes.*"

"Five thousand dollars' worth of shoes."

She waved her hand. "You have to pay for quality."

"And you ran into the gate again."

She slipped back into her seat. "It was because of an animal this time."

"Right." Exasperation wrinkled his face. "You have to *do* something with your life."

"With my fabulous literature degree?" She rolled her eyes.

"*You* chose your major," he snapped.

"But I didn't choose my school."

"Sure you did." He frowned. "You chose Mother's alma mater."

"I wanted Yale." She bit her lip.

"With our history there—" his black eyebrows formed a straight line "—you didn't get in?"

"I *was* accepted." Of course her brother would think that she hadn't had the grades, that she hadn't been smart enough. "I test very well."

Gray rattled his drink. "I don't understand."

"Father wouldn't allow me to go to Yale because

I wasn't a *serious student*." She stared at her food, not wanting to see the pity on Gray's face.

"I didn't know. I would have argued for you. Helped you." Gray tipped up her chin with his finger, forcing her to stare into sympathy-filled eyes. "But that doesn't mean you couldn't have had a different degree program."

Arguing with Father for months on end had sucked the motivation right out of her.

"So, you're working for me." He tapped her nose.

It was something he'd done when she was young, when she'd been upset. He'd been good at cheering her up. She tried to smile. "I could lay low until Mother convinces Father that this is ridiculous."

"You work for me, or you leave." He forked a piece of enchilada into his mouth. "Since I haven't finished the build-out on my office space, we'll work out of the house. You start tomorrow."

He would make her leave? "Can't you tell Father I work for you, but I don't actually do anything?"

"No." Pity filled his face again. "We start at seven thirty. That means you're up, moving and have eaten your breakfast."

"Lovely." She had to keep this from happening.

He pointed at her plate. "Are you going to eat that?"

Her appetite was gone. "It's all yours."

She headed into the library and refilled her margarita glass. Lord let her catch a horrible disease by tomorrow.

KADEN STEPPED INTO the Fitzgerald House kitchen and sniffed. Then sniffed again. His mouth watered at the scent of peppers, limes, tomatoes and onions.

Nathan waved from the table. "You got my message."

"Hey, Kaden." Abby set a dish on the table. "Grab a chair."

He took a seat across from Issy, hoping she would get comfortable with him.

Gray and his sister came in through the swinging door. Damn, Courtney was gorgeous. His system absorbed the hit of her beauty like Kevlar absorbed the energy of a bullet.

Courtney's gaze slipped over to him. She looked shell-shocked. Then her smile emerged like a mask. Odd. She hadn't smiled much last night.

Gray sat next to Kaden and slapped him on the back. "Good to see you again."

"Thanks."

"Kaden's taking on Nigel's duties while he's recuperating," Abby called over. "He'll stay in the carriage house apartment."

Cheryl pulled out pans of enchiladas from the oven and nodded to Kaden. "It will be nice to have you nearby."

Courtney's pretty mouth dropped open. "Don't you have a job?"

"I'm...between assignments."

Her lips pursed, making an almost perfect pink

circle. She touched a line forming above her eyebrows and it disappeared. "You're a handyman?"

She made it sound like it was worse than selling drugs on the street.

"I learned from the best," he said. "My granddad."

Gray glared at his sister. "Abby will feel better knowing you're handling Nigel's work."

Kaden turned away from Courtney's derision and back to Issy. "I saw the beautiful mural in your old bedroom. Did you paint it?"

She giggled. "Daddy did."

Josh stuck his thumb to his chest. "I helped."

"It's wonderful." And pink. Very pink.

"Daddy's painting a mural in our new house," she whispered.

"Your daddy's very talented," Kaden said.

She tipped her head against her father's chest. "I love Daddy."

How could Heather have ever put this little girl in jeopardy?

"Eat," Abby insisted. "Your next course is almost up."

They dug in. Kaden asked Issy about school, but Josh answered for her.

Courtney caught his eye from across the table and winked at him. Winked? What was going on? Then she put her hand on Josh's arm and asked, "How did you learn to draw so well?"

Courtney and Josh tucked their heads together, leaving Kaden free to talk to Issy. He envied Courtney's ease with the kids.

"So when do you go to kindergarten?" he asked Issy.

"Not 'til I'm…" She held up her hand, fingers spread out.

Her father rubbed the girl's back.

"Five?" Kaden asked, to keep the conversation going.

She nodded and ate more of the mouthwatering food Abby and Cheryl kept bringing to the table.

What else could he ask a kid? "Josh says you're getting a puppy when you move."

Issy nodded. "Like Carly."

He shook his head. "Who's Carly?"

Nathan explained, "My brother's dog."

"Love Carly," Issy whispered. The kid never spoke very loud.

"That should be nice."

"We won't get a dog that big, right, short stuff?" her father said.

The girl tipped her head at her father and batted her eyes. "Maybe."

Everyone at the table broke out laughing. Even Courtney. He frowned. She hadn't laughed the previous night. She'd worn a stunned expression on her beautiful face. Now it was more…sultry. He'd never described a woman that way.

With a head full of ebony curls and brilliant blue eyes, Kaden imagined Courtney had flaunted her own childhood cuteness. She'd probably wrapped adults around her finger back then and men now.

Gray and Nathan talked about the restaurant construction. Courtney chatted away with Josh.

Kaden was stumped. How did you talk to a kid? What else could they talk about?

"Josh, no drawing at the table." Cheryl brought something fragrant to the table. *"Pollo verde."*

"What's going on?" he asked Abby.

"There's an engagement party in the ballroom."

"That's why we're eating here," Nathan added. "Abby and Cheryl always make enough to feed the crew so we benefit."

"And Mrs. Gonzalez gave me some of her family recipes." Abby wiggled her eyebrows. "The *pollo verde* is hers."

Gonzalez? His body went on alert. Gonzalez family members were lieutenants in the Salvez cartel. The father, Jose, had worked his way up to underboss. Was it possible cartel members were in the Fitzgerald House ballroom celebrating?

He touched the gun under his shirt. He couldn't overlook the possibility that Hector Salvez might be upstairs with Heather Bole. His heart pounded.

Kaden slid away from the table. "Excuse me."

Stepping next to Abby, he whispered, "Nigel said

one of my jobs will be to set up for events. Do you mind if I peek into the ballroom?"

Her reddish-blond eyebrows snapped together. "Sure."

"Third floor?"

She nodded.

"Let me take you up," Cheryl volunteered. "I can see how things are going."

"Thanks."

Cheryl led him to a back stairway. As they neared the third floor, she asked, "Does this have to do with Issy?"

What could he reveal? "*Gonzalez* is a name associated with the case. It's a long shot, but it's possible Salvez, Bole's partner, is here."

Cheryl swallowed. "Do you think Heather is here?"

"Only one way to find out."

In the service hallway, trays of stainless steel covers and dirty dishes were neatly stacked on carts. The muffled clinking of silverware and the hum of voices came through the door. "How many guests?"

"The estimate was one hundred." She swung open the door.

"Will I be able to see most of them from here?"

"About half. We can stop here and then go around to the ballroom doors."

Stepping inside, he scanned the ballroom, looking for any of the faces he'd memorized from the

Mexican cartels operating in Georgia. He didn't recognize anyone. And no sign of Bole, either.

"Let's check from the entrance," he said.

The main doors were open. And at least one man looked familiar.

There were two tables of adults near the back, with two older men at each table. No one noticed as he zoomed in with his phone camera.

"That's all I needed."

Now he had to wait to see the actual photos. And he wasn't good at waiting.

COURTNEY SWIRLED HER GLASS, but her margarita was gone. The glass clinked as she set it on the courtyard table.

Look what her life had come to. She couldn't remember ever drinking alone. All because of dear old Dad. Gray insisted she be ready to work at seven thirty—in the morning. Back home she wouldn't get up until nine or later.

She missed her friends, missed Boston and missed a home where she didn't have to think about getting up at dawn. "Damn it! Why is my life so screwed up?"

Footsteps echoed along the path. They stopped on the other side of the hedge and a hand reached through. A deep voice asked, "Everything all right?"

The handyman.

"Just…getting away from the lovebirds." She jerked her head up to Gray and Abby's window.

Kaden came around the plants and scanned the area. "Were you talking…to yourself?"

Here was someone to take her mind off her troubles. The soft lighting in Bess's garden set a seductive mood. It barely lit her quarry, the hot Mr. Kaden Farrell.

She shook her hair so it cascaded over one shoulder. She excelled at wrapping men around her finger. "My life is in a bit of an upheaval right now."

His eyebrows lowered. "That's hard to imagine."

She moved closer, swinging her hips. "I'm bored. I don't suppose you know of any nightclubs or someplace we could have some fun?"

She set her hand on his chest. His muscles bunched under her fingers. She smoothed her hand up to his shoulder. Nice.

"I don't have fun." He caught her hand and pushed it away.

She stumbled into his body and looked up into his icy blue eyes.

His gaze flicked down to her lips and stayed there.

Her stomach fluttered. The hum of attraction was so much nicer than wallowing about having to work for Gray. She licked her upper lip. His nostrils flared. She stood on her toes so he wouldn't have to bend too low to kiss her.

He stepped back. "Stop."

Kaden was rejecting her? A handyman? She wanted to curl into a ball and hide. Instead, she whispered, "Stop?"

"I'm not here to entertain you." He set a heavy hand on her shoulder, keeping her from moving closer.

"But we could… You're a long way from Atlanta. Don't you want…" *Me?* She never stumbled and stammered.

"It's late and I need to…rest."

He was making excuses? This couldn't be happening. A handyman!

"No one ignores me," she whispered. Louder, she snapped, "Just…just…stay out of my way."

He pointed at her. "You've got it."

A man had never looked at her with that kind of…animosity. The bushes rustled as he stomped away.

She slumped against the nearby palm tree. Why was her life out of control? She'd been ready to kiss him, and he'd shut her down.

The jerk! No man did that. Not to her. Somehow, she would figure out how to bring Mr. Kaden Farrell to heel.

And then she would treat him like the dog he was.

CHAPTER FOUR

KADEN WHEELED HIS bag around the spot where Courtney had come on to him. Unbelievable. Just one more reason to ignore the way his body reacted to her.

Courtney was *bored*.

He was *not* here to distract a spoiled rich girl, even if she was gorgeous.

Hell. He'd almost kissed Courtney. She'd pressed up on her toes and her lush lips had been a whisper away.

He didn't need a distraction like her. This undercover assignment was too important. He needed 100 percent of his energy focused on capturing Heather Bole. That meant ignoring Courtney.

He used the key Abby had given him to unlock the carriage house side door. The lock was so flimsy, he could have opened it with his credit card.

After trucking his bags upstairs and down the hall, he unlocked another flimsy lock. Home for the next little while.

The B and B's cleaning crew had been through the apartment. Everything was spotless and smelled clean—not bleach, but something tangy.

Granddad had been thrilled Kaden was helping at the B and B. He wanted Kaden to take care of the Fitzgeralds. And he no longer felt guilty about occupying a Carleton House guest room.

After unpacking, he set his computer on the kitchen table. As much as he would like to use the second bedroom as an office, the pink mural would be too distracting.

He opened the file of pictures he'd taken last night. Zooming in, he focused on scars and visible tattoos, trying to match the faces with known drug dealers or cartel members. Nothing.

But he forwarded the file to the team. They could run the pictures against their database, just in case his memory was failing him.

He rolled his neck and the vertebrae cracked. He'd visited his grandfather. Packed and moved. Checked faces. Now what? He always had a backlog of tasks needing his attention at the Bureau. This not working was…unsettling.

Time to check on what Abby needed.

He headed down the stairs. Muffled voices and hammer strikes echoed through the wall. Nathan's crew was working on the restaurant.

Curious, he headed around the building and ducked through the open door. Letting his eyes adjust to the dim light, he waited. Nathan and three men walked a frame into place on the wall that looked out to the courtyard.

"Be with you in a minute," Nathan grunted as they shifted, leveled and added shims.

Kaden relaxed as Nathan's team worked together.

Screw guns squealed. Then they set glass doors into tracks in the framing.

"Got this?" Nathan asked one of the crew.

"Yup," the man drawled.

Nathan swiped off his hat, pushed back his hair and jammed his cap back on. Then he headed to where Kaden leaned against a pillar.

"Great idea, having windows looking into the courtyard." Kaden nodded at the windows. "People will love looking out while they eat."

"Abby can open them, too." Nathan took a slug of water and splashed some on his neck. "And Bess is extending the patio, so there can be outdoor seating. It was Nigel's idea."

"My grandfather's?"

"Yes." Nathan stared at him. "But I doubt you came by to talk about Abby's patio windows," he whispered. "Anything pop in the photos you took?"

"No." Kaden kept his voice low. "I didn't recognize anyone, but I sent the photos to the team."

"Good."

The crew laughed, opening and closing the windows.

Nathan called over, "Guys, there's another set of doors to install."

"Sure thing, boss," someone hollered.

"Anything you need?" Nathan asked.

Kaden jerked his head to the ceiling. "I've moved in."

"That's a relief." Nathan's shoulders relaxed a little.

"Are you replacing the locks on the exterior door and apartment?" Kaden asked.

Nathan frowned. "Why?"

"Flimsy. I could open them with a credit card." And if he could, any felon would know the trick.

"I'll take a look," Nathan said.

Kaden waved his hand. "What kind of security is going in the restaurant?"

Nathan's knees popped as he stood up. "I can show you the plans."

"Thanks," Kaden said. "I'd also like to add cameras around the B and B."

"You really think Heather will show up?" Nathan's hands formed fists.

He hoped not. Not with the company she was keeping. Everywhere Salvez went, he left a trail of bodies. "If she does, I want to be forewarned."

Nathan's tan face paled. "I'll do what's necessary to keep Issy safe."

Kaden clasped his shoulder. "Is there some way to ensure Abby and her sisters don't get suspicious if I add extra cameras?"

Nathan paced. "I'll…figure out something to tell them."

"FBI will provide the cameras and software. I'll place the equipment. Can you tell Abby I've done security installations in Atlanta?"

"Sure."

Kaden left Nathan and headed across the courtyard to the Fitzgerald House kitchen, already creating an inventory of the equipment he needed. Roger should be able to overnight what was required unless he wanted Kaden to tap the Savannah department. He snorted. Not a chance. His boss wanted Kaden's presence in Savannah kept quiet.

He knocked on the door and stepped into a heavenly smelling kitchen. He picked out BBQ, sugar, spices and something earthy.

Abby sat at the table with an open notebook. "Did you get settled?"

He nodded. "Not much to unpack."

She put down her pen. "What can I do for you?"

"Can you let me know what my granddad was working on?"

"Absolutely." Her green eyes lit up. "Let me show you Nigel's system."

She moved to a set of cubbyholes next to the back door and pulled out a wad of paper. "We leave notes for Nigel here. He has a workshop in the first basement."

Kaden followed Abby down the stairs and waited for her to open the room. A table saw occupied the corner. Along the wall, batteries charged next to electric drills and screwdrivers. Even through the scent of sawed wood, he caught a hint of Granddad's aftershave, that odd combination of sandalwood, ambergris and verbena. Calm swept over him like a hug.

Above a counter, tools hung in their pegboard outlines. The shelving held various wood trims and paint cans labeled in his granddad's bold print. He picked up a can—Julia Grant. The next was labeled Rosalynn Carter. He frowned. "What are these?"

Abby laughed. "My mama named the Fitzgerald House rooms after presidents' wives. My sisters and I named Carleton House rooms after Savannah squares."

"Right." He set the can back on the shelf.

"You'll need a master key card. It will open all the rooms in Fitzgerald and Carleton Houses." Abby made a note on the tablet she always carried. "I'll get those."

"Thanks." He stroked a finger down an ornate gilded picture frame set in a vise.

"Nigel was repairing that." Abby stepped next to the worktable. "I don't know what we'll do without him around."

"I know what you mean." He checked the bulletin board.

Paint J Kennedy bathroom
Clean gutters FH CH
Reorg Bess's storage

Okay. He might have to check with Granddad on some of these. But cleaning the gutters gave him a chance to check for camera angles.

Abby straightened her shoulders. "Let's get you set up."

In the kitchen, he sorted through the notes in Granddad's box. Kaden had worried about not having enough work? Problem solved.

"DID YOU CALL the plumber?" Gray called to Courtney from his office. "I need confirmation he'll meet me this afternoon at two."

"Not yet." She rolled her eyes, not that her brother could see.

Courtney sat at a small desk in Gray and Abby's sitting area. She flicked a finger at the printout of people to contact. He'd only given it to her thirty minutes ago. Her plan was to get through the day with minimal effort.

"I need to know they're coming," Gray called to her.

Channeling Christina Applegate in *Don't Tell Mom the Babysitter's Dead*, she lied, "I'm on it."

She turned back to her phone and glared at Gwen's Facebook feed. Her BFF had posted a ton of party pictures. Gavin, the man who for the last month had begged Courtney for a date, had his arm wrapped around Gwen's shoulders.

Courtney gritted her teeth. How could Gwen? Courtney had refused to date Gavin. His family was on the fringe of their social group. Gwen should have respected the rules they'd set on who they would date.

When she opened Instagram, more pics of Gavin and Gwen filled her feed. Her BFF hadn't even called for advice. Courtney would have told Gwen "hands off." She closed the app. Gwen and Gavin deserved each other.

Picking up Gray's list, she looked at all the people she had to call. Sucking in a breath, she dialed the first contact and waited until a man answered. "Hi, I'm calling for Gray Smythe. He wants to confirm that you'll be at—" she rattled off the office address written on the top of the page "—this afternoon at two."

"This afternoon? Are you sure?" the man asked. There was a rustle on the other end of the phone. "I've got the walk-through scheduled for…next week."

"Gray wants you there today," Courtney said.

"I guess I can be there, once I shuffle some jobs."

She then confirmed that all the vendors on the list would arrive in the afternoon.

"Done," she called to her brother.

Next she tackled boxing up the files Gray was moving to his new offices. Abby and Gray really needed servants to handle menial tasks.

She pulled open the first case and grabbed a stack of files. How much money was she making for each handful? She grabbed another and the file case tipped. She bumped the drawer closed with her hip, opened the next drawer and unloaded half of the files.

"I'm out of boxes," she said to Gray from his office doorway.

Gray didn't glance up from his computer. "There's a case next to the bookshelf."

She headed back to the sitting area. "Not here."

"You have to put the boxes together."

Courtney knelt, not an easy feat in her sheath dress. She hadn't brought clothes for this kind of activity. She ripped off the plastic wrap, then pulled out white and blue pieces of cardboard. The instructions were simple. All she needed to do was pull up flaps and fold things in.

She tugged, folded, manipulated and…voilà—a box. She grinned. "Not so hard."

Next was the lid. Slot A fitted into hole B. Easy peasy. This wasn't as hard as trying to find the perfect lipstick. She could do this.

Bringing over her first completed box, she pulled open another file drawer. After she'd tossed in the files, she grabbed the box through the handles she'd punched out. *Lift with your legs.*

Cardboard screeched against cardboard. Files and papers spilled out the bottom. "Shit. Shit. Shit."

"What?" Gray yelled.

"Nothing." She sank to the floor. *Riiipp.* The back seam of her beautiful dress gave way. "Damn it, damn it."

"What the hell is going on out here?" Her brother glowered from the doorway.

"I ripped my dress!"

"Your dress?" He pointed at the mess on the floor. "What about my files?"

"The box was defective." She kicked it.

Gray stomped over and picked up the box. With a few quick moves, he reassembled the box and handed it to her. "You have to pull up the bottom to make the base."

"I followed the directions." Hadn't she?

He rolled his eyes and assembled two more boxes. "Can you handle the lids?"

"Yes." She yanked the last box out of his hand. "I have to change first."

"Wear something more...appropriate."

Courtney stomped downstairs and flung herself on her bed. This was her normal daywear. A nice dress, in case she stopped for lunch or drinks. Was she supposed to take her fashion cues from the Fitzgeralds? If so, she'd be wearing shorts and tank tops.

Give her a cocktail party or a fund-raiser. That was her milieu. Not filing or making phone calls. Well, phone calls she could handle. But it grated on her nerves to have Gray telling her what to do.

Sighing, she stared longingly at the tiny patio off the bedroom. Could she take a minute and read a few pages of her book?

A shadow passed on the other side of the hedge. Kaden. Carrying a ladder around the back of the house.

She glared. Never had one man made her so

mad. She'd made all her signature moves; placed her hand on his chest, slithered close and stood on her toes, knowing her hair would flow free. Most men thrust their fingers through it.

Kaden had pushed her away. That would not do. She tapped her lips. Within one week that man would beg to kiss her. Then *she* would push *him* away.

She shimmied the dress over her hips. Who would sew the rip? Was she going to have to throw it away? Hanging it up, she shoved it to the back of the closet. She would deal with it later.

In her suitcase, she found sparkling white shorts more appropriate for walking the beach on Martha's Vineyard. It was that or jeans and those were as tight as the sheath that had ripped. Then she dug out a red-and-white boat shirt with elbow-length sleeves. She didn't look in the mirror. It would have to do. She didn't have clothes for working for her brother. And right now she didn't have a credit card to buy more.

Back in the sitting area, she plugged in her earbuds and flipped Beyoncé onto her phone. It was a sad reminder that she'd been to her concert, not with the sweaty, drunken masses, but in a lovely suite. Would she ever get to another concert? Rocking and swaying, she tossed papers and files into the boxes Gray had put together. Once she emptied all the file cases, she spotted a bin full of blueprints. Gray would want those moved, right?

She unrolled and folded each until they fit in the boxes. It was cumbersome, slow work.

"What the hell are you doing?" Gray's deep voice interrupted "Love Drought," the story of her life.

"Packing your files like you asked."

He rushed over and tugged the papers she'd folded out of her hand. "Why are you folding blueprints?"

"Because they're too long to fit in the box."

"I'll move them in the blueprint stand." He threw up his hands. "Roll them back up and make sure all the sheets for each project are together."

"Yes, master."

Gray glared. "I need the Rosemount warehouse files."

She pointed at all the boxes. "I packed your files."

"They were alphabetized. You should be able to find everything, right?"

Alphabetized? She could almost feel the blood drain out of her face. "Sure."

"Rosemount files first, please." He looked at the neat pile she'd made of his blueprints and rubbed his forehead.

How was she supposed to know this? Courtney popped the lid off the first box she'd packed. There was River Street. Rosemount should be behind that, right?

But the next file was Carleton House. She chewed her lip.

Ripping open box after box, she scanned file names. She should have noticed the organization. No Rosemount. Until she came to the box where she'd tossed the spilled files. Of course. She popped the lid and the first file was Rosemount Bids. Excellent.

But there weren't any papers in the file. The next file was labeled Rosemount Project Plan. And another, Invoices. The papers had scattered and she hadn't refiled them.

She pulled out stacks of loose paper and folders and made a semicircle around her on the floor. How she wished it were the children at the South Side library and not stupid papers.

She could do this. She wasn't dumb.

Most of the papers had notes in Gray's blunt handwriting. When she could decipher the contents, she set the papers on top of the proper file. After sorting, there was still a stack she couldn't figure out.

"Where are my files?" Gray called from the other room.

"All over the floor," she muttered, then yelled, "Coming."

She stuffed the identified papers inside the correct files and grabbed the stack of unfiled papers. With a toss of her head, she entered Gray's office. "They were in the box that exploded."

She set the almost-empty Rosemount files on Gray's desk. The stack of unfiled papers was taller than the file folders. "I couldn't figure out what projects these papers came from."

He flipped open the file marked Bids and picked up the single paper she'd filed. His jaw clenched. "Go through that stack and find everything from Simon Electric."

She pulled an armchair up to his desk and started flipping. This would take forever. "Why don't you hire a secretary?"

He tipped his head. "That's why you're here."

"I thought I could—" she waved her hand around the room "—help you decorate, pick paint colors. That kind of thing."

"I don't need someone to do that. I need help with paperwork."

Great. She pulled out a bill from Simon Electric and handed it to him.

"Keep looking." He snatched it from her. "There's more."

Was this how she was going to spend the rest of her days? Mother needed to fix this.

Gray wrote the file name on each piece of correspondence. She refiled it. Mindless. Boring. Even the sandwiches Abby brought over didn't ease the tension in the room.

After lunch, Gray dusted the crumbs off his hands. "Come on. Let's walk over to the office site. The plumber should be there soon."

"Walk?"

He nodded. "It's not far. One of the joys of working and living in Savannah."

"But why do I need to go there?"

"In case I need you to let in a sub." Gray shook his head. "Come on."

As they headed through the courtyard, the heat and humidity made her stagger. She sucked in a breath and pulled her hair off her neck. "How can you stand the temperature?"

Gray frowned. "You'll get used to it."

"No way." She tried to keep up with his long strides, already sweating. Why hadn't she worn a sleeveless top? With each step, the fringe of her Jimmy Choo sandals slapped her feet. "Can you slow down? I'm going to melt if you keep up this pace."

He slowed. A little. "I thought you were in better shape."

"I'm in great shape, but I'm wearing heels." A Pilates instructor came to the house three times a week.

Hopefully Marcus had contacted her instructor. Father would freak if he had to pay for classes when she wasn't even there. It would be one more lecture to endure.

"Is Father having trouble with money?" she blurted out. Everything inside her tilted like the earth's axis had jolted.

Gray stopped in the middle of one of Savannah's many squares. "What?"

"Is that why he's worried about my credit card bills? Are we broke?" That would be worse than having her cards taken away for a few weeks.

He crossed his arms. "As far as I know, he's doing quite well."

She grabbed his arm. "Would he tell you?"

Gray rubbed his temple. "Yes."

"Okay." She caught her lip between her teeth, then heard Mother's voice in her head. *Don't bite your lip.* She would ask Mother tonight if they were destitute.

Gray checked his phone. "We need to hurry."

They turned the corner. Four men blocked the sidewalk in front of a building.

"What the…?" Gray hurried toward the group.

"What's going on, Smythe?" one of the men asked.

"Why are you all here?" Gray shook out a key and opened the door. Their work boots clomped on the building's concrete floor.

This wasn't an office. She turned. It was one big empty room.

The man wearing a Dorchester Electric T-shirt said, "I got a call from your secretary to be here at two."

She stood a little taller; she wasn't a secretary.

"I only wanted the plumber." Gray's blue eyes blazed a path right to her. "Who else did you call?"

"Everyone on the list you handed me." Her teeth

chomped on her bottom lip. "You told me to call and ask them to be here this afternoon."

"Just Walters Plumbing. Hey, Walt. Everyone, I'll be right with you." Gray slapped a hand on his jean-clad thigh. He grabbed Courtney's arm and pulled her outside. "How could you get this wrong?"

"You handed me a list with a bunch of names to call."

He exhaled. "Call the security company. They aren't here yet. Tell him to stick to the original schedule." He shoved a folder at her.

Her face burned as she searched through the file. "I'm...sorry."

"Right." He shook his head. "When you're done, go back and finish the filing."

She tugged her phone out of her purse. Another man walked into the building with King George Security on the pocket of his polo shirt. Yikes. No need to call him now. The phone would probably ring while the man talked to Gray. She slunk out before her brother could howl at her again.

By the time she made it back to the carriage house, her feet were doing the howling. So much for not expending energy on her first day on the job. She'd ripped a new dress, had blisters on her feet and when Gray returned he was going to yell. At her.

If this was what working was like, she didn't want to participate. She wanted a massage.

She kicked a box. *Ouch!*

She'd have to pull everything out so Gray didn't yell about the mess she'd made. Damn it. She wanted to rest. Instead, she had to alphabetize.

KADEN CHECKED "hallway paint touch-up" off his grandfather's list. He'd also touched up paint in a bedroom, changed lightbulbs, and moved tables and chairs for an afternoon event in the ballroom. This certainly wasn't a retirement job. He'd worked straight through lunch, trying to catch up on the small tasks necessary to keep the B and B in pristine shape. He wanted to check off enough tasks to justify planning the security system. Then he needed to make sure Abby didn't get suspicious.

But for right now, it was time to reattach the trellis over at the Carleton carriage house. He'd already located the trellis dangling from the fascia. Vines covered with purple flowers twisted and wrapped around the wooden structure on the full two-story trellis. It sure was pretty. Granddad probably knew the name of the flowers. He didn't.

Kaden had other skills. He could ID whether white powder was cocaine, heroin or cornstarch, and whether a baggie contained oregano or marijuana.

He picked up a tool belt, stroking the leather. It looked old enough to be the same one Granddad had worn when Kaden was a kid. Pride and sorrow weighed on his chest. He hated the idea that Granddad was aging.

He tightened the belt low on his hips, making sure it didn't interfere with access to the gun clipped at the small of his back. He preferred a shoulder holster, but with his handyman cover and the heat, wearing a jacket wasn't feasible. This way, his shirt covered his weapon. A little uncomfortable, but he would not face Bole and Salvez unarmed.

The trellis fix shouldn't take long. Then he planned to map out the security-camera placements. Once that was complete, he'd check in on his grandfather.

His running shoes slipped as he climbed the ladder he'd set up earlier. The task force's assistant was sending down his work boots and more clothes, otherwise he'd eventually have to work in dress shirts and suit pants. As he neared the second-story window, movement caught his eye.

Courtney. She danced to whatever music played through her earbuds. Papers and file boxes covered the floor. She sang "Shake It Off" and wiggled her mighty fine ass. Black curls flew around her shoulders and chest. His heart pounded as she tipped back her head and her crushable curls rained down the middle of her back.

With her flashing blue eyes and a face that could launch ships, Courtney was a fantasy. She'd flirted with him, but only because she was bored. If she was so bored, why was she in Savannah? He swallowed. She'd told him to stay away and that's what he planned to do.

But he lingered by the window. His breath came a little faster as her lithe body twisted and spun. *Get a grip, Farrell.* He tore his gaze away and headed to the top of the ladder. His animal attraction would not overcome his brain. He wanted more in a woman than a pretty face.

He pounded in new nails to anchor the trellis to the wooden fascia and tested his work. That shouldn't pull free.

Before he started his descent, he checked the view from behind the trellis. Since the vines hadn't fully covered the two-story latticework, he could hide a camera here. Someone would have to get really close to see the equipment. From this vantage point, it would cover a large portion of the gardens. Perfect.

As he moved past the window, he glanced in. Two blue eyes stared out at him. He slipped, gripping the sides of the ladder to keep from falling two stories.

She opened the window and planted her elbows on the windowsill. "What are you doing?"

He wouldn't look down her shirt. No way. But his gaze dropped as he readjusted his hold on the ladder. He spotted a hint of two lovely breasts. His mouth went as dry as cardboard. "The trellis was loose."

He yanked his gaze back up to where it belonged.

She raised her eyebrows over those amazing Caribbean blue eyes. Her knowing half smile drilled into his gut like a bullet through a paper target. Bull's-eye.

"Aren't you handy?" She shoved a mass of hair over her shoulder, and murmured, "Did you get a good look?"

"A good look?" His tongue stumbled over the words.

A knowing smile curled on her lips.

"I'm sorry." His sweating hands slipped on the metal ladder. "That was rude."

"I don't mind. As long as I get to look back."

He frowned. This was a 180-degree attitude change from last night. She was playing him like a cat with a mouse.

"I'm sorry, too." She set a butt cheek on the window ledge. "I shouldn't have reacted so…poorly last night. I'd just talked to my mother."

"That's why you were upset?"

She shrugged and her curls slipped over her shoulder. And down to her breast.

He couldn't stop staring at the curl.

"I need to get back to work." She hit the last word like it was an evil thing. Waving, she said, "I'll see you around."

"Yup." But she'd already turned away from him.

He hurried down the ladder and heaved in deep breaths. He couldn't waste time figuring out Courtney's motivation.

Moving around the property, he identified locations for the surveillance cameras.

"Nathan?" he called, stepping into the half-completed, sun-lit restaurant.

"Back here." Nathan waved him into the empty kitchen where he was gluing down trim.

A tray of sandwiches sat on one of the stainless steel counters and Kaden's stomach growled.

Nathan laughed. "Hungry?"

"Yeah."

"Abby keeps us plied with food. Go ahead."

He took a thick ham-and-cheese sandwich. He hadn't eaten this well—ever.

"What's up?"

Kaden rolled out the landscape drawings he'd found in Granddad's workshop. He'd marked the camera placements. Pointing to the northern corner of Fitzgerald House, he said, "I'll mount cameras under the roof, keeping them hidden."

"Good." Nathan grabbed a sandwich, too. "Are you sure this is necessary?"

"This is a big property, and cameras will make protecting Issy easier. Heather and the people we believe she's with are dangerous."

"I'll clear everything with Abby." Nathan shook his head. "I hate thinking Heather might try to take Issy away from me."

"So let's be prepared enough that I can put her away. I've already talked to my superior and the equipment is on its way."

"I won't mention that fact to the Fitzgeralds."

"I just need the opportunity to place the cameras." Kaden rolled up the plans. "I'll tell Abby that we talked about me helping with the security."

"Great."

Kaden headed back to the Fitzgerald House kitchen. Abby waved as he walked in the door.

He pulled a new work slip from his grandfather's cubbyhole. While he filled a coffee mug, he said, "Nathan and I were just talking about the security cameras you're adding around the restaurant. Since I've had experience, do you mind if I help him?"

"Not at all." Abby grinned. "Anything to make sure Nathan meets the restaurant-opening deadline."

The kitchen door banged open. Kaden jerked, slopping hot coffee on his hand.

Gray.

Abby touched her husband's cheek, a frown creasing her forehead. "What's wrong?"

Gray inhaled, twice. "My sister just cost me about a thousand dollars, if I'm lucky."

"How?"

Kaden focused on adding milk to his coffee, but couldn't help his curiosity. What had Courtney done? When he'd been on the ladder, she'd been sorting files.

"Instead of just calling the plumber to meet me at the office space, she called *all* the subs. They'll probably charge me for the wasted time."

"It's only her first day," Abby said.

"Yeah." Gray swiped Abby's coffee cup and took a swig. "What else can she screw up?"

Abby stroked his arm. "Maybe working for her brother isn't the best job in the world for her."

Kaden raised an eyebrow. Why did Courtney *need* to work?

Gray shoved a hand through his hair. "Maybe she should work for you."

"Doing what?" his wife asked. "Housekeeping?"

Gray rubbed his wife's back. "Hard to imagine."

Kaden kept his head from nodding. Courtney was a beautiful, rich, spoiled woman who probably didn't know what to do with a sponge.

Gray nodded to Kaden. "How's your day going?"

"Good. I'm catching up on Granddad's backlog."

"Kaden is going to help Nathan with the restaurant security," Abby said.

"You've worked with security systems?" Gray said.

"Yes."

"Maybe over a beer I could tap your knowledge on security for my warehouse and office?" Gray grinned. "I've had problems at the River Street condos."

First working as a handyman and now security? "You can always bounce ideas off me."

"Thanks. I'll take you up on that offer." Gray got his own mug of coffee and brushed a kiss on

Abby's forehead. "I'd better see what Courtney has messed up this afternoon."

"Don't be too hard on her." She walked him to the door. "Do you want to join us for dinner, Kaden? Seven again? Cheryl and Nathan will be here, too."

And the benefits of this case multiplied. Abby hadn't blinked about him working on the security system, and he was getting another meal. "Sounds good."

DONE. COURTNEY PUSHED the last box over to the stack by the wall and checked the time. Eight hours plus. She was done, too.

For the rest of the evening she planned to curl up with a book and a glass of wine. Unfortunately, Gray said they were eating at Fitzgerald House— again. At least Issy and Josh would be there. When she talked with the kids, she didn't have to worry about what they were thinking. Not like the hot handyman.

He may have pushed her away last night, but he'd checked her out today. She flipped her hair back. She could handle him.

She needed affirmation that she wasn't losing her touch with men on top of her father destroying her life. If she lost her ability to control the male species, her life was officially over.

Her friends didn't care she'd disappeared. Gwen had taken up with the man Courtney had refused to date. Courtney was stuck in Savannah *working*. What circle of hell would Dante consider this?

She freshened her makeup and brushed her hair, smoothing the skin between her eyebrows. If she didn't stop frowning she would need Botox. She shivered, hating the idea of needles piercing her face. Somehow this was Kaden's fault—or Gray's, or her father's.

Grabbing her sun hat, book and a glass of wine, she headed to the carriage house's private patio. She could at least escape to Italy with the hero and heroine of this book. Since she wouldn't be flying off to Venice without her father reinstating her credit cards, she'd have to do it through fiction.

Twenty pages later, the hero was hiring a gondola. Goody. She'd been waiting for the characters' first kiss.

"Hey." Gray rapped the glass tabletop. "It's after seven. Abby's waiting for us."

Gray brought her back to Savannah and reality. She wasn't in sultry Venice or even familiar Boston. Tears backed up in her eyes. "Already?"

"Let's go," Gray said.

She left the book in her room and hurried to Gray's side. She should probably apologize again. "Are you still mad?"

He stopped, pulled in a deep breath and exhaled. Twice.

Uh-oh. Father did the same thing. She widened her eyes, going for her most innocent look.

"Don't," he warned. "I know your tricks."

She swallowed, but the lump in her throat didn't move.

"You cost me money today. I have to pay for the time the subs wasted coming to the office."

"I thought you wanted me to call everyone on the list." She bit her lip.

"If you're not sure of things, you have to ask questions." He waved her next to him and they headed to Fitzgerald House. "Maybe working for me isn't the answer."

"What?" It had to be. Her hands shook, so she hid them behind her back. "Give me another chance. Please."

He shook his head and sighed. "I don't know, brat."

"It was my first day, Gray-ray." Her life was imploding.

She was using the nickname she'd called Gray when she was four and begging for a job she didn't want. "Please."

He didn't look at her, just held the door. "We'll see…"

She forced her feet to shuffle into the kitchen. If her finishing-school instructor set a book on her head right now, it would crash to the ground and be trampled by the people around her.

Hearing male voices, she straightened, but it was harder than normal. Curling into a ball sounded like more fun than dinner with people who knew she was useless.

When Gray swept Abby into a kiss, everyone called out his name. No one noticed her or said hi. Her breath caught. What was she doing wrong?

Since the adults ignored her, she headed to the kids, who were playing a board game in the sitting area. "What's this game?"

"Quarto." Josh handed a wooden piece to Issy. "You have to get four pieces the same all in a row." He pointed. "Either tall. Short. Round. Square. Light. Or dark. I pick what piece Issy has to use and she picks what I have to play."

Issy shrugged. "Josh always wins."

"It sounds like fun." Courtney examined the board and rubbed her hands together. A strategy game. "Issy, do you want help?"

Issy's brown eyes sparkled. "Yes."

Josh grinned and wiggled in his chair. "I can beat you both."

Courtney scooted around and sat with Issy. "Let's see what we have."

The door opened. Kaden walked in. Everyone greeted *him*.

She swallowed and shook out her hair. It didn't matter that no one wanted her here.

"That looks fun." Kaden stepped close, staring at the board.

Josh explained the rules again.

It gave Courtney time to figure out where to

place the piece. Issy pointed at one of the sixteen spaces on the board and Courtney nodded. Now there were three round pieces in a row. Josh would have to block so they didn't win. She and Issy selected a square piece to hand to Josh.

Kaden stood behind Josh. Was that to make her nervous or was he watching the game? Or maybe he was checking out her cleavage. Again.

Josh started to place the piece on the board, but Kaden, the jerk, knelt next to the boy. "Hang on. They'll win if you do that."

The two of them whispered to each other. Josh nodded his head so hard, his hair whipped around. "I missed that."

Courtney scooped Issy onto her lap. "Guess we don't get the easy win, pumpkin."

Kaden glanced at her and grinned, a dimple flashing in his cheek.

Oh, my. He'd never smiled *at* her. Wow. She might have to change his moniker to Hottie Handyman.

Issy tucked her head under Courtney's chin and giggled. Courtney wrapped her arms around the little girl. Contentment streamed over her like warm massage oil. This was better than a massage. Her perfect job would include playing with kids.

Not happening. She didn't have early childhood training or teaching skills. All she had was a love for children and two months of nanny experience in high school for her cousins. Father wouldn't agree that babysitting was a *worthwhile* job.

The boys picked their spot and handed them a piece. She and Issy whispered their strategy and Issy placed the piece. And they continued with the game.

"Hey, you four," Abby called. "Dinner."

"We're one piece away from winning," Courtney complained.

"What?" Kaden frowned at the board.

Issy bounced up and down. Courtney and Issy had two ways to win and Josh would only be able to block one.

"She's right, kid." Kaden stared at Courtney, an assessing look in his eyes. "I didn't see that coming."

Courtney wiggled her eyebrows. "We did."

Josh sighed and held up his fist for his sister. "Good game."

The little girl wrapped her arms around Courtney. "We won."

"That's really fun." Kaden helped Josh put the pieces in the box. "We'll get them next time."

Them?

"Issy, hop up," her father called.

Issy tugged on Courtney's hand. "Sit with me."

Courtney let Issy pull her to the table. The little girl was the only one who wanted her here. God, she missed her friends. Missed the easy life. When she helped Issy into a chair, she looked up. Kaden watched her, a frown marring his smooth forehead.

"How was your first day at work?" Cheryl asked Courtney as she served Josh a pork chop.

She shot a look at Gray, but his face was blank. "I—I guess okay."

Abby glanced at her husband, her eyebrows arched. Great. *Awesome Abby* knew about her problems.

"Cut please," Issy sang.

"Sure." At least Courtney couldn't screw that up.

"So who won the game?" Nathan asked.

Issy set her head on Courtney's arm. "Us."

"What?" Abby asked.

"You're kidding," Dolley said.

Could they be more insulting?

"You beat the champ?" Nathan asked his daughter, a smile breaking over his face. "No one beats Josh at Quarto."

Josh pouted.

"We beat Josh *and* Kaden," Courtney said.

Kaden nodded in her direction. But there wasn't a smile there. She couldn't fathom why he wasn't behaving like other men. She forced her face muscles to relax. Being stuck in Savannah would add ten years to her looks.

For the rest of dinner she chatted with Issy. When everyone finished, she pushed away from the table.

"Color?" Issy asked her.

"Sure." Courtney started to move back to the sitting area.

Gray grabbed her arm as she moved next to him. "Help with the dishes."

"Dishes?"

Her brother shook his head. "They aren't going to magically place themselves in the dishwasher."

"But…"

His eyes went cold. "Help clean up."

"Sorry, Issy," she whispered. "Later."

"You could thank Abby and Cheryl for the delicious dinner, too," Gray said.

Why was her brother so mean? Her face burned. "Th-thank you."

Abby and Cheryl nodded.

Everyone knew where everything went. Even Kaden. She hung back, then tried to imitate Bess and Dolley. She brought her plate, wineglass and silverware over to the counter. She bent to set her plate in the rack, but a hand on her shoulder stopped her.

Kaden jerked his thumb to the back of the kitchen. "You need to scrape your plate over there."

She looked around. "Where?"

He grabbed another plate with leftover food on it. "Follow me."

He used a fork to scrape stuff into a barrel. Yuck. She tipped her plate, trying to shake everything off.

He rolled his eyes, and then used a fork to get the

remains. "A farmer picks up the scraps and feeds it to his livestock."

"That's just…gross." She didn't want to know this stuff. She wanted to go to her happy place, either playing with Issy and Josh, or reading her book. But she trudged back to the massive dishwashers and stuck her plate and the others inside.

"I think that's it." Abby hung a towel on a rack.

"Great dinner," Kaden said. "Thank you."

And he walked away. Without giving Courtney a glance or a goodbye.

Gray took the opportunity to hug his wife. "Fabulous, as usual."

Nathan did the same to Cheryl and she blushed about thirteen shades of pink.

"Thank you again," Courtney added, tapping her feet. Had anyone in their family ever thanked Marcus or the cook for a meal? She was sick of not understanding how people expected her to behave.

"Can we play again?" Josh asked.

Cheryl shook her head. "Time to head home."

"We'll play another time." Courtney ruffled his hair. The kids were the only bright spot in her life in exile.

She followed the Foresters to the door.

"Courtney, hang on a minute," Gray called.

Gray and Abby sat at the table. Her brother pointed to a chair.

This felt like the time she'd ended up in the principal's office in grade school for pulling a girl's hair. Instead of sitting, she stood behind the chair, holding on to the rounded back. "Yes?"

"Clerical work isn't your strength." Gray's blue eyes locked on hers.

"It was my first day. I already said I was sorry." Hadn't she?

"Maybe part of the problem is I'm your brother," Gray said. "Maybe it's better if I'm not your boss."

"But…" What would she do now?

Abby was close enough to pat her arm.

Courtney pulled away from her sister-in-law's touch and tucked her trembling hands behind her back. Did her brother have to humiliate her in front of his overachieving wife? "I'll…do better."

Gray shook his head. "If you don't like what you're doing, you won't."

She didn't like the *idea* of work.

Sympathy filled Abby's green eyes. "Why don't we try you in the B and B?"

"Here?" Courtney locked her knees so her legs didn't give way. "In the kitchen? I don't know anything about cooking."

"No." Abby shook her head. "In housekeeping."

Cleaning? Her legs went limp. The chair squeaked as she pulled it over the tiles and collapsed into the seat. "I don't know how."

Sympathy filled Gray's face. "You'll learn."

"Marion will train you," Abby said.

Courtney grabbed Gray's hand. "Call Father. Ask him to let me go back to my real life."

"Working is good for you." He squeezed her fingers. "You need to make something of your life."

"I have! I'm a pretty little ornament," she snapped. "I'm exactly what Father made of me and *now* he wants me to change. How is that possible?"

Pity filled Abby's and Gray's faces.

She couldn't take it. She yanked her gaze so it landed on the table.

"Is that all you want to be?" Abby asked.

Did she? Her life was a train wreck right now. Her lip quivered. "I don't…"

Gray leaned forward. "Then do something about it."

"This is all Daddy expected of me." Courtney sniffed. God, she couldn't cry in front of them. "If he could have sent me to finishing school instead of college, he would have."

"Prove him wrong." Gray slapped the table and she jumped. "You've got a brain in that pretty head."

"Cleaning toilets will prove him wrong?" She couldn't stop the tremor that raced over her body.

"It's a start," he insisted.

"I'll talk to Marion." The pity hadn't left Abby's face. "You should be here by seven."

"Fine. Great." Courtney pushed away from the table. She had to get out of here.

Her body shook like it was twenty below. The door banged behind her. She stumbled through the courtyard, bumping past Kaden.

"Courtney," he called. "What's wrong?"

She ignored him. *Everything was wrong. Everything.*

CHAPTER FIVE

"SOMETHING'S BLOCKING THE view on the left," Kaden called to Boyd, the FBI agent Roger had sent to help install the security equipment.

"I… Yup. Got it," Boyd replied from up on the ladder. "Try again."

Kaden moved around the courtyard, watching his actions on his iPad. This was the last camera they'd installed. And the coverage was just what he'd envisioned.

Boyd clattered down the aluminum ladder. "That good?"

"Excellent." Kaden nodded. "Thanks for coming down with the equipment."

"You know how Roger is." Boyd raised his eyebrows. "He didn't want you calling his ex for assistance."

"I know." Roger and his ex-wife's problems better not get in Kaden's way. "Have a safe drive back."

"I don't need to leave yet. I could stay another night and check the visibility."

"We did that the last two nights."

"I was hoping the work would last longer." Boyd sighed. "This B and B is incredible. I could be your backup and stay."

Kaden shook his head. Two people might look suspicious. "Sorry, not my call."

"You sure? The Statesboro authorities spotted Salvez near campus. That's only an hour from here."

"I know." Which made getting the cameras and software up and running a priority.

"Apparently, one of Salvez's cousins goes to school there." Boyd raised an eyebrow. "Think the kid is in the family business?"

"Probably." But they had bigger fish to fry, namely Salvez and Bole.

"I think you need me here." Boyd packed up his toolbox. "If something changes, mention my name first?"

"Sure."

"We could check the facial recognition software again?" Boyd wasn't giving up.

"It's working perfectly."

"What was the name of the woman you practiced on?" Boyd looked around the courtyard. "She lives on site, right?"

Kaden's hands formed fists. It had been a mistake to test the software using Courtney's picture. Boyd needed to stay far away from her. "I never said, and she's just visiting."

"She's hot."

She's trouble. And troubled. Boyd's reaction to her shouldn't make him...jealous. Ridiculous.

The last time he'd been close to her, she'd

pushed past him in the courtyard looking like her best friend had died. Courtney wasn't working for her brother anymore, either. She was working in the B and B.

But he didn't have time to worry about Courtney. His job was to set a trap for Heather.

After walking Boyd to his car, Kaden put the ladder away. He'd better check on any fires Abby needed him to put out.

Keeping the B and B in repair was fun. He could see why his grandfather enjoyed working with the sisters. Their work ethic rivaled his. And they smiled and laughed...a lot.

When he stepped into the kitchen, Courtney was slumped at the table. She stared into her mug, her lips pinched together as if she was holding back tears.

She glanced up. Sadness, shock and then cunning crossed her face. She did a slow scan of his body and a half smile played across her lips.

Every muscle in his body strained toward her. His head, the big one, had to take control. She wasn't his type.

"Hel-l-lo." The way she spun out the word sounded like an invitation to strip her naked.

Her fantasy-inspiring black hair curled down her back. Her blue eyes sparkled. She had a body full of curves and angles that would take a lifetime to explore. And there was a brain in there, too. Otherwise she and Issy wouldn't have beaten him and Josh at Quarto. Besides Granddad, no one beat him in strategy games, and here was this—this…princess having done just that.

She flipped her hair over her shoulder. "How's your day going?"

Why was she flirting with him?

"Busy." He pulled out the work slips from his granddad's cubbyhole.

Move planters on front porch—call Bess for location.

Check 2nd flr railing main staircase left side—needs to be tightened—Marion.

Oil door hinges—ballroom woman's bathroom—Marion.

Set up 2 buffet tables and a dozen chairs by fire pit—Abby.

Refinish end table in Julia Tyler room—Marion.

This should keep him busy. He headed for the swinging door, passing right by Courtney.

"How's your grandfather?" She swirled a spoon in her mug.

He should keep going, but he stopped. "Complaining that he wants to move home. But he's all right. Half the women at the rehab center are in love with him."

"He is handsome." She tapped the small spoon

against the side of her cup and placed it on the table. "Apparently you take after him."

His stupid body went on alert, as if he was on surveillance and had spotted a suspect. "I thought you were working in the B and B now?"

"I am." A ridge formed between her eyebrows. "Break time."

"I don't usually see staff taking breaks."

She exhaled and smoothed out her forehead. She did that a lot. "Marion suggested it."

He leaned a hip against the table. "Did you do something to upset her?"

Courtney released another deep breath, her top clung to her breasts like his hands might—if he was interested. She had to know what her sigh did to her breasts tucked into that form-fitting top. He forced his gaze back to her face. Of course, that was mesmerizing, too.

"I used the wrong kind of cleaner on the woodwork." Her shrug had her hair falling back to her chest, and a curl looped itself around one breast.

Jesus, Mary and Joseph. It took effort to rip his gaze back up to her face. "Were you working in the Tyler room?"

"I never remember the room names." She shrugged again. At least this shrug displaced the curl. "Why can't they use room numbers?"

"That wouldn't be as interesting."

"Of course not." She tipped her head. "How did you know where I was working?"

"Marion wants me to refinish an end table."

She let her head drop to the chair back with a thunk. "I'm not cut out for this."

He grimaced at the sound. "For what?"

"Work." Her head popped up. Distress filled her blue eyes.

He wanted to ease her pain. Stupid idea. "What did you do back in Boston?"

"Nothing." Her voice was small. "Sometimes I helped my mother with her charities."

"How do you fill your days?" Shock poured into his voice.

She looked around. "No one knows this."

Interesting. "What?"

"I volunteer at a library so I can read to kids." She placed a finger to her lips. "Don't tell anyone."

Reading to kids and not announcing to the world that she was doing it didn't fit his image of Courtney. Wouldn't she want people to know what a saint she was? "Maybe you should work in a library."

"I wish. But I'd have to go back to school."

"Then why not do that?"

She grimaced. "I can't."

"You won't." Kaden shook his head. Courtney's lack of ambition reminded him of his mother. She'd always taken the easy path. That comparison should halt his drooling over Courtney.

She looked at the clock and sighed. "I'd better get back. Maybe Marion's cooled down by now."

"Good luck." He headed to the basement.

What he was learning about Courtney didn't add up. But it didn't matter. There was only time for one puzzle in his life—Heather.

MAYBE COURTNEY *SHOULD* check out Savannah's library system. She missed reading to her kids back in Boston.

Wrapping the top sheet around the duvet, she smoothed the bedding, just like Marion had taught her. She hoped.

All she had to do was get through the rest of the day without another accident. Then she had a day off. A day to have fun. She couldn't even smile at the idea. How much fun could she have without money or friends?

Pressing out one more wrinkle, she chewed her lip and stepped away. That looked right.

If only this was the one bed she had to make—but she had five more to go. And when she was done, she had to help set up for a party in the ballroom.

She *attended* parties. She didn't set up for them. At least no one from Boston could witness her *working*.

When would she get back home? Mother

hadn't returned her call yesterday, but she'd sent a short text.

Your father got the bill on the damage to your car.

Whoops. Even though her father had already found out she'd hit the gate, her mother's note didn't bode well for returning to Boston soon.

She headed to the other bedrooms, and began emptying wastebaskets and making beds. At least making beds shouldn't ruin her manicure. She tugged off the dirty sheets. And snapped a nail.

Fate hated her.

After jamming her cart into the linen closet, she plodded up to the ballroom.

Issy and Josh sat on the floor outside the main doors. Their backpacks were open and toys were spread across the carpet.

"What are you two doing?" she asked.

"Mom's setting up for the wedding tonight. We need to *stay out of trouble*."

She smiled at the way his voice drew out the last syllables. "Are you staying out of trouble?"

"I'd rather be fishing." He shrugged. "Other kids get to fish."

She sat on the floor, even though she was wearing her current go-to shorts. They were no longer the pristine white they'd been when she'd packed them back in Boston.

Weird. Since arriving in Savannah, she'd spent more time on the floor than she had as a child. "Do you have friends who fish every day?"

"Naw. But their parents don't work weekends, either."

Issy scooched a little closer and set her head on Courtney's arm. "Read to me?"

The girl's voice always sounded a little like she was singing. "I need to work, too."

Issy handed her a book. "Please?"

It was a Little Golden Book. "Real fast."

But it wasn't fast. Issy examined each picture, discussing every princess's dress and crown.

"I thought I heard your voice." Bess swung open the ballroom door. "Can you come help?"

It might have been phrased as a question, but Bess's demand was obvious. Resentment bubbled inside Courtney like steam during a facial. Now that she worked for the Fitzgeralds, everyone bossed her around.

She pushed up from the floor. "I need to go."

"We didn't finish." The girl grabbed her hand.

Bess tapped her toe.

"Josh, will you finish reading the book?" Courtney begged.

"Yeah. Come here, sis." He might have sounded frustrated, but there was love in the way he said *sis*.

Once upon a time, Grayson had shown that kind of affection for her. Now, he didn't even like her.

"Sorry," Courtney mumbled as she brushed past Bess. "It's hard to say no to Issy and Josh."

"They're easy to love." Bess's frown melted into a smile. "Let me show you what I need."

Kaden pushed a cart loaded with tables through the service door. His muscles bulged as he picked up tables and rolled them into the center of the room.

Why did the hottest guy she'd met in years have to be a handyman? What would Father think about her having a crush on a man with limited income potential?

Couldn't happen. Father wouldn't consider Kaden *worthy* of dating his daughter. But a Savannah fling before she headed back to Boston? She grinned. That might be fun.

Courtney spread white tablecloths on the tables that Kaden jostled into place. She kept glancing his way, but he ignored her. Her eyes prickled. Since leaving Boston, she'd become invisible.

Bess had her spread smaller pink linens on the white tablecloths she'd already laid. By the time she'd covered half the tables, her arms ached from whipping the cloths in the air.

"Great, Courtney. Now the tall arrangements go in the middle of each table." Bess shoved her long red ponytail over her shoulder and pointed to boxes of flowers stretching the length of the ballroom wall. It would take forever.

Issy's mother, Cheryl, and another woman decorated large buffet tables. Their laughter carried across the room.

Could she be more alone? Her brother barely tolerated her. Abby wasn't thrilled she was working at the B and B. Marion was mad. Kaden ignored her and Bess ordered her around. She sighed and headed to the first box. Maybe making beds was easier.

Courtney could barely see around the pink gerberas and bird-of-paradise arrangement she held. Small pompom-like flowers, resembling little alien beings, brushed her nose. Didn't the bride know this combination was garish? She placed the first arrangement, sloshing water on the tablecloth. Whoops.

"Hang on," Bess called. "I forgot the mirrors." She glared at the water spot on the tablecloth. "At least that will be covered. Pick it up again—carefully."

While Courtney held the flowers, Bess slid a mirror in the center of the table and Courtney set the arrangement down with a crack.

"Careful," Bess barked.

"The damn vase was slipping," Courtney snapped back.

"Just…don't be so rough." Bess chewed her lip. "Instead of the vases, why don't you set out the mirrors?"

"Sure." Everyone thought she was incompetent. Stupid ugly vase.

She shook her head, hoping her face wasn't bright red. It didn't matter what they thought. She wouldn't be in Savannah long enough to care.

She snatched up a couple of mirrors and set them on the closest tables, making sure her back was turned in case a tear slipped down her cheek. She wanted to be where she knew the rules, where she wasn't viewed as some sort of…liability.

Since Gray had come to Savannah, everything had changed. She hated it. Hated her father for forcing her to work. Her mother for failing to change Father's mind. Hated the way Gray and the Fitzgeralds looked at her like she was…useless. Hated Kaden because he wasn't attracted to her. She hated her life.

Wallowing, she worked around the edges of the room, alone. But she didn't have a choice—she had to work her way into the center. Then it was back to spreading tablecloths. Even when her mother hosted charity dinners, she'd never helped decorate.

She carried the box of mirrors closer to the tables where she'd just laid the tablecloths. Kaden arrived with a load of chairs. *How many people are coming to this wedding?*

"Abby says about two hundred," Kaden said.

Shoot. She'd better watch what came out of her mouth. Courtney bent and grabbed more mirrors.

Cold metal smacked into her. The mirrors flew, crashing in a thousand pieces. She landed on her ass. Pain radiated up to her side. "Ooh!"

"God, I'm sorry." Kaden dropped the chairs he'd rammed into her. They clattered to the floor. "Are you hurt?"

Courtney took a breath. "I'm. Not. Sure."

"Where did I hit you?" His blue eyes filled with worry.

"Side." She pointed, struggling to breathe.

He ran his hand over each rib. His fingers brushed her breast and he didn't react. She'd had doctors give her exams with less clinical intensity. "I don't think anything's broken."

How would he know?

"Damn." Bess looked at the broken glass. "Everyone okay?"

"I bumped her," Kaden said. "I'm sorry. I'll pay for the mirrors."

Bess set her hand on his shoulder. "Don't worry about that."

Wait. Courtney grimaced. She was the injured party.

"She doesn't have any broken ribs." He pushed up from the floor and held out his hand.

"How many mirrors broke?" Bess asked.

Courtney took Kaden's hand. "Two, I think."

"Get this cleaned up," Bess said to her. "Grab a

broom and make sure you get all the shards. We don't want people who dance barefoot to get cut."

Kaden touched her elbow. "You're sure you're okay?"

No, she wasn't okay. Bess expected her to keep working? "I guess."

"Good. We've only got an hour." Bess tiptoed around the glass. "I wonder who gets the seven years bad luck, Kaden. You or Courtney?"

He laughed.

Courtney winced as she walked to the service door to retrieve a broom. All she'd wanted was an accident-free afternoon. Instead, she got seven more years of bad luck.

"WHAT'S WITH THE jacket and slacks?" Granddad pushed away his scrambled eggs. "You trying to impress someone?"

"I have a couple of visits to make." Kaden checked the time. "Thought I'd go in professional mode."

He'd dedicated this morning to checking on Granddad, talking to Issy's psychologist and visiting Issy's day care. He didn't like the fact that the little girl was vulnerable at places he couldn't control.

"You'll be miserable." Granddad pushed up from the table. "This isn't Atlanta. It's going to be hot."

Kaden held back a snort and eased Nigel's walker

next to him. Life was different down here, but it was hot in Atlanta, too. As they left the cafeteria, Kaden slowed his pace so he didn't get ahead of his grandfather.

"Are you keeping up with the Fitzgerald House work?" Granddad asked.

"Barely. Courtney keeps me busy."

"Who's Courtney?"

"A walking demolition crew." That wasn't kind. "She's Gray's sister and is working for Marion. Screws up something every day she works."

"Marion and Abby won't tolerate that for long." Nigel grimaced. "What's she done?"

"Monday, she pulled up the runner on the stairs. Tuesday, she gouged a wall." He ticked things off on his fingers. "Wednesday, she broke a pane of glass in a French door."

"No way." Nigel shook his head.

"Oh, yes." Today was Thursday. What new disaster would occur?

"Is she clumsy?" Granddad turned the corner and headed to the sunroom.

"Clueless." But…he couldn't stop thinking about her.

Each time his path crossed hers, he had to force his body to keep from breaching her personal space. When he'd smacked the chairs into her, running his hands over her fascinating body had been—enjoyable. More than enjoyable. He couldn't remember the last woman he'd touched intimately.

More a comment on his dedication to work than on his love life.

But last night he'd dreamed of touching Courtney.

"How's your case going?" Granddad kept his voice low.

"I've installed the security cameras at the B and B. Otherwise, quiet."

There were rumblings that Bole and Salvez had met with one of the Madré cartel's lieutenants back in Atlanta.

Obviously, Heather was moving up in the drug dealing world. Maybe she'd taken out her old partner. Maybe Salvez had done that for her. Kaden wanted them both behind bars. If nothing else, it was criminal that Heather allowed her daughter to be near that kind of life.

"Keep Isabella safe." His grandfather settled into a chair in the sunroom. "She's precious."

"I will." Kaden pulled over a footrest. "You sure you don't want to nap before your PT?"

"Spending time in my room makes me feel like I've got one foot in my grave."

Kaden's heart jolted. "Your room is there so you can rest."

"I'll rest out here." Nigel pulled up his bad leg and set it on the footrest. "I could go home now."

"The doctors haven't cleared you to return home." Kaden asked, "How would you get around the bungalow?"

"I'd manage." Granddad rubbed his thigh. "I want to see my house."

"I'll run down there after my appointments and grab your mail."

"Doris brought the mail yesterday." One of the neighbors.

Kaden asked, "Do you want me to check your house?"

"Doris is handling it." Granddad sighed. "It's been weeks since I've heard the water through my window. I don't sleep well without it."

"To get home, you need to heal." But maybe he could spring his grandfather for an afternoon. He'd check with the staff.

Whenever Kaden ran into Josh, the boy asked about fishing. Maybe Granddad could handle a little fishing off the dock. Josh and Issy could come along. His fingers clenched at the thought of being responsible for the safety of the kids.

"Nigel." A woman in a wheelchair rolled into the room and headed right for his grandfather. A heavy knee brace encased her leg, making it stick out like a torpedo. "I missed you at breakfast."

"Grandson stopped by." Nigel made introductions. Smiling at Kaden, he touched his heart.

"I love you, too," Kaden whispered, brushing a kiss on his grandfather's head. "I've got to go."

He was still smiling as he entered the psychologist's office. After greeting Dr. Rebecca, he opened the folder he'd been authorized to show her. "The pictures are…graphic. But Nathan hoped they might help you with Issy's care."

The doctor pushed back her salt-and-pepper hair and examined the crime scene photos. With each picture, her face grew paler.

When she flipped to the one with the blood trails on the floor under the body, he explained, "We think the victim fell on Issy. Somehow she ended up underneath him and was dragged out."

The doc swallowed, then shoved the last picture into the folder and pushed it back to him as if it was toxic. "It explains the pictures she draws."

He set the folder on his lap. "There were three bodies at the crime scene."

"No children, please, God," the doctor whispered.

"No."

She curled her arms around her stomach. "From what Issy's been able to communicate, her other papa was a victim."

"Yes. Magnussen. Has she said who shot who?" This would be an incredible break.

"I haven't asked." Her eyes went cold. "A four-year-old can't be clear on cause and effect."

"Too bad." He tapped his fingers. Any facts could help. "I'd like you to ask her at your next session."

"What you'd *like* me to ask and what's good for Issy aren't compatible." Her eyes narrowed. "I won't interrogate a child. She's just getting over her nightmares and starting to speak."

He held up his hands. "But..."

"No." She straightened. "You can go to Nathan, but I would strongly—*strongly* recommend that she not be questioned."

The doctor reminded him of a she-wolf protecting her den of cubs. Not something Kaden's mother would have done. He regrouped and pulled out his card. "If she gives you any information on the murder of three people, I would appreciate a call."

"If—*if* she volunteers something, and since Nathan has authorized me to discuss Issy with you, I'll call."

It was all he could ask for. Except an eyewitness who wasn't four years old and traumatized. Dealing with minors was impossible. He held out his hand. "Thank you. And I need you to keep the fact that I'm with the FBI secret."

"Of course."

He texted Nathan he was on the way to the day care. Nathan would meet him there.

"How was Dr. Rebecca?" Nathan asked, when Kaden approached the day care door.

Kaden searched for the right description. "Protective."

"I'm glad." Nathan smiled.

The director led them back to a crowded office. After introductions, he and Nathan each took a chair.

Kaden's knees banged against the desk as he sat. "Have you thought of building shelves to give yourself extra room?"

"That's what I thought the first time I walked in here." Nathan pulled out a pencil. "Do you have paper?"

The director pushed over a pad.

"I would dump the credenza and build shelving around your file cabinets." He made a quick sketch.

Kaden watched as Nathan's vision came to life. "You could also extend to the corner."

Nathan handed him the pencil and Kaden added the remaining details. His shoulders relaxed as he drew.

The director looked a little shocked as she took in the drawing. "It would solve the small space issue."

Nathan flashed a grin at her. "Maybe we could barter tuition for carpentry work."

"We'll talk." The director looked up. "How can I help you?"

Nathan nodded to Kaden. He pulled out pictures of Bole and Salvez. "It's possible Issy's mother, Heather Bole, might try to take Isabella. Bole has been seen with this man recently."

The director stared at the photos. "May I have copies of these? I'll make sure the teachers are all aware. We'll keep them at the front desk."

"Those are for you," Kaden said. "I'd also like to review your security."

"And what is your connection to all this?" The director waved her hand.

"I'm here to capture Heather Bole, Issy's mother." Nathan nodded.

"Who do you work for?"

"The FBI." He flashed his badge. "But that needs to be kept secret."

Her eyes widened. "Of course. Let me show you our security."

After the walk-through, Kaden said, "Your doors are strong enough. But anyone can enter the lobby. Once in the lobby, a perp could force the receptionist to open the interior door."

"I've asked the owner to put a keypad on the external door," the director said. "She's thinking about it. We have a panic button at the front desk, but it only notifies the back rooms."

The security was adequate, but Kaden hated having Issy in day care all day.

He and Nathan left together. Mission accomplished. He could turn off his FBI persona and become handyman again. Time to find out what Courtney had destroyed this morning.

COURTNEY JERKED THE cart filled with breakfast dishes to a stop. She had a goal for this Thursday. Same goal as yesterday. Get through without another screwup. She couldn't stand the looks that passed between Marion and the Fitzgeralds whenever something happened.

She set her hand on the swinging door.

Someone inside the kitchen said, "I don't suppose you could use Courtney's help in the greenhouse?"

She froze. That was a Fitzgerald. Talking about *her*. She leaned closer.

"Are you kidding? I have thousands of dollars' worth of orchids in there." That had to be Bess. "You've talked about the *Courtney path of destruction*. I won't have her near my plants."

Courtney's face heated in embarrassment. She couldn't help the accidents that had occurred during the week. She hadn't been bred to change beds and clean up other people's messes.

"Is she improving at all?" Was that Dolley's voice?

"The broken mirrors before last weekend's wedding weren't her fault. Kaden ran into her," Abby said.

She knew her sister-in-law's voice the best. At least Abby recognized *everything* wasn't her fault.

"That was a mess. Any chance you can find a use for her, Dolley?"

"No way!"

Mother and Father didn't want her in Boston. No one from her circle of friends bothered to call or text. Her brother had pawned her off on the Fitzgeralds. They didn't want her, either.

She bit her lip. Why couldn't she head home?

There she could lock herself in the library. She'd read, relax. Be happy.

"Those dishes don't belong in the hallway." Marion walked toward her.

Courtney blinked. "I…"

"Let's go." Marion pushed open the door and held it.

The dishes rattled as she guided the cart into the kitchen. She stared straight ahead, pretending not to notice the witches gathered at the table. The sisters stopped talking. Right. Now they had nothing to say.

Josh's mom was with them, too. It wasn't enough that the Fitzgerald sisters thought she was worthless. Cheryl did, too.

She dumped the scraps into the appropriate can. She wasn't going to make that mistake again. Let the pigs enjoy the B and B's leftovers. Then she sprayed and loaded dishes, ignoring the group at the table.

"I'll have to bring Josh and Issy here for tonight's event," Cheryl said. "Nathan has his dyslexia group and my regular sitter is having surgery."

Courtney turned and moved toward the table. "I'll watch them."

"What?" Cheryl's eyebrows went straight up into her hairline.

Oh, God, what had she done? Hadn't the women just been reciting all her screwups? What parent would let her watch their precious kids after hearing all that?

But she was good with Josh and Issy. She stood a little taller. "I'll watch them tonight. I'm not on the schedule."

Cheryl's brown eyes were huge and round in her thin face. "I know the kids love playing with you—"

"I was a nanny for my cousins when I was in high school," she interrupted. She refused to be rejected for the one thing she knew how to do. "Actually, I stayed with them when their parents were in Europe. Two summers." The words flew out of her mouth.

"You were a nanny?" Disbelief painted Dolley's face.

"Yes." No Fitzgerald would make her feel inferior. "I'm good at it. And I didn't leave a *path of destruction*."

Abby's mouth dropped open. Bess looked at her hands and Dolley gave a small nod.

"What time do you need me?" she asked Cheryl, wanting to spend time with the kids.

"Nathan has a meeting at five, so four thirty?" Cheryl said. "I can't pay much—"

"I'll be there. You don't need to pay me. I can't wait." She turned back to the dishes, her movements more confident.

Finally something to look forward to in this hot, humid, horrible place.

COURTNEY SHOULDERED HER bag and called out, "I don't know when I'll be home."

Of course, no one answered. The place was empty. Gray was at Fitzgerald House, probably drooling over his wife—or his wife's food—or helping with the wine tasting.

She rubbed her forehead, smoothing away the ever-present grooves. Not tonight. Tonight she would have fun with Josh and Isabella.

After climbing the carriage house stairs, she knocked at the second-story door. This was the first time she'd been inside this building, even though the restaurant was almost complete. A restaurant Gray was financing for Abby.

Resentment began to boil, but petered out. Hating took so much energy and tonight was for the kids.

The door popped open.

"Hi, Miss Courtney," Josh said.

"Hi." She stepped into a room that was slightly cooler, but not by much. A sofa faced a flat-screen TV. Dolls and cars covered the floor. A rocking chair was set in the corner.

Nathan came into the living room, Issy hanging on his back like a monkey with her arms around his neck. "I don't know where Issy's gone."

The little girl giggled.

"I hear her." Nathan turned, pretending to look for his daughter. "Where could she be? Courtney, have you seen her?"

Issy grinned and shook her head.

"I don't know where she is." Courtney smiled.

Josh rolled his eyes. "Look behind you, Papa."

Nathan spun so hard, Issy's legs swung wide. He tugged her around to his chest and hugged her. "Found her!"

"Daddy!" she squealed.

"I've got to go, but you be good for Courtney." He tossed her in the air and set her on her feet. "Dinner's in the oven. Phone numbers are on the fridge. And Cheryl detailed out their evening routine."

Issy ran to Courtney and hugged her knees. Courtney picked her up, setting her on her hip. "We've got it."

"You help Courtney." Nathan picked up Josh and tossed him in the air, too. "And be good."

Josh laughed as his father tickled him. "I will."

"I'm not sure who'll be home first," Nathan said. "My meeting usually goes until around nine."

"Don't worry." She winked at the kids. "We'll try not to burn down the carriage house."

Nathan jerked, and then dimples popped out as he smiled. "Sounds like a solid plan."

She could see why Cheryl and Bess had been attracted to the twin brothers. They were handsome.

"Let's check what's for dinner." Courtney pulled out a dish of enchiladas. "This looks good."

"I chopped the lettuce and tomatoes." Josh

grabbed them from the fridge while she poured their milk. Then they all sat at the table.

The kids put their hands together. They were going to pray? Okay.

"Josh, will you lead us?" she asked.

He said a prayer she'd never heard. And they all said "Amen" together.

"What did you do at school today?" She dished portions onto each plate.

Josh bounced in his seat. "Zach threw up. All over the swing."

Courtney grimaced. "That's not a conversation for the dinner table."

"It looked like this." Josh opened his mouth and gave them a view of his chewed-up dinner.

Issy cried, "Yuck."

"Josh," Courtney warned.

But it was hard to scold the little boy, who grinned at her. "What about you, Issy?"

"I pet a bunny."

"We got to play with him, too." Josh crunched on lettuce. "I fed the bunny lettuce."

The kids talked about wanting a bunny. And then the puppy they were going to get when their house was finished, but how the puppy could hurt the bunny.

Courtney had forgotten how kids' conversations swirled around. Only a little food ended up on the floor from Josh swinging his fork as he talked.

"Did you have a pet?" Josh asked.

Courtney set the last plate in the dishwasher. "My brother had a dog."

Her parents assumed one pet in the family was all they needed, ignoring the fact that she'd wanted a kitten.

"Mr. Gray is your brother, right?"

She nodded and wiped the table. "Yes, he's my older brother."

"I'm Issy's older brother."

The little girl gave him a hug.

"Yes, you are." Courtney looked around the kitchen. Why was it more satisfying cleaning here than at the B and B? "I think that's good."

She checked the schedule. Cheryl suggested starting to get them into the shower or bath around seven thirty. They had plenty of time for fun. "I brought art supplies."

"Where?" Josh demanded.

She brought her bag into the living room and sat on the sofa in front of the coffee table. "Would you like to make your mom a bouquet of flowers?"

Josh shook his head. "We're not 'llowed to pick Miss Bess's flowers."

"Of course not. This will be a permanent bouquet." She pulled out tissue paper, pipe cleaners, scissors and a clear vase she'd gotten from the B and B.

She let them pick the colors for their flowers. Issy picked pink and purple tissues. Josh chose primary colors. Then she helped them fold the paper. "Good job, Issy. Press hard."

They worked together to place the pipe cleaners. Then she cut Issy's folded tissue papers into a fringe while Josh cut his own. "You can round the edges."

"I want to do that." Josh tucked his lip between his teeth as he cut.

"Sure." Courtney swept up the scraps and dumped them into the vase.

"Pretty," Issy said.

"Just like you." Courtney tapped her nose. "You're such a pretty girl."

Her stomach twisted. Mother and Father's words had come out of her mouth. The words that had made Courtney believe her only value was as a pretty little ornament. Appalled, she blurted out, "You're smart, too."

Issy smiled and nodded.

"Now the magic happens." Courtney held each pipe cleaner stem and showed the kids how to pull the folded tissue petals open.

"I can do that." Josh grabbed his first flower and immediately tore the tissue. He wailed, "It ripped."

"That's okay. Just be more careful."

"My mom will hate it." Josh frowned at Issy's flower. The girl was treating the paper as if it was glass. "She'll like Issy's more."

"It's going to look beautiful," Courtney said.

"Just pull the paper apart slowly. No one will see that tiny tear."

They each made three flowers. There were more rips, but Josh admitted, "You can't see the tears."

"I told you." Courtney folded the pipe cleaners so the flowers filled the vase. "What do you think?"

"I like my colors the best," Josh said.

"Mine are pretty." Issy patted the pink and purple flowers she'd made.

"They're all beautiful. Where should we put them?" Courtney asked.

"Mom puts flowers on the kitchen table," Josh said.

Issy nodded.

"Then that's where they should go."

Issy pulled out a bright yellow place mat and Josh set the vase in the middle.

"That looks gorgeous." And homey. It was nothing like the Smythe mansion, where exotic flowers graced most rooms. This was kid-friendly and fun.

There was a knock on the kitchen door.

"Mr. Kaden!" Josh tugged a chair from under the table and pulled it over to flip open the deadbolt lock.

"Hey. You're supposed to ask who's at the door." Kaden picked up Josh from the chair and set him on the floor.

"I knew it was you." Josh frowned.

"You can't just open the door. It's not safe."

Kaden moved the chair back to the table, finally noticing Courtney. "Oh."

Oh? That's all she got? She started to flip back her hair, let him see what he kept ignoring, but when they'd started to work on the flowers, she'd pulled it back into a messy bun. Not a good look for her. She tugged the binder out of her hair, hoping it didn't look like a rat's nest.

Kaden asked, "Is Nathan here?"

"He's at a meeting," she said.

Issy sidled up to Courtney's legs and wrapped her arms around them.

She patted the little girl's head. "Is there something you needed?" she asked Kaden.

"Nathan wanted my opinion on…something." His eyes slid sideways.

The man just lied to her. "Ahhh. *Something.* Well, he'll be back after nine."

Josh tugged on Kaden's hand. "Let's play Quarto."

"I…"

"Come on," Josh said. "You promised that the next time you came over, you'd play with me."

"But Courtney's here." Kaden backed up.

"We'll play her and Issy." Josh tugged harder. "We'll win this time. Men against the girls."

"Women," Courtney amended. Picking up Issy, she whispered, "Maybe Mr. Kaden's afraid he'll lose to smart women."

A smile flashed across Kaden's face. "And maybe the guys will win."

NAN DIXON 157

Josh ran to his room and came back with the bat-tered game box. He'd set out half the pieces by the time Issy and Courtney sat on the living room floor.

"We'll start." Josh grabbed a piece.

"No. We'll make this fair. Like when my grand-dad and I play chess." Kaden took a dark piece and a light piece and mixed them behind his back. Then he thrust his closed hands toward Issy. "Choose."

Issy pointed at his right hand.

"Light. Ladies will hand us a piece first."

"Fine." Josh slouched onto the sofa.

Courtney let Issy pick the first piece. Strategy didn't matter at the start.

How she wished she'd worn her blue sundress. It made her eyes pop. She hated Kaden seeing her in shorts and a T-shirt. She'd just thought these clothes would be easier with the kids.

She'd showered before coming here, and hadn't bothered reapplying her makeup. Now she wanted to grab her purse and head to the bathroom to put on her armor. A little makeup would give her the boost she needed to deal with Kaden.

She touched her forehead. Oh, Lord. Furrows. She was creating furrows!

Josh set their first piece on the board and then he and Kaden selected the next one for them. Issy held it above the board, hovering over each spot until they both agreed on the placement.

As they played, Kaden studied the board, chatted with Josh, talked to Issy, but didn't talk to or even look Courtney in the eyes.

Was this part of her seven years of bad luck? Her attractiveness was gone?

Issy stared at her, concern filling her mocha-coffee eyes. "Okay?"

"I'm good." Issy was so sensitive. Courtney squeezed the little girl in a hug. "Don't worry."

Kaden *finally* locked his icy blue gaze on her. It was like falling into a Swiss mountain lake.

"Miss Courtney, we need a piece." Josh's impatience dragged her up from drowning in Kaden's stare.

"Umm, sure." She surveyed the board and found the path to another win.

Issy picked up the correct piece. Wonderful. She flashed a grin at Josh and Kaden. With the pieces remaining, she and Issy were assured a victory.

Kaden frowned, studying the board. His mouth dropped open. "Not again."

Standing and twirling Issy, Courtney sang, "We are the champions. We are the champions."

"Champion, champion." Issy sang with her.

"No." Josh knocked the board.

"Don't be a sore loser." Kaden grimaced.

"I want to play again." A pout filled Josh's voice.

Courtney checked the time. "You'll have to play with Mr. Kaden. Issy needs her bath."

Josh rolled his eyes. "Maybe I'll finally win."

Kaden pulled the pieces off the board. "Not if I can help it. I need to figure out why we keep losing."

"Because we're smarter," Courtney whispered to Issy as they headed to the bathroom.

She relaxed while helping Issy. Then she helped Josh start his shower while Kaden read to Issy. It was nice to hear his deep voice as she picked up dirty clothes and turned down their bunk beds, but why was he still here? *They* certainly weren't friends.

Her heart ached a little. Sometimes even when she'd been with her friends in Boston, she'd felt so alone. In Savannah, she was even more isolated. Her best friends were six and four.

Josh finished his shower and she supervised his teeth brushing.

"Bedtime," she said.

"I want to play another game," Josh whined.

"Sorry. Another time." Courtney called, "Issy. Bedtime."

Kaden carried Issy into the bedroom. "Which one is yours?"

Issy pointed at the lower bunk. It had a bright pink comforter. He settled her onto the pillow like she was a priceless vase.

"Night, kids," Kaden said as he left the room.

"Story?" Issy asked.

"Story, please." Josh scrambled up the built-in stairs to his bunk. "My papa makes them up, 'cuz he has trouble reading. You can, too."

Trouble reading? Right. Cheryl had said Nathan was going to a dyslexia meeting.

"Okay." Courtney shut off the lamp next to the bed and the soft glow of the night-light filled the room. She sat on Issy's bed. What could she tell them?

"Once upon a time there was a beautiful young girl named—Becca. Everyone thought her life was perfect, but it wasn't. Her friends were jealous of her beauty and the fact that she lived in a mansion. They only pretended to like her so they could play with her toys."

"Yuck." Josh blew a raspberry. "I want a story with boys in it."

"Just wait." Courtney brushed back Issy's hair. "There was a…a lake on the mansion's property that Becca liked to look at, even though she wasn't supposed to get dirty."

"Does she fall in the water and a boy saves her?" Josh asked.

"Becca knows how to swim and can save herself." Courtney tried to shape a story that would blow away the stereotypes that had hurt her growing up. "One day, she was lonely and sad. Her best friend told another friend that Becca was stuck up. That she only played with Becca because she had all the American Girl dolls."

"Dolls are stupid," Josh snorted.

"No, they're not," Courtney said. "Dolls are toys just like your *Star Wars* figurines."

Josh didn't come back with another comment.

Courtney took a breath. "The words hurt Becca. She told her mother, but her mother was planning a party. Her brother was playing baseball, so of course her father watched him. And they didn't invite her to come to the game. Girls in her family didn't go to baseball games." She swallowed. "Becca didn't want to watch a bunch of boys play baseball, anyway."

"I like baseball. My papa plays with me and Issy."

"You're lucky." Why couldn't her father have been more like Nathan?

"No one in the house wanted to talk or play with Becca. None of her friends could come over. Becca decided to sit under the willow tree next to the lake. It was her quiet spot. She liked to read books there, but she was feeling so sad, she didn't bring a book."

"I love stories." Issy stroked Courtney's hand.

"I do, too." Courtney held Issy's hand. "But Becca wasn't alone. There was a boy fishing from her favorite thinking spot. And he had a dog with him. She wasn't allowed to have a pet."

"I like to fish," Josh mumbled. "And Issy and I get a puppy."

"Puppy." Issy nodded.

Courtney tucked the sheet up to Issy's chin. "Becca told the boy he couldn't be on the property."

"She's mean." Josh rolled over and looked down to the bottom bunk.

"It's all she knows," Courtney said. "The boy, James, introduced Becca to the puppy. The dog's name was...Theo."

"Weird name," Josh mumbled.

"It's short for Theodore." What should happen next? "Becca knew no one was supposed to be on the grounds, but the boy asked her to fish with him. She wasn't supposed to get dirty, but James was having fun. And the dog licked her face."

"Fishing's fun." Josh's voice grew softer. "I catch big fish."

"James showed Becca how to thread a worm on the hook. She didn't like doing it, but if she wanted to fish, she had to bait her own hook."

"Worms," Issy sang, her eyes shut.

Courtney lowered her voice. "They spent the morning fishing and Becca caught her first fish. James showed her how to reel the fish in, but she pulled the fish out of the water on her own. She was very proud of herself."

"Do they eat it?" Josh yawned. "I ate the first fish I caught."

So did her brother after Father showed him how to fish from the small lake on the estate. She'd sat alone on the grass, watching Father and Gray laugh.

Courtney stood. Stretching to the top bunk, she touched Josh's cheek. "No, they threw it back."

"Too bad." His words slurred as his eyes closed.

"Night," she whispered.

"Tell us more tomorrow," Josh muttered.

"Sure." She backed away from the bed. What kind of adventures could her two make-believe children get into?

Turning, she jolted. Kaden leaned against the wall.

She'd forgotten about him. Her exhale was a little shaky. She should have read a book and not made up such a silly story.

Kaden walked down the hall ahead of her.

"I thought you left," she whispered.

"I wanted to make sure you locked up behind me." He headed into the kitchen.

Her eyes dropped down to his butt. Nice. She'd never really admired a man's butt before. But there was something about Kaden. And it wasn't just that she wanted him to notice her.

He turned and caught her staring. He raised an eyebrow. Her cheeks burned with embarrassment. Great.

"Will you be taking care of the kids often?" he asked.

She shrugged. "I volunteered to help tonight."

He nodded, but lines deepened around his mouth.

"Why?" She clenched her fingers to keep from reaching out and smoothing away his worry lines.

"Nathan's planning on installing a new security door, but right now, anyone could break into the carriage house through the side door."

"Okay." What was with Kaden and locked doors?

His face was so serious. His concern was over-the-top.

He tapped the wooden door. "Make sure this is locked."

"Got it." She crossed her arms and waited for him to leave.

Kaden stared into her eyes and the room shrank. She caught a whiff of a clean pine scent and inhaled. Aftershave? He didn't strike her as a man who wore cologne.

"Were you the little girl?" His voice was a deep caress.

"What?"

He swept a wisp of hair off her face. "Were you that unhappy girl?"

She didn't want to talk. Didn't want to move. She wanted him to touch her. "I—I was making up a story for the kids."

"Right." He tucked a curl back behind her ear, and a single finger stroked her cheek. His blue eyes locked on hers as he brushed her lower lip with his thumb. "I'm so sorry."

Her breath stuck in her chest. Tingles zipped from her lip straight to her core. Finally, Kaden was going to kiss her. She'd prove she hadn't lost everything.

His eyes weren't glacial anymore. But there wasn't only heat in his eyes. They were filled with pity.

Pity. Not lust. No way.

She was Courtney Smythe of the Boston Smythes. Her father and brother wielded power like gods. This handyman, with no real power, acted just like them. Like if he spoke, minions would scurry to do his bidding.

Courtney had held the same kind of power in Boston, but here? Here, she was nothing.

He cupped her cheek. Was he going to give her a pity kiss? No way.

She pulled away from the attraction tugging her closer. "There's nothing to be sorry about. I had a wonderful childhood," she lied.

"Right." He took a step backward and tapped the door with his knuckles. "Lock this."

He was through the door before she could insist her childhood was happy. She'd had everything. Well, not a pet. Or her father's attention. Or her mother's support.

But everyone wanted to be her. *Everyone.*

Just not her.

CHAPTER SIX

KADEN SHOULDN'T HAVE touched Courtney last night. Shouldn't have stroked her soft skin. Hell, if she hadn't stepped away, he'd have kissed her.

He wiped the end table he'd sanded, and then spread on some stain. A table Courtney had ruined. Shouldn't that thought dull this...lust building inside him?

Not happening. Last night while Courtney had told her story to the kids, she hadn't worn her entitled-heiress facade. Her words had oozed with loneliness and pain. Who was she? The lonely girl or the woman who expected men to worship at her feet?

The desolate tone in her voice had cracked his heart. But he was still here to do a *job*, not Courtney Smythe.

He'd known her kind of loneliness. As good as Granddad had been, when Kaden had first arrived in Tybee, he'd mourned his brother and parents and the only life he'd known. And he'd blamed himself for his brother's death. The guilt had driven him to avoid other kids, fearing he might hurt them, too.

Granddad had forced him to play sports, and participate in school activities. But Kaden had always kept himself just a little separate. That way he wouldn't fail another kid like he'd failed Kaleb.

After finishing the staining, he called Roger and caught up.

"There weren't any hits on the pictures you sent," Roger said. "And the meth supply chain is back up and running."

"That's not good. Any word on Bole?" Kaden asked.

"Marty from the task force was over in Vidalia, checking out a lead. He swears he caught sight of her in a bar. When he tried to get to her, she vanished."

Vidalia. Around eighty miles from Savannah. "She's close. It's like they're circling the area."

"We're hearing rumblings that Bole is consolidating her power. Now that things are calming down, she might take her daughter back."

"I'm ready for her."

"Any sightings?" Roger asked.

"No. But the cameras are all operational." He needed to delete the Courtney alerts, but whenever he started to…he stopped. He liked knowing where she was. "If Bole shows up, I'll catch her."

"Any concerns?" Roger asked.

"Issy's day care security isn't as tight as I would like it."

"Then figure out how to tighten it up," Roger barked. "If we lose Issy, we lose Bole."

"I'll try." But he didn't have any idea how to keep Issy safe at the day care center.

Roger said, "Stay vigilant."

That was a good reminder. It was easy to be lulled by Fitzgerald hospitality. He was losing his edge. Abby or Cheryl kept him fed. His bed was almost too comfortable. He'd caught up on sleep down here. And Granddad was healing. He'd even started to feel sorry for the poor little rich girl, Courtney. He headed up the stairs to the main floor. Time to see what else was on the to-do list.

People were talking in the kitchen. He stopped to ID the voices. Abby and Marion. Then he pushed through the swinging door.

"Hey, Kaden." Marion smiled at him, but she looked weary. "How's it going?"

"Not bad. The end table should be ready in another day."

"Good. Good." Marion looked at Abby. "I added more repairs to your list."

"I'll get to it." He decided to pour a cup of coffee before grabbing the work slips that seemed to have multiplied in his granddad's box.

"That girl is not cut out for this work," Marion said to Abby. "She knocked a heavy picture frame off the wall. Broke the glass and frame. Picture's fine."

They had to be talking about Courtney. Every day, he had to repair, fix or touch up something that Courtney seemed to be responsible for ruining.

Abby rubbed her temple. "Gray wants her to work."

"She's eatin' up your profit."

"Maybe she's good at something else." Abby sighed.

"Gift shop?" Marion suggested.

"There isn't enough traffic to warrant paying a person to sit in the shop." Abby tapped the table.

"And I wouldn't put her in charge of money," Marion said. "She might know how to spend it, but I don't think she has a clue what all her mishaps and thoughtlessness are doing to you."

Kaden shouldn't eavesdrop. He grabbed the pile of slips. Sure enough, the top slip said he was to grab a picture out of the second-floor maid's closet for repair.

"I don't know where I can put her." Abby held her head.

Was Kaden the only person who recognized Courtney should be working with kids? Hadn't Abby noticed the way she was with Issy and Josh at the meals they'd shared?

He inhaled. That was the answer. Have Josh and Isabella stay on site with Courtney. Then he'd be able to keep his eye on everyone. His security would alert him if Heather or her new partner showed up.

The idea settled over him like a warm blanket on a cool night. It felt right.

He stuffed the notes in his pocket and headed out to talk to Nathan.

"You want me to take care of Issy and Josh full-time?" Courtney asked Nathan. Her breath caught.

Someone *wanted* her around? The metal edge of the patio chair dug into her fingers as she clutched it.

"It would help Cheryl and me out." Nathan slapped his hand on his thigh and sawdust flew. "On top of work, I'm trying to remodel the house before our wedding. Cheryl and Abby are crazy busy with the B and B and getting the restaurant up and running. Having you watch the kids here would save us time."

"But…I work for Abby." Not that she was any good at housekeeping. But according to her mother, Father had softened after learning she was working for his *favorite daughter-in-law.*

Babysitting wouldn't qualify as a job in her father's eyes. Even if she called herself a nanny, she could picture her father's frowning face and hear him say "Babysitting is something a kid could do."

"It'll take a few days to get everyone notified." Nathan ran his hand through his hair. "But all the kids talked about this morning was how much fun they had with you last night."

"I had fun, too." The most fun she'd had in weeks, maybe even months. That included her time in Boston.

Except, Kaden's almost-kiss had been awful. And frustrating. Not fun. She hadn't sunk so low that she would accept a *pity* kiss from any man.

"I have to think about this," she said.

Nathan grabbed her hand. His brown eyes glittered with gold sparks. "You're good with the kids. Think hard, will you?"

She would. "I adore them."

Nathan named a wage that was higher than what she was making at the B and B. "If we ever need you at night, we'd compensate you for that. If you're available."

The only people she knew in Savannah were the Fitzgeralds and the B and B staff. None of them had ever asked her to stop for a drink or take in a movie.

"I don't do much at night," she admitted. Besides read. "Let me think about your offer."

"Please say yes. The kids really like you." Nathan headed back into the restaurant.

She set her foot on the chair, letting her head rest on her hand. Her mother would be appalled. Feet should remain on the ground.

When she exhaled, her breath shook. Nanny position? Glorified babysitting?

But seeing Josh and Issy every day...

She tossed her hair over her shoulders. So what if her father disapproved. She wouldn't tell him where she was working, just that she *was* working. She could let Father think she still worked in the B and B.

Her fingers tapped a rhythm on her thigh. What would she do with the children all day? Did Savannah have a zoo or a children's museum? Was there a library nearby?

They could start a book-reading chart. Each book

would get them a star and stars would earn them rewards. Her cousins had loved that when she'd initiated it. How would she drive them around? Could they walk—in this heat? Did Issy take naps?

There were so many things she needed to check on. What did they eat for lunch? Her skills in the kitchen were poor—oh, what was she saying? They were nonexistent. Even when she'd taken care of her cousins, their cook had been around. And Issy and Josh had a mother who cooked for Abby Fitzgerald, the Kitchen Queen.

Footsteps echoed on the flagstone garden paths.

Courtney let her feet slip to the ground.

"I'm heading over for lunch, are you interested?" Gray stopped next to the table.

This was her day off. The last place she wanted to be was the B and B, but it was a chance to talk to Abby. Could she do that with her brother listening to every word? "Sure."

"There you are." Abby turned at the slap of the door. A grin spread across her face as Gray pulled her in for a kiss.

Really? When she'd come in for iced tea a couple of hours ago, they'd been smooching in the carriage house kitchen. They needed to tone it down.

Gray set Abby back on her feet. "What's for lunch?"

"There's sandwiches or salad on the table." Abby checked the time.

He headed to the food. "Thanks. I'm starving."

"I'll be right back," Abby said. "I need to take the trays over to Nathan's crew."

Courtney had done that last week. It seemed strange that Abby fed workers who were being paid to build her restaurant. Shouldn't they bring their own lunches?

Ghad. If she accepted Nathan and Cheryl's offer would she be expected to bring her own lunch?

Gray set down his half-eaten sandwich. "I'll help."

"No, no, sit. I can make a couple of trips." Abby waved him back to the table.

"I—" Gray began.

"I'll help," Courtney interrupted. Helping would give her a chance to ask Abby about quitting.

"You?" Abby's mouth dropped open.

"You?" Gray's eyebrows shot up.

"Sure." Did they have to be so surprised?

Courtney gathered one tray and Abby the other. "There must be a lot of guys working today."

"They're so close to finishing. I want to make sure everyone is fed and happy."

Courtney waited until they were walking through the courtyard. "Umm, Abby?"

"Yes?"

"How much notice do you need for me to quit working at the B and B?" Notice. That's what it was called, right?

"You're quitting?" Was that relief in Abby's voice?

"Nathan offered me a nanny position for Issy and Josh."

Abby stopped and stared at her. "He did?"

Courtney nodded. "I'm not…adept at cleaning, but I really adore being with the kids."

Abby raised her eyebrows. "That's the truth, although there weren't any disasters yesterday, right?"

A broken glass, but she'd tucked it in the garbage before anyone saw. "None."

"Let me check with Marion, but I think you can quit right away." Abby pushed open the carriage house door.

"Okay, good." Courtney sighed. Now to come up with a plan on what to do with the kids each day.

THE SECURITY SIGNAL BUZZED. Bole? Kaden snatched the tablet from his granddad's workbench and opened the recognition software while racing up the stairs.

It was Courtney, Issy and Josh. They were in the courtyard. He let loose the breath he'd been holding and returned to the workshop.

Courtney was now taking care of the kids. It was great having her on site, but she and the kids kept setting off the alerts.

He pushed back through the workshop door. If he was honest, he liked watching Courtney with Issy and Josh. When she was with the kids, her smile was free, not calculating like when she flirted with him. Why couldn't she drop the pretense and show him who she really was?

But understanding Courtney wasn't why he was in Savannah.

He kept his eye on the cameras. Even though it was Saturday, Courtney and the kids headed down the courtyard paths. He couldn't help but enjoy the rear view of Courtney's great ass. After they passed Abby and Gray's home, he lost sight of them. Where were they going? Should he add more cameras on that side of the property?

Nathan said he would show Heather's picture to Courtney, but had he gotten a chance? Kaden needed to know. He tapped the lid on the varnish can, stuffed a copy of Heather's picture in his pocket and took the steps two at a time. What were they doing?

The good thing about working undercover at the B and B was he could wander where needed and no one questioned him. Plus, Bess had asked him to move some pots. He had an excuse to head over to her greenhouse and find out if that was where Courtney had taken the kids.

The rain last night had left the plants scattered with dew. Color peeked from among the lush greens in the gardens and the splash of the frog fountain was a soothing backdrop of tranquility.

A few guests lingered over coffee in the courtyard. He nodded in greeting, knowing he needed to keep up the facade of being an approachable

B and B employee, but he hurried by so no one engaged him in conversation. It happened all too frequently. No wonder his granddad loved working here. Fitzgerald hospitality set everyone at ease.

Turning the corner of Abby and Gray's house, he headed up the small hill. Even here, palms and flowers surrounded Bess's greenhouse.

The glass building had a vaulted roofline. Windows were open on the top and sides. Inside, the kids and Courtney talked to Bess.

He opened the door and walked through an entryway into the main room. Humidity and the smell of dirt and flowers hit him like a punch. Racks and racks of exotic-looking plants stretched halfway to the ceiling. They were the same kind of weird flowering plants that had been in his room in Carleton House.

Bess knelt in front of the kids and held a plant with waxy white flowers.

"Hi, Mr. Kaden." A grin creased Josh's face. "We're learning about orchids. I get to draw them."

Courtney turned, her deep blue eyes wide open. Issy gave him a little wave. Bess smiled.

"That's great." To Bess, he said, "Thought I could move those pots for you."

"Give me a minute." Bess turned back to the kids. "An orchid needs to attract pollinators, so they use color, shape or smell. Moths pollinate most white orchids. The white flower lets them be found by night-flying insects."

"Cool," Josh said.

"Cool," Issy repeated.

Courtney cringed. "There are bugs in here?"

"Necessary for the plants." Bess pointed down an aisle. "I set up a table and chairs for you. And I've added flowers that I thought you'd like to draw. Why don't you go ahead and check them out?"

The kids and Courtney headed to the table.

Bess came over to him. "Let me show you which pots I want to transfer to the Fitzgerald House porch and which to Carleton House."

As they moved through the greenhouse, he said, "This was a great idea for the kids. Nice of you to think about it."

"I didn't come up with this idea—Courtney did."

"She did?" His eyebrows popped up.

"Yeah. I didn't give her that much credit, either." Bess shrugged. "Too much bad blood between her and my family."

He moved eight pots of red and yellow flowers to their respective porches. Then he hauled eight more back into the greenhouse. "Anything else you need?"

"I'm good." Bess called over to the kids, "Do you want to see me propagate an orchid?"

Josh and Issy scrambled over to Bess's workbench.

Courtney hung back.

He had to know if she was aware of what Heather looked like. "Can I talk to you for a minute?"

She checked the kids and then nodded. "What's up?"

He didn't want the kids overhearing them, so he tipped his head toward the entry. "Since I'm around the B and B all the time, Nathan gave me a picture of Issy's mother. He wants to know if I see her hanging around."

Courtney glanced over at Issy. "He started to say something yesterday, but Issy walked into the kitchen. I didn't get a chance to look at the picture."

"I've been carrying an extra photo around," he lied. "Just in case I see someone who doesn't look like a guest."

She unfolded the paper and stared. "Do you think she's still blond?"

Good question. "I assumed so."

She pointed at Heather's dark roots. "She could have gone back to her natural color."

"Hmm." She might have. He'd better have the specialist run simulations of Heather as a brunette and redhead.

Courtney looked over at Issy. "Maybe she wanted to look more like her daughter, but whoever was coloring her hair used too harsh a brand. It looks incredibly dry."

And…there was the Courtney who didn't see below the surface. Kaden shook his head. "I'll let you know if I spot her."

"I should give you my number." Courtney held out her hand for his phone. "I can enter it for you."

"Oh, I'll enter it." He couldn't let her see he already had her cell phone number. He pretended to open screens. "Go ahead."

Courtney rattled it off. She looked up and her fake smile appeared. Running a finger down his bare arm, she said, "Feel free to use it. Anytime."

Her touch hit him like a karate kick to the chest. He should be stepping back, but his feet were rooted to the floor.

"Miss Courtney, come see," Josh called.

Just like the night he'd almost kissed her, she stepped away. He inhaled, sharp and quick.

"Coming." She stared up at him through thick black eyelashes. And winked.

The blood deserted his head and sank lower into his body.

Courtney straightened and touched her chest, reminding him of Granddad's signal. "I'll let you or Nathan know if I see this woman. I won't let anything happen to Issy."

She turned back to the kids and his gaze dropped to watch her ass as she put a little extra sway into her step.

Who was Courtney? She criticized another woman's hair coloring, and couldn't clean worth spit. She seemed at odds with her brother and didn't fit in with adults, but she loved Josh and Issy and thought of fun activities to keep them not only entertained, but also educated. She was smart enough to keep beating him and Josh in a game of strategy.

Who was the real Courtney, and could she keep Issy safe?

THERE WAS KADEN. Again.

Courtney caught the kids' hands and crossed from Fitzgerald House into Johnson Square.

Every time she and the children left the apartment, Kaden materialized. While Bess had taught the kids about orchids, he'd been in and out of the greenhouse. Whenever she was outside with the kids, he was close. She'd even spotted him when she and Issy and had walked Josh to his bus stop, or waited for him at the end of the school day.

If she didn't know better, she'd think the guy was a stalker. It was as if he'd bugged the apartment and knew whenever they left.

His mixed messages—all business and then looking at her with eyes so hot she feared her body would melt—were confusing. Maybe she'd played her seduction games too long. This thing with Kaden wasn't fun anymore. It was better to stay focused on the kids.

"Hang on," Kaden yelled, jogging toward them. "Where are you heading to today?"

"The library," Josh answered. "The book lady is reading."

Issy nodded.

"Issy likes going," Josh added.

"Josh," Courtney said. "You weren't going to talk for Issy, right?"

"Yeah." Josh stubbed the toe of his sneaker on the cobblestones. Too often he acted as Issy's voice. The little girl was quiet and Josh…wasn't.

"I'll walk with you," Kaden said.

This was—odd.

"Don't you have work to do?" she asked.

Kaden's stack of requests from Marion and the Fitzgerald sisters was probably a little shorter now that she wasn't breaking or destroying things, but she was amazed by the effort expended to keep up the B and B.

"I have to run an errand." He waved his hand in the general direction they were walking.

Where? She frowned, then relaxed the furrows between her eyebrows. Her face wasn't going to survive Savannah.

"How was the park yesterday?" he asked, walking next to Josh.

"Balloons." Issy tipped up her face, smiling. "I petted a lamb."

"What was a lamb doing in the park?" he asked.

"They had a small petting zoo set up," Courtney explained. Issy had been entranced.

"I wanted to go." Josh stubbed the toe of his sneaker again, this time on the sidewalk. "They had pony rides."

"I'll check to see if they come back," Courtney promised.

Josh slipped his hand out of hers and grabbed Kaden's. He tugged. "When are we going fishing?"

"I don't remember promising to take you fishing," Kaden said.

"On Italian night," Josh insisted.

Courtney snickered. "I think you *talked* about fishing, but Mr. Kaden didn't promise to take you anywhere."

Josh looked at Kaden. "It would be a reward, since I gotta go to school."

"Have to," she said, correcting him. "And why does that matter?"

"'Cuz maybe we can go after I come home from school. Usually I help my papa with the new house on weekends." Josh stuck out his chest. "I'm the best clean-up man he's ever seen."

"I'll bet you are." Courtney stroked his blond curls. The kid was so darn cute.

"And that's why I should get to go fishing." He tugged on Kaden's arm. "Right?"

Kaden looked a little shell-shocked. "Umm…"

"Josh, don't hound him."

"But—"

"No."

"Then can we go, Miss Courtney? Issy loves to fish." Josh wasn't letting go of his fishing idea.

"I'd have to talk to your parents about going to the river or beach."

"What?" Alarm filled Kaden's voice. His reaction was…extreme.

"I'd want Cheryl and Nathan to be okay with me taking the kids to the beach," she said.

"Where would you go?" Kaden stopped in the center of the sidewalk and caught her hand in a viselike grip. "Issy is safer at the B and B."

She pulled her hand out of his hold and crossed her arms. "I don't know where we'd go. And of course Issy will be safe. I can swim. Actually I was on the swim team in high school." She'd quit because she hadn't been good enough to get Daddy's attention. What difference did it make if she came in second most meets? Smythes should always take first.

Kaden frowned.

"I've qualified for all my lifesaving certifications." She'd intended to become a lifeguard at the country club in high school. Her father had nixed that idea. Smythes didn't work at the clubs they attended. He'd also refused to let her work at the community pool.

"I'll—I'll go with you," Kaden blurted out. "Let me talk to Abby. We can set something up next week."

Josh jumped up and gave Kaden a high five. "Yes!"

No. She didn't want Kaden tagging along on their adventure day.

Issy hugged Kaden's knees. "Fun."

"We…shouldn't pull you away from your work," Courtney said.

"I'll be fine. This will be fun. I promised to take my granddad out. He needs time off from the rehab center." Kaden stopped at the entrance to the library. He brushed her arm and added, "I'll talk to you later about logistics."

That wasn't what she wanted. But the kids were grinning and bouncing up and down. Fishing? Really?

Kaden's hot-and-cold routine made her spin. And not in a good way.

KADEN ANGLED THE camera so Courtney's image filled the screen. Alone, she didn't flip her hair or fake a smile. She turned another page as she read in the garden. Most evenings, she was in the exact same seat, ending her day with a glass of wine and a book. He worried his obsession with her was... getting weird.

He'd overreacted this afternoon. The idea of Courtney and the kids being on the river or at the beach and Heather showing up had him volunteering to come with them.

His cell rang. Roger. He shut off the camera view and set his laptop on the bed next to him before answering. "Anything new?"

"Bole used a credit card over at Hilton Head."

Two hours away. Kaden rolled his shoulders. She was staying close. "I want to warn the kid's sitter about her."

"She has Heather's picture and the cover story

of Nathan being worried the mother would take the kid, right?"

"Yes, but that's not the full story."

"If more people at the B and B find out what you're doing, Margaret might get wind you're there in an official capacity," Roger warned. "Knowing my ex, she'd take over the case. Is that what you want?"

Kaden was used to working undercover. And he didn't want to be edged out of this case. But was Roger more concerned with his ex-wife and jurisdiction than catching Bole and Salvez?

"The nanny deserves to know." Kaden gritted his teeth. Courtney was planning too many excursions for the kids. "She doesn't just keep them locked in their apartment."

"Then figure out a way to stay close. That's why you're at the B and B."

"Do you want me to date the sitter?" Kaden snapped.

"How pretty is she?"

Very. "That's not the point."

"Keep your cover in place." Roger hung up.

Kaden reopened his laptop and stared at Courtney in the courtyard. She read while sipping wine.

The tightness in his gut eased. The Bureau was using Isabella as bait to capture Bole. He needed to stay close to Issy. And Courtney spent most waking hours with the child. By dating Courtney, he could get close. Very, very close.

CHAPTER SEVEN

"THAT'S WONDERFUL," COURTNEY said to Issy as the little girl added another shade of reddish-brown to her drawing. "Is it a...?"

Josh leaned over. "Dog."

"Woof, woof," Issy barked.

"And a beautiful one." Courtney set a book on the edge of the paper as it fluttered in the breeze. After they'd walked Josh home from the bus stop and had a snack, they'd decided to draw in the garden.

Josh was working on his own picture.

"That's a beautiful orchid," Courtney said. "The blue looks just like the one Bess showed us."

Josh grinned. "Thanks."

Courtney drew morning glories. She would never be the artist six-year-old Josh was, and that was okay. Apparently she was good at telling stories. Who knew?

A shadow darkened the table and Kaden's familiar piney scent sneaked up on her.

"Hey," she said, faking nonchalance.

He peered at the papers. "These look like they should be framed."

Josh thrust his picture in Kaden's face. "I did this one."

"Excellent."

Issy tipped her head and gave Kaden a shy smile, then held out her paper. "Puppy."

"It's very nice." Kaden set his hand on Courtney's shoulder.

She froze. Kaden never touched her.

"I talked to Abby and if you want to take the kids fishing—" he knelt next to her chair, his arm resting on her leg "—I could go with you this Saturday after I set up for the wedding. Are you sitting for the kids?"

"Yes!" Josh launched out of his chair. "Yes, yes, yes!"

"I am watching them." Courtney chewed her lip. "But I haven't asked Cheryl or Nathan about taking them on this big of an outing."

"I did." Josh grabbed her hand. "We've talked about fishing for days and days. Weeks."

"*You've* talked about it," she said.

"It'll be fun." Kaden invaded her space and sucked up all the oxygen. "We can use my granddad's boat and afterward head to Tybee for lunch and swimming."

"It sounds like you have the whole day planned." If Kaden was offering, he could bait the kids' hooks.

He covered her fingers. "It will be a lot of fun for the kids." He lowered his voice. "And we could have some fun, too."

She blinked, but Kaden was still there kneeling at her feet and smiling up at her.

How long had she tried to get his attention? Now he was volunteering to spend a day with her and the kids?

"Please," Josh said.

"Please," Issy repeated.

"It'll be great." Kaden grinned, and a dimple flashed from his left cheek. She was a sucker for a dimpled man kneeling at her feet.

"Okay." She checked the forecast on her phone. Hot as usual. "Saturday."

Josh spun in a circle. Issy nodded. Kaden grinned, a second dimple appearing on his right cheek.

She rolled her shoulders, trying to relieve the chill running down her back. Why did Kaden want to spend a day with her and the children? What was in it for him?

COURTNEY TUCKED THE bag Cheryl had packed into the back of Cheryl's SUV. The bag contained lunch, snacks and everything they needed for a *week* at the beach, let alone a single day. Courtney wasn't sure why they needed calamine lotion, much less two bottles.

Kaden pulled his SUV into the parking lot.

"Mr. Nigel!" Josh ran over to Kaden's vehicle.

The window rolled down and Nigel leaned out. "Good to see you, Josh. Issy."

"Hi, Nigel." She wasn't sure they'd ever been formally introduced. "I'm Courtney."

"Gray's sister."

She nodded. This day was going to be…strange. The only bright spot in this confusing day was that the kids were so excited.

Kaden climbed out of his car. He was wearing board shorts showing off lean legs, a T-shirt that clung to his muscles and a ball cap. He looked incredible.

"Everyone ready?" he asked, rubbing her shoulders. Ever since Kaden had offered to take them fishing, he hadn't stopped touching her.

"I'm ready," Josh yelled.

Issy nodded.

She didn't know how to relate to Kaden anymore. When he'd rejected her flirtations, it had been easy. But now he was acting as if he had the right to touch her. Did this mean something? Her head reeled. Maybe after their fishing trip, she'd understand what game he was playing. His switch had been too abrupt.

"Follow me." Kaden patted her arm.

"Everyone into your seats," she called to the kids.

Issy and Josh scrambled into Cheryl's SUV. She double-checked that they were buckled.

"Don't drive too fast," she called to Kaden.

"I won't." He waved.

She headed to the driver's seat. She didn't want anything happening to the kids or Cheryl's vehicle. Ironic, when she'd smashed the fender on her convertible half a dozen times and had never cared. Being responsible for Issy and Josh changed everything.

She followed as Kaden drove slowly around the squares. Finally they were on a causeway flanked with water and marshes.

"Are we there?" Josh asked.

"I don't know," she answered.

Josh bounced in his seat. "I can't wait."

Courtney laughed. "I can tell."

"On Mr. Dan's sailboat on the Fourth of July," Josh said, "we went all the way to the Atlantic! I caught the biggest fish."

"I think I've heard about that fish." About two dozen times.

Kaden's signal blinked that they should turn. She chewed on her lower lip. Right into the swamp?

"The houses are on stilts," Josh called from the back seat as they turned onto a road carved into the marshland. "Why?"

"Maybe because of hurricanes?" she said, guessing. "You'll have to ask Nigel."

Kaden pulled into a long drive next to a small bungalow built on stilts. She parked behind his SUV. By the time she had the kids and bags out of the car, Kaden had his granddad into a wheelchair and had pulled out a walker. She took a deep breath of soupy, humid air. Dirt, water and decomposing vegetation filled her nose.

"Welcome to my home." Nigel waved his hand.

"It's cool!" Josh grabbed the walker, swinging

himself on it like it was monkey bars. "Why's your house on stilts?"

"Careful on the walker, Josh." Kaden pushed the chair across the driveway, the shells crunching under the wheels. "If there's a hurricane storm surge, the water won't ruin the houses."

He and Josh talked about storms washing through the lower levels of houses.

"Kids, one more trip to the bathroom," Courtney said.

Josh stared down the long dock that stretched to the water. "I want to see the boat."

"Bathroom first," she said.

"You have to do what Miss Courtney says." Kaden stopped the wheelchair at the foot of the stairs up to the house. "Can you bring over the walker?"

"Sure." Josh pushed it to the base of the stairs.

Nigel took the walker handles and Kaden eased him to his feet. Then the two men worked their way up each step. What a lot of work just to get into the house.

She held the kids back so they didn't get underfoot. Then they followed Nigel and Kaden into the bungalow.

"The bathroom's there." Nigel pointed. He headed down the hallway and into a bedroom.

Kaden opened a closet and pulled a key from a hook on the wall. "I'll get the boat cover off."

Josh ran down the hall. "I'm first."

Issy and Courtney wandered into Nigel's living room. Different shades of blue fabric—sky blue, ocean blue—covered the furniture. A huge picture window with a seat looked down on a dock. Tall reeds surrounded the long stretch of boards.

Bookshelves filled the room. She checked out the titles. Classics were next to a volume of Shakespeare's complete works, nestled next to volumes of thrillers and a couple of romance books.

Pictures of Kaden as a child dotted the shelves. There was one of him in a basketball uniform and another with him on one knee in a baseball uniform.

On another shelf were pictures of Nigel. In many of the photos, he had his arm around a lovely-looking woman. And there were pictures of a young girl, too. Kaden's mom? Young Nigel and Kaden had the same blue eyes, but Kaden didn't smile as much as his grandfather. Apparently Kaden had been the same stick-in-the-mud back when he was growing up.

But he'd smiled more lately. At her. Her shoulders itched. She didn't trust the drastic change in him.

"I'm gonna help Mr. Kaden with the boat." Josh shot out of the house, the screen door slamming.

"Wait!" She hurried after him. No way would he fall in the water while she was responsible.

As Josh ran down the long dock, she yelled, "Kaden!"

He looked back at her from the two-level dock.

A boat lift hung above the uppermost dock. That meant the boat dangled more than ten feet in the air. And Kaden was up there tugging a tarp off it.

Courtney pointed. "Watch him, please."

Kaden climbed down. "Got it."

She didn't move until Josh stood next to Kaden.

Back in the house, she helped Issy go to the bathroom. She should have made Josh stay here with her. Josh was a slippery six-year-old. Was Kaden keeping track of him?

She picked up Issy and tried to speed up the process of washing hands. Then she carried her out of the bathroom.

Issy touched Courtney's forehead, her lips tucked between her small teeth.

"Yes, sweetheart?" Courtney asked.

"No worry," Issy said.

"I'll try." Impossible. She stared at the boat, but couldn't see Josh. "Nigel, do you need help getting down to the boat?"

Nigel moved out of his bedroom. "Unfortunately."

She drew in a breath. "What can we do?"

Nigel headed to the door, slower than Boston's snow removal equipment during a blizzard. "I'll need help getting down the da—" he stopped. "Darn stairs."

"I'll help," Issy whispered.

On the porch, Issy steadied the walker. Courtney

supported Nigel as he placed one foot at a time on the steps. He needed a ramp.

Nigel settled into the wheelchair with a sigh and held out his arms to Issy. "Want a ride?"

The girl nodded.

Courtney set Issy on Nigel's lap, stealing glances down to where Kaden and Josh climbed all over the boat, still suspended in the air. She grabbed the bags next to the cars.

"Can you hold this?" She settled the lightest bag on Issy's lap. Then she slung another bag over the handles of the wheelchair and picked up the picnic basket. "Let's see what the guys are doing."

But she couldn't push the chair and hold the basket at the same time, so she exchanged the basket for the bag Issy held.

As she jiggled the chair so it climbed onto the wooden walkway, she glanced down to the dock. Josh's head popped up inside the boat. Okay, she could at least see him. But if he fell, she was too far away to save him. The dock ran forever.

"Josh, be careful," she called.

"I'm helping," the boy called back.

Why hadn't Kaden lowered the boat into the water to remove the cover? She rushed the chair down the uneven boards of the dock. The bag banged against her legs.

Josh climbed on the edge of the boat, rolling the tarp up as he walked.

"Josh, stop!" she called.

He turned and stumbled, his arms windmilling as he tried to balance.

"Josh!" He was going to fall into the water. A long, long drop.

She scurried around the wheelchair, her boat shoes pounding on the wooden dock. Her heart bashed inside her chest.

Kaden snatched Josh just as he tipped backward. The little boy's sneakers squealed as Kaden dragged him across the hull. "I've got him."

"You shouldn't have to catch him!" Courtney clambered up a ladder onto the wide platform. She poked Kaden in the chest. "Six-year-olds can't walk on the edge of a boat when it's dangling this high above the water."

"I was right here." Kaden set Josh on the dock. "And I never fell as a kid."

"How old were you when you climbed all over the boat?" She'd seen the pictures in the house and pointed at the kids. "Six?"

He opened his mouth, then stopped and paused. "Eight."

Nigel called from the walkway. "Point to Courtney."

Issy buried her face in Nigel's chest. Courtney needed to deal with Josh before she could comfort Issy.

She ran her hands along Josh's arms and waist. "Are you okay, honey?"

"That was cool." Josh grinned.

"Not cool." She glared at Kaden. "He shouldn't have been on the dock without a life jacket."

"I was watching." But Kaden avoided her scowl.

She waved at the wheelchair and bags. "Life jackets are back there."

"Give me a minute and I'll lower the boat," Kaden growled.

"Life jackets," she insisted. "Now."

Kaden grumbled, but jogged back and pushed Nigel and Issy to the bottom level of the two-tiered dock. He dug in the bag and pulled out life jackets, handing the largest one up to Courtney.

What if Josh had fallen in and hit his head? "New rule, kids. No one on the dock without a life jacket."

"They rub my neck," Josh complained.

"Too bad." She knelt in front of him, shaking out the leg straps. "If you want to fish, you wear a jacket."

Josh sighed. "Fine."

Once she'd zipped up Josh, Courtney hopped down to the lower level and did the same for Issy. The electric squeal of the boat lift echoed across the marsh as Kaden lowered the boat.

"Josh, come down here with me."

He pouted a little but did as she asked.

"Maybe this was a bad idea," she murmured.

"I'll be good. I'll be good." Josh tugged her face so they were eye-to-eye. "Look. I'm wearing my life jacket."

The trouble wasn't Josh, it was Kaden. Would he pay enough attention to keep the kids safe?

Kaden pulled the boat around to the lower level. "Can you hold the boat steady?"

Courtney grabbed the side. Kaden half helped, half lifted Nigel into the boat and settled him next to the driver's seat. Courtney handed him the bags and picnic basket, and finally guided the kids from the dock into Kaden's arms.

Then it was her turn.

Kaden held out his hand. Their eyes locked as he helped her into the boat. It rocked as she stepped in and she crashed into his chest. Unwanted warmth spread through her like she was sinking into a hot mud bath.

His piney scent infused the air. A shudder racked her body and she clutched his hand.

A man had never made her so *aware* before. This wasn't the way of the world. She made men want *her*. Now it was Kaden who pulled her in. Kaden who made her want to stare into his steel-blue eyes. Kaden who made her breath catch.

When had the roles in the game reversed?

"Everything okay?" he asked.

She jerked her hand from his and staggered away from him. "Why?"

"You've got those lines between your eyebrows that mean you're worried."

She slapped a hand to her forehead. "I'm fine."

"Not just fine." He pulled her hand away from

her face and stepped close enough to whisper in her ear. "You're beautiful."

His lips brushed against her ear as he pulled away.

She shivered. This was what she wanted. Kaden falling under her spell. But her stomach jittered in confusion.

"Are we going fishin' or what?" Nigel called.

"Just getting settled." He rubbed his thumb over her cheek.

She stumbled over to the children. The boat rocked, knocking her onto the bench seat.

Kaden turned the key, checked the gauges and flipped a switch. A humming filled the air.

"Everyone seated?" Kaden asked.

Nigel looked around. "Good to go."

Josh bounced a little in his seat but held on to the edge of the boat. "Yes!"

"We're ready," Courtney said, tugging Issy onto her lap.

The engine roared. Kaden backed away from the dock and headed along a path within the marshy weeds.

"Are you sure we won't ground?" She clutched Issy on her lap, and double-checked that Josh was holding on. Her hair whipped around their faces.

Nigel half turned in his seat. "We're in Turner Creek and heading to where it empties into the Wilmington."

Kaden grinned. "We've had good luck fishing there."

Courtney tipped her face into the wind and inhaled. A brackish aroma filled her nose. It wasn't
necessarily pleasant, but it wasn't obnoxious. As an
added bonus, it obliterated Kaden's scent.

Flying through the marshy water wasn't the type
of sailing Father and Gray always shared, but there
was a freedom in letting her hair tangle and swirl
about her head. It would be a rat's nest by the end of
the day, but who cared. She was with the kids and
they were smiling. Nigel and Kaden were smiling.

Issy smoothed out the ridges above her eyebrow.

So why was she frowning?

Kaden Farrell.

"You've got one." Kaden caught Issy's fishing pole
as it dipped in the water. "Hang on."

The little girl giggled and climbed onto his lap.
They held her pole together.

Whoa. He wrapped his arms around her as if she
was a live bomb. Why didn't Issy sense he wasn't
comfortable around kids? He cuddled her close and
she tucked her head under his chin. Total trust.

He released a shaky breath. Maybe being around
the kids wasn't so bad.

Josh stared into the water at Issy's line. "It's big."

"Go, Issy." Courtney glanced up from the book
she was reading. She'd hidden her brilliant blue

eyes behind massive sunglasses. "Josh, don't lean over so far."

"We could use some help here." Kaden swung the fish over the edge of the boat toward Courtney, dangling it above her lap. The woman needed some messing up. Although there wasn't much to mess up right now. Not clothes, at least.

She'd stripped off her shirt and shorts and exposed a bikini that showed every luscious curve on her body. He'd probably drooled as she'd stroked sunscreen over her skin.

He wanted to touch her. Wanted to do *more* than touch. Ever since he'd blurted to Roger that he should date her, he couldn't help but think about ways they could stay connected, most of them in bed. Against the wall or in the shower would be fine, too. Having her fall into him as she'd stepped into the boat had been both pleasure and pain. And he hadn't been able to resist running his lips along the edge of her ear.

"Can you take the fish off her hook, Courtney?" Kaden teased.

Granddad snorted, tucked his hat lower over his face and went back to sleep.

"No." Courtney tipped down her sunglasses and stared at him. "Unless it's sushi, ceviche or cooked, I don't touch fish."

She twisted away and turned the page, pretending to ignore them. But she kept a watchful eye on both kids. And him.

Kaden unhooked the fish and tossed it in the bucket. The boat got quiet. He and the kids fished, Granddad napped and Courtney read.

"Time to reapply sunscreen," Courtney called a half hour later.

Josh complained, but handed his pole to Kaden. Issy did the same—no complaints.

Courtney had been right. Not that he wanted to admit that. He shouldn't have let Josh walk on the edge of the boat without a life jacket. Hell, he should have lowered the boat first. But when he'd come to live with his grandfather, he'd loved being up that high.

At seven, he'd always worn a life jacket on the dock. He'd had to be strong enough to tackle the salt marsh currents before he was allowed on the dock without one.

He pulled another black drum fish off Issy's hook and tossed it in the bucket. "That's a nice fish."

Issy held her bare hook up and he baited it. Courtney hadn't bothered to respond the last few times he'd joked about her helping.

"*I'm* supposed to catch the biggest fish." Josh pouted.

"You need to be quiet and not bob your line up and down." Kaden kept his voice low.

"It's boring when they're not biting." Josh frowned, but turned back to his own line.

Courtney pulled out a notebook and began writing.

"What are you working on?" Kaden asked.

Her head popped up hard enough to shake the hair she'd clipped to the top of her head. "Just some notes."

"Our story?" Josh asked.

She reached over and chucked his chin. "Yes."

"What's next?" Josh asked.

"I'm working on that." Her cheeks brightened in a blush.

Why was she embarrassed about working on a story for the kids?

"More," Issy said.

Courtney bit her lip. "Maybe if you behave for our entire adventure day."

"Just…tell us what their next adventure will be," Josh persisted.

"Next adventure?" Kaden asked.

"They have adventure days just like us." Josh bounced a little. "They found a puppy and saved it, 'cuz it was starvin'."

"They made cookies—" Issy said.

"And took them to a sad man," Josh said.

"Josh." Courtney raised her eyebrows. "You promised not to finish Issy's sentences."

Josh heaved out a sigh. "And they met twins."

Courtney amazed him. How could someone so focused on herself be so good with kids?

"What's next?" Josh asked.

"They go to the zoo." She chewed on her pen.

"Lions escape!" Josh yelled.

"The fish won't bite if you're loud," Kaden reminded him.

"I've never been to the zoo." Issy moved her fishing pole up and down from Kaden's lap.

Courtney leaned forward. "Is there a zoo in Savannah?"

Kaden shook his head. "But I went to a marine zoo when I was a kid."

"That would be fun." She slid back in her seat. "We'll have to figure something out."

"You're not going to keep running around with the kids, are you?" He wanted her locked down at the B and B.

"They need to learn about their city," Courtney said. "And we love our adventure days."

Damn. He needed to keep getting himself invited on their outings. Between the B and B, his grandfather and reviewing task force material, he was running out of hours in the day. And Courtney was suspicious. Of him.

He would have to get even closer. Forget all the little touches he'd started. Time to take this attraction to the next level. He exhaled. For the job. To capture Bole.

Courtney bent over her notes. Her skimpy blue

bikini fired up fantasies of him tearing it off with his teeth.

The first week he'd met Courtney, the idea of getting close to her would have been offensive. Now it sounded like a dream come true.

COURTNEY UNLATCHED ISSY'S seat belt and scooped up the sleeping girl. Turning to Kaden, she whispered, "Thanks for taking the kids fishing."

"I had fun. When I dropped Granddad off at the rehab center, he said he enjoyed it, too." Kaden helped Josh with the bags and poles as they climbed the stairs to the Foresters' apartment. He whispered, "I wouldn't mind joining your next adventure day."

His breath on the back of her neck sent shivers through her body. "How can you get away from work?"

He shrugged. She was his work. "I'll manage."

At the top of the stairs, she unlocked the apartment door. "Thanks for hauling everything up here."

She moved to the bedroom and set Issy on her bunk. The little girl didn't always take a nap, but she was tired.

Josh turned on the shower. She walked back to the living room, expecting it to be empty, but there was Kaden.

He glanced up. "I mean it. I like being with the kids—and you."

"I don't get it. You despise me."

"I don't despise you." He closed the distance between them. "Trust me on that."

Trust him? Trust was such a foreign concept.

With his finger, he tipped up her chin and stared down at her.

She hated looking up at people. Especially men who tried to intimidate her with their height. But this wasn't intimidation. Kaden's stare had her quivering. She'd never been breathless around a man.

"I have a hard time getting to know people." His hand slipped down and cupped her shoulder. "I think it comes from being taken from my parents when I was a kid."

Taken from his parents? "I'm sorry."

"I'm not. I got to live with my granddad." His right hand cupped her other shoulder. He tugged her close, his hands stroking down her back.

She was burning up. Had the air-conditioning quit working? Each breath came faster and dragged in the scents of marsh, sunscreen and pine that lingered whenever Kaden was around.

He's going to kiss me.

She should stop him. But he was reeling her in.

She slapped a hand on his chest. "What are you doing?"

"If I have to explain—" his half smile was just this side of cocky "—I'm losing my touch."

His hand covered her fingers and a final step put his body flush with hers.

Her breath caught in her chest and her fingers clenched his hand like it was a lifeline. She couldn't remember the last time she'd actually let a man kiss her. It wasn't part of her game. Her gaze locked on his pulse fluttering in his neck.

With his palm he angled her head.

She wanted to stare at the floor, at the wall, at anything but his eyes. They seared her like the blue flames of a gas fire—too hot to touch, but oh, so pretty to look at. "Maybe we—"

His mouth covered hers. Firm lips possessed her mouth, controlled it. His tongue stroked hers. Sweet. Strong. Heaven.

Everything hard of Kaden was pressed against everything soft of her. She cupped his magnificent butt and groaned. He pulled up her leg and wrapped it around his hip. *OMG*. His hand stroked a fire up and down her back.

"Yeah," he whispered, his breath hot in her ear.

"What are we doing now?" Josh called as he exited the bathroom.

She stumbled away from Kaden. What *was* she doing? She was responsible for the kids.

"Don't shout." She touched her swollen lips. "Issy's asleep."

Her swimsuit cover-up was rucked up to her waist. She tugged it down, slipping farther away from Kaden. Her legs wobbled and she sank onto the sofa. She'd never had a kiss that…amazing.

Kaden stared out the window, his fists leaning on the sill.

Josh hopped up next to her. "Can I finish watching my movie?"

She checked the time, relieved she didn't have to think of an activity when all she could think about was Kaden's lips and hands. "Thirty minutes."

Josh clicked the remote buttons faster than she could follow. "Can you watch with me, Mr. Kaden?"

"I'd better check if they…need anything at the B and B." Kaden hurried to the door.

That was it? He was going to kiss and run?

This was why she stayed in control. This was why she treated men as a game.

At the door he turned. His eyes were glazed and his mouth hung open. He gave a small shake of his head, like he was clearing away fog. "I'll—I'll call you tonight."

She heaved a sigh, cuddled Josh and settled in to watch Nemo be found.

Maybe Kaden had been affected by what just happened. Thank goodness. She would hate to be the only one confused.

WHAT THE HELL was that?

Kaden headed down the steps, inhaling, but he couldn't clear away Courtney's sinful scent.

When his lips had touched hers, he'd forgotten there were kids in the apartment. Forgotten he was here to capture Bole. He'd only wanted to kiss Courtney deeper, touch more of her skin and hear her sexy sigh.

He'd lost control. He *never* lost control.

When she'd stumbled away from him, his damn knees had gone weak. It was all he could do not to reach out and haul her back.

To help find his focus, he recited the FBI oath of office—

I, Kaden Farrell, do solemnly swear that I will support and defend the Constitution of the United States against all enemies, foreign and domestic; that I will bear true faith and allegiance to the same; that I take this obligation freely, without any mental reservation or purpose of evasion, and that I will well and faithfully discharge the duties of the office on which I am about to enter. So help me God.

He had a job to do—capture Bole. That mission demanded he stay close to Issy. If being with Courtney helped him accomplish that, he would do what was necessary to bring Heather Bole to justice and keep the little girl safe.

Had Courtney been as blown away by their kiss?

Probably not. Toying with guys was what she did.

He stumbled, grabbing the railing. Courtney had rocked his world.

His phone rang. He cleared his throat and answered, "Hey, Roger."

"Local police shut down a meth house. There were a couple of fingerprints that were flagged—one of Salvez's cousins and Bole's. I need you to head to Claxton. Check out the scene."

"Will do." Less than an hour from Savannah.

Courtney and the kids were safe right now, but with Bole circling the area, he couldn't let Courtney wander around without him keeping watch. Now that they'd kissed, hopefully she wouldn't question if he came with her and the kids on their outings. Guilt weighed on his shoulders. He told her she could trust him.

He'd lied.

CHAPTER EIGHT

"YOU'RE COURTNEY, RIGHT?" A woman with curly brown hair stopped next to her table.

"Yes." Courtney slipped a bookmark in her book and let her feet drop from the courtyard chair she'd propped them on. It was one of her days off. When she looked up at the woman, she couldn't help but scan the area for Kaden.

Ever since the kiss, Kaden had vanished. No phone call. No sightings.

What a jerk.

Maybe if she took the kids off the property, he'd finally show up.

"I'm Maggie. I don't think we've met." The woman shook Courtney's hand. "I'm on the housekeeping staff. I usually work at Carleton House."

"Sure." The brunette looked familiar. Sort of. She was a little older than Courtney and could use a facial—but Courtney couldn't judge. It had been weeks since she'd seen the inside of a spa.

"May I?" Maggie asked.

She nodded. Maggie was the first person who'd actually sought her out.

Maggie pulled out a chair, the metal scraping against the stone terrace. "I—I understand you've been taking care of Cheryl's kids."

Courtney couldn't help smiling. "Yes."

Maggie bit her lip. "Could you take on one more?"

"More?"

"My daughter. She's six, the same as Josh." Maggie leaned forward, her words rushing out. "My mother usually watches her, but my sister's having twins. My mom will head to Charleston to help her out. Could you watch Daria for the three or four weeks my mother is gone?" Maggie touched her arm. "She's in school, so it won't be a ton of hours."

"But I take care of the kids at Cheryl and Nathan's apartment."

And she didn't know how much longer she would be in Savannah. She swallowed. Mother hadn't made any headway with Father. In her last conversation with dear old Dad, he'd maligned her job. As expected he'd insisted caring for children was not worthy of a Smythe.

"It's impossible to find short-term care. She's really sweet. She won't be any trouble. And she and Josh go to the same school."

Courtney rubbed her forehead and found those darn ridges forming. "I…I don't know."

"What if I talk to Cheryl? See if she's okay with Daria joining you and the kids?" The woman took her hand. "I'm desperate."

"Three or four weeks?" It might be fun. And good for Josh and Issy. "If Cheryl doesn't have a problem, I'll do it."

"You're a life saver. My sister doesn't expect to deliver until around Labor Day."

Courtney could handle another child for a few weeks, especially since Josh and Daria were in school. She might have to limit their adventure days with a third child. They'd need to walk everywhere. "If Cheryl is okay with it, sure."

"Thank you." Maggie gave her a hug. "I'm going to find Cheryl right now."

It was possible that Cheryl would say no, although Courtney didn't think that would happen. She ran back to her room and grabbed her idea notebook. How could she keep *three* kids occupied?

Forsyth Park was usually fun. They'd gone to the playground once, but they could go again. Maybe even take a picnic. They could tour the gardens and identify flowers. Maybe Bess could come along. Or they could do the same here in Bess's gardens.

She noted other ideas; painting in the courtyard, making playdough. Play instruments? That might disturb Abby's guests.

She could do this. She could handle three kids. *Maybe.*

Courtney headed to Fitzgerald House to grab a cup of coffee. Her body must be adjusting to the heat. It didn't bother her to drink hot beverages when the air was as hot as the liquid in her cup. Even her hair was starting to frizz...a bit. She hadn't been able to waste money on her normal hair products.

In the kitchen, Abby, Cheryl and Maggie were

huddled around the table. Issy played in the sitting area.

"Hey, Issy," Courtney whispered.

Issy gave her a sunshine-filled smile. "Hi."

"Perfect," Abby called to Courtney. "We're discussing where the day care should go. Come join us."

Courtney's mouth dropped open. "Day care?"

"Maggie asked me about you watching Daria in the apartment," Cheryl said.

"And opening a day care on the property evolved from there." Abby tapped her pen on her ever-present to-do list. "This is a great idea. Nathan's checking out the empty space on the first floor of the carriage house. I hope it will work."

"Wait, *you're* opening a day care?" Courtney headed to the table, her hands clenched into fists.

Josh and Issy were her responsibility, and Abby was taking over their care? If she lost this job, she would never get back to Boston. Back to her life.

"No." Abby waved her over to the group that was stealing her job. "*You're* opening a day care."

Courtney's heart thumped double-time. "*I'm* opening a day care?"

Cheryl and Maggie grinned, nodding their heads like they were bobblehead dolls.

"It's a great idea," Cheryl said. "So many of the staff have kids. They have trouble with the B and B's odd hours. You've been really flexible with Josh and Issy."

"But…" She sank into a chair across from Abby. "I don't know anything about running a—a day care."

The kitchen door opened and Nathan joined the group. "I think it will work. The day care can use the north door. We'll build a couple of bathrooms and you can get three good-sized rooms back there along with a small reception area, an office and storage. Luckily, we poured all the floors when we started on your restaurant."

Courtney's head spun so hard, she was worried it would fly off. "I don't know anything about running a day care," she repeated.

"I built some in Atlanta," Nathan said. "We'll pull up the regs. You'll need to get licensed."

"Dolley texted. She'll help with that." Abby made a note on her list. "I don't know why we didn't think of this earlier."

"But…" Courtney stopped, not knowing what to say. Regulations? Kids? Offices? She wouldn't be here that long. And what did licensing entail?

Everyone talked around her, over her, making plans.

Issy climbed on her lap and patted her cheek.

Kaden pushed open the swinging door and stopped. "Sorry, I didn't mean to interrupt. I was just checking for any requests."

Abby waved him in. "You're not interrupting."

Kaden nodded to Courtney but dodged her gaze. Had they really kissed three days ago?

Why hadn't he called? Was she a terrible kisser? Courtney jerked her head in his direction. No way would she show she was upset with being in the same room with him. Better to ignore the best kiss of her life and the man who was responsible. She straightened her spine and gave Issy a tight hug.

"Do you have a lot going on right now, Kaden?" Nathan asked.

"Not too much."

"My crews are stretched thin," Nathan said. "Maybe Kaden can help pull the day care together?"

"Great idea." Abby nodded. *Everyone* nodded. Courtney shook her head. Kaden frowned.

Abby explained, "We're putting a day care in the carriage house."

"You're starting a day care?" Kaden took the chair next to Courtney, his shoulder bumping hers. He shifted his arm across the back of her chair.

She scooted her bottom to the front of the chair so they didn't touch. She cleared her throat. "I'm—"

"It will be for Fitzgerald House employees," Abby interrupted, "to start."

"Courtney's been so flexible with the odd hours I work," Cheryl added.

"That's perfect," Kaden agreed with more enthusiasm than seemed reasonable.

"Why?" Courtney asked him. What was a day care to Kaden?

"Umm, that way you don't have to take the kids

very far. You'll have…everything you need right here at the B and B."

"We can make the food here or in the restaurant once we open," Abby said. "The cleaning crew can be responsible for the day care, too." Everyone tossed out ideas. Everyone but Courtney.

Dolley pushed through the swinging door. "I got your message and contacted our attorney. She's pulling the regs and promised to get back to me this afternoon."

Courtney swallowed. Her head wasn't spinning anymore. It had been tossed into the gale of a massive New England nor'easter. Why did everyone assume she was on board? Shouldn't someone ask what she wanted? Did she want to do this?

Kaden leaned in and whispered, "Are you okay?"

"No." Her stomach churned. This was not her life's dream.

But being with Josh and Issy was the happiest she'd been in years. If she didn't take this on, someone else would be taking care of them.

She sighed. Apparently, she was opening a day care center.

KADEN STARED AT the text that Roger had just sent.

Salvez used credit card at Savannah airport car rental—2 days ago

Shit. Why had it taken so long to get the intel? His hammer clattered to the floor of the day care.

After two days, Salvez and Bole could be anywhere. At least there hadn't been any facial recognition alerts. Maybe Bole wasn't even with Salvez.

He wanted to lock up Courtney and the kids and not let them out until Bole was in custody. But that wasn't going to happen. Courtney wasn't talking to him. He'd screwed up by not calling her after the kiss, but he'd been at the Claxton scene until three in the morning. Best thing he could do was help finish the day care. Then Courtney and the kids would be in one spot. He hammered a little faster.

Josh stuck his head in through the door. "Wow!"

"You shouldn't be in here." Kaden didn't need any distractions, and this was a work zone. With his record, someone would get hurt.

"Miss Abby sent us over." Josh bounded into the room with a basket. "We brought lunch."

"Fine." He hadn't worried about meals in a while. "Just stay on that side of the room."

Issy came into the room with cups. Courtney brought up the rear, not looking at him.

"Be careful," he warned.

All the progress he'd made going fishing with Courtney and the kids and they were back to coolness because he couldn't keep his head. He should have called Courtney the next morning, but how could he have explained that he'd been at a meth house? Roger's ex-wife had been on the scene.

She'd grilled him on encroaching on her territory. He'd only been partially honest when he'd told her he was in Savannah for his grandfather's recovery.

At some point he had to deal with the elephant in the room. If he and Courtney didn't get back to something more normal, he might have trouble staying close enough to the kids to catch Heather. That wasn't an option. Granddad was getting better. His cover for hanging around the B and B was going to disappear soon.

"Where's Daddy?" Issy whispered.

"Picking up supplies," Kaden said.

In the two days since the day care idea had surfaced, they'd gone through the regs with the lawyer, figured out the layout with an architect and roughed in rooms. The plumber was coming tomorrow for the bathrooms, handwashing station and small kitchen.

"Look at this." Courtney turned around. "I can't believe the space is coming together so fast."

Neither could Kaden. When the Fitzgeralds and Foresters made up their minds, they charged ahead. "They know all the right people to make things happen."

If he hadn't been watching Courtney's face, he wouldn't have seen her slight grimace. Why? Knowing what was going on behind that gorgeous face didn't affect the job he had to do, but he was…curious.

Josh skipped over to the wall Kaden was securing and wove between the studs.

"Don't," he called.

Josh grabbed an unsecured stud. The framing Kaden had just swung into place wobbled.

"Watch out!" Courtney leaped toward Josh and yanked him out of the path.

Kaden grabbed the frame and caught it before it crashed to the floor.

Issy screamed, then crumpled into a ball, whimpering.

"Everyone freeze!" His jaw clenched hard enough to grind his teeth to dust.

This is why he couldn't be around kids. Someone always got hurt. He lowered the framing to the floor.

Courtney ignored his order. She hurried to Issy and pulled her into a hug. Josh slunk closer to Courtney and his sister.

"It's dangerous in here. Let's eat in the courtyard." Courtney held out her hand for Josh. She scowled at Kaden.

He wasn't the bad guy here. "Once I get this hammered in place."

Because nailing the studs together would give him time to settle and a chance to work off his tension. He pounded as Courtney and the kids headed outside. When there were no more loose studs, he anchored the wall in place. No more excuses not to join Courtney and the kids.

He dusted off his clothes. Should he head to his apartment to clean up?

What was he thinking? This wasn't a date.

Wait. Maybe he should ask Courtney out. It would deal with the elephant in the room and ensure he could stay close to Issy.

Courtney and the kids sat at the closest courtyard table. Sandwiches and watermelon slices filled paper plates.

"Here." Courtney handed him some sort of wipe and he cleaned his hands.

"Thanks."

She had the kids on each side of her. He took the chair opposite and picked up a sandwich. Turkey. Tasty.

"What did you guys do today?" he asked.

"We picked out instruments. I chose the drums," Josh said. "Issy wanted the triangles and chimes. Miss Courtney found other stuff."

Issy's smile crept across her face. Good, maybe the accident hadn't traumatized her.

"So you'll have music classes?" he asked Courtney.

She tugged the meat out of her sandwich and took a bite of just turkey. "It's good for children to learn rhythm and hear music. And dance."

"But drums?" he asked. "Won't they be—"

"Cool," Courtney insisted.

Loud.

"They won't come until…" Josh looked up at Courtney.

"Two weeks," she added.

How strange that the woman he'd thought was beautiful—but useless—had morphed into this calm caretaker. She no longer wore haute couture around the B and B, but appropriate shorts and tops. He pushed away the memory of trailing his lips along the soft skin behind her ear. "What else do you have planned?"

"I'm working on a schedule." Courtney picked at her sandwich.

"Papa's putting together play equipment." Josh bounced so hard, his chair scraped the stone. "We get to help."

"To be licensed, the children have to be outside for at least one and a half hours a day. I have to keep lesson plans on site." Courtney took a deep breath that pulled her top snug against her breasts. "There's a lot of rules."

"The attorney told you all this?"

She flinched. "I did the research. It's my responsibility, after all."

"Of course." Again, he'd misjudged her.

He wanted to know her better and that wasn't a euphemism for getting her in the sack. But how did you ask out a woman who was justifiably mad at you *and* who always had two curious children shadowing her steps?

Josh kept up a running dialogue of all the plans

they were making. Issy would nod or hum. And Courtney added tidbits when she could get a word in. Kaden didn't try.

After lunch, Issy and Josh headed over to the fountain. He and Courtney packed up the leftovers. "How many kids are lined up?" he asked.

"Right now, five. But because the schedules vary, I'll only have all five on Fridays."

"So you'll have Saturday and Sunday off?"

She shook her head. "Sunday and Monday, assuming I find an assistant. But that schedule won't start for two weeks."

He tucked the last of the garbage into the basket and moved around the table to whisper in her ear. "Then I think we should celebrate your last Saturdays off. Want to do something?"

She closed the lid on the picnic hamper. "But I won't have Josh and Issy."

He set his hand on her shoulder and let it slide down her back, enjoying her little shiver. "I didn't mean the kids and you. I meant *you*. And me."

She blinked and her deep blue eyes flashed. "I thought…"

He squeezed her waist. "You thought?"

"I…" She shook her head and curls tumbled around her shoulders.

He wanted to crush her hair in his hand and yank her mouth to his. But the kids were staring.

She shuffled back and his hand slipped away

from her warmth. "I thought you'd decided to ignore what had happened."

"Not possible to ignore that kind of attraction. I'm sorry I didn't call that night. I had to…run errands and didn't get back until late." He stroked a finger down her soft cheek. "Saturday?"

Her breath came out in small puffs, making him grin. "That would be lovely."

Mission accomplished. Now where could he take someone like Courtney, who was used to everything being the best?

"WHERE DO YOU and Cheryl like to eat?" Kaden asked Nathan as they framed in another wall.

"You mean like a date?" Nathan bolted the frame to the floor and stepped away.

"Yeah."

Nathan grinned. "Cheryl's as talented as Abby in the kitchen, so I like home. But if you want a little bit of fancy, go to The Old Pinke House. If you want a little fun, head to Kevin Barry's pub, most nights they have music. Plus, it's a nice walk along the river. If you're into seafood try Chive. It's walking distance from here."

"Great." Pinke House. Barry's. Chive. He'd check out their reviews. "Thanks."

"Who's the lucky lady?" Nathan asked.

Kaden pulled up the next framed wall they were placing. Would telling Nathan who he was taking out affect her job or his? "Someone I met."

"Well, have fun." Nathan nodded. "How's Nigel?"

"Good. They're talking about him transitioning back home." Granddad would need to get to his PT appointments once he was out of the rehab center. Right now, it was easier to monitor both his grandfather and Issy from Savannah. Tybee would be problematic.

Nathan wedged his end of the frame into place. "How much longer can you stay here?"

"I'm fine for now." If something didn't happen soon, he might have to return to Atlanta, but he didn't want to leave Savannah. Leave his granddad. Leave the B and B.

Strange. He'd spent his adult life searching out and destroying criminals. Now he'd been lulled away from what was important by the Fitzgeralds' haven of hospitality.

He slammed a nail in place a little harder than necessary. Time to get his priorities straight. Hanging around Fitzgerald House wouldn't stop the flood of drugs ruining peoples' lives.

"Have you heard anything more about where Heather might be?"

"She used a credit card near Hilton Head, but Salvez used one at the Savannah airport two days ago."

"Here?" Panic edged Nathan's voice. "Are they in Savannah?"

"We don't know. That makes getting the day care ready a top priority. We can keep Issy in one place."

Nathan paced. "Maybe I should take the kids and Cheryl away."

And remove the FBI's bait?

"I'll talk to my superior," Kaden said, stalling, "but the best way to keep from worrying is to catch Bole. That will be easier if Issy is here."

"Let me know what he thinks." Nathan rolled his shoulders. "But my number one concern is my family."

"Understood."

After they placed the walls, Kaden headed to his apartment. He stared at his phone, needing to call Roger.

He was torn. Should he recommend Nathan take his family away? He might lose the chance of catching Bole and Salvez, but Issy would be safe.

Until Bole came back.

Better to tighten up security and capture the scumbags.

He called Roger and caught him at the office. "Roger, any word on Bole?"

"Nothing."

"The father wants to take the family out of town."

Roger swore. "What did you tell him?"

"It would only delay capturing Bole." Kaden rubbed his neck. "That it was better to use Issy to pull her out."

"Agreed."

"But I'd like backup."

"I'll see what I can do. We're shorthanded up

here and the Atlanta police actually asked for our help on an upcoming raid."

Kaden rolled his shoulders, but the tension didn't ease. "What about pulling in the Savannah office?"

"No frigging way!"

Kaden didn't break the silence after Roger's outburst.

"Are you worried you'll fail?" Roger asked. "Is this because of the twin boys you lost?"

"No." His failures were always waiting to slap him in the face.

Any child under his care wasn't safe. Hadn't Josh slipped on the boat when they were at Granddad's place? And today, Josh had almost pulled a wall down on top of himself.

But the worst? His brother, Kaleb.

He'd been told to watch his sweet, two-year-old brother, but for once they'd had a television and Kaden couldn't be bothered. His brother had found a packet of what he now knew was heroin and eaten it. His fault.

"Do you think I'll fail? Do you want to replace me?" The kids were too much responsibility.

He was good at saving people from drugs…in general. It was when things became personal. Now that he knew Issy and she was comfortable with him, would his presence cause her harm? He gritted his teeth hard enough that Roger probably heard the grinding.

"I don't want to replace you. Everyone knows

you're Nigel's grandson. I'm worried about your lack of confidence. You're one of my best agents."

"Thanks. But think about sending backup." Kaden heaved out a sigh. "And send me anything new we have on the Salvez family."

"Will do."

Once he hung up, Kaden flipped through the cameras. A couple of guests sat in the garden. One of the staff hauled a tray over to Carleton House. Everything looked normal.

He pushed away from the table he used as a desk. There should be more he could do. He wanted to crack this case. Down here surrounded by everything that was sweet and nice in life, he was losing his edge. When he checked the time, it was after six, and Courtney had transferred Issy's care back to Nathan.

Kaden could run to the gym and lift weights. Work out the frustration building inside him.

The run along Oglethorpe was more a pedestrian dodge and weave. He finally cut up Bull to get to Broughton.

The attendant had him sign in then handed him a locker key and a towel. "It's quiet today."

"Good." Kaden needed quiet.

He worked his way through his routine, starting with hand weights and moving from there to legs and finally ending on the rowing machine. But his anxiety level didn't decrease. It ramped up. Where were the promised endorphins?

He headed back to his locker. Before he was next to the door, he heard the camera alert on his phone going off. Shit.

He jammed the key in the locker and yanked his phone out. He typed in the password, holding his breath.

Possible identification: Heather Bole. 45% probability.

He hustled to the front door and tossed the key on the desk. Back on the street he ran, at the same time pulling up Nathan's phone number. "I just had an alert Heather might be in the courtyard," he gasped. "Camera outside the restaurant."

"Damn. My mother just called. A woman called the business number looking for me. She wanted to know where I lived," Nathan said. "Mom didn't give her any information and the woman wouldn't leave a name or number. It's got to be Heather."

Kaden sprinted down Bull, hoping people would see his desperation and clear a path. "The last place she saw you was the restaurant, right? When she dropped off Issy."

"Yes." There was rustling on Nathan's end of the conversation. "I don't see her in the courtyard. Do you want me to go check?"

Kaden turned left on Oglethorpe and hopped around a couple waiting at the crosswalk. Couldn't people see he had to move? He sped up, swiping at the sweat stinging his eyes.

"I'm a block away," he gasped. "Go down the back way. Don't let her know where you live. If she's there, keep her talking."

All he had was his phone. His weapon was locked in his apartment. Heather wouldn't expect a B and B guest to try to capture her, right? Surprise was always an advantage.

He slapped his guest card against the reader and entered the back garden. Slowing, he pretended to scroll through his phone. But he was checking the B and B cameras.

Guests sat at a courtyard table. Nathan stood by the restaurant door, scanning the area. Gray and Courtney walked out of the Carleton carriage house, probably heading over to Fitzgerald House and the alert buzzed for Courtney. Everything normal. No Heather.

He swore. If he'd stayed at the B and B, he might have caught her. This might have been over. He met Nathan by the carriage house.

"I couldn't find her." Nathan's voice was low.

"Let me check with the guests in the courtyard." Kaden took a couple of calming breaths and headed over to the couple. "Excuse me."

They looked up.

"I'm wondering if you saw a woman in the courtyard. We were supposed to meet here," he lied.

The woman frowned. "Let's see, since we sat down I saw one of the staff head over to the other house."

"A woman peered into that building." The man

pointed behind his companion's back at the carriage house restaurant.

"Was she blond?" Kaden asked. The definition on the screen hadn't picked up her hair color.

"Maybe." The man frowned. "She didn't stay long."

"Thanks. I must have missed her. Oh. Do you know how much I missed her by?"

"Ten, fifteen minutes?" He held up his drink. "Enough to drink half a glass of Abby's great wine."

"Thanks." He would check the street. Maybe she was hanging around the front of the B and B. But if she didn't know Nathan lived here, why would she stick around?

He headed back to Nathan. "Take the Fitzgerald House parking lot and north side of the building, I'll take the Carleton House lot and the south."

"When she dropped off Issy," Nathan said, "she left in a pickup with dark tinted windows."

They parted company. Kaden started for the parking lot. Each morning he ran the license plates of the cars parked in the lots. Maybe he needed to run them morning and night. He snapped pictures of the plates. Then he worked his way around Carleton House and walked the remaining block back to Fitzgerald House, checking the vehicles parked in the street. He was grasping at straws.

Nathan met him on the sidewalk. "Nothing. She must have called my mother after she left."

"It's possible she'll come back tomorrow."

"Tomorrow's Saturday."

He was so off his game. "Monday then."

Nathan pulled off his ball cap and shoved his hand through his hair. "I don't want Heather any-where near Issy."

"Neither do I. I'll stick closer to Courtney and the kids on Monday. And all next week." He would talk to Roger again about bringing in backup.

Courtney needed to know what was going on, but Roger hadn't given him the okay. At mini-mum, Nathan could warn her someone looking like Heather had been spotted at the B and B.

He'd already made enough mistakes in Savan-nah. Time to get his head in the game and catch a drug dealer.

THE LOGISTICS OF opening her child care center crammed Courtney's brain. Well, the *Fitzgerald House* center, but everyone assumed she was in charge. The Fitzgeralds were paying for all the equipment and construction, but she was respon-sible for the program, staff and collecting revenue. She was also back on the Fitzgerald payroll.

Making one more note, she shut the laptop Gray had lent her. If she'd known she would be here this long, she'd have brought her own computer. It didn't seem worthwhile to have Mother ship it down now. How much longer would she be ban-ished to Savannah?

Courtney waited for the resentment against her father to rear up and make her stomach ache. But there was…nothing. Everything was changing. No ache to return home swelled inside her. She had no desire to see the so-called friends who hadn't contacted her. She'd been so busy researching all the Georgia regulations and figuring out how to comply with them, she hadn't even talked to her mother for almost a week.

"I'm going to grab some lunch," Gray said. "Are you hungry?"

Even her relationship with Gray had mellowed. "That would be great."

"They're installing the last of the play equipment today." Gray held the door and they headed into the courtyard.

"Wonderful. I'll check it out after lunch." She touched her brother's arm. "Thank you for putting up with me."

He stopped in the center of the walkway. "Putting up with you?"

She swallowed. "I shouldn't have come down here without asking."

"I'm glad you did." He wrapped an arm around her shoulder. "This has given us a…new beginning."

She bumped his chest, not concerned when he mussed her hair. "I think you're right."

"Stay as long as you like." He left his arm around her shoulder. "I like who you've become, brat."

"I wish we could have had this kind of relationship when you lived in Boston." Tears welled in her eyes. "Maybe I wouldn't have been such a—a bitch."

"I don't know." He chuckled. "You're still pretty uppity."

She jammed an elbow into his gut. "And you aren't?"

They were laughing as they entered the Fitzgerald House kitchen. Abby looked over and her grin wasn't just for Gray. It included Courtney. "Got any food for hungry workers, innkeeper?" Gray said.

"Maybe." Abby winked. "Depends on what kind of payment you have in mind."

Gray swept his wife off her feet and planted a kiss on Abby that had Courtney blushing.

Would Kaden kiss her again tonight? Would it be the way Gray kissed Abby? As if the only thing in the world that mattered was being with her?

Courtney hadn't evoked those kind of emotions in men—ever. She was the untouchable woman. No one hungered for her. They wanted to conquer her. Once they had, they moved on. Or she did.

But watching Gray and Abby, she wanted someone to want her like that just once in her life.

"Get a room, you two," she muttered and headed to the table where Abby had set out pasta salad and a tray of sandwiches.

"We have one," Gray quipped.

"Eat your lunch." Abby pushed him away. "I have to prep for tonight's event."

"Where's Cheryl?" Gray asked, grabbing a glass and combining lemonade and iced tea.

"She'll be back. Nathan wanted her to stop at the new house and make flooring decisions."

"Did she say anything about Heather possibly stopping at the B and B on Friday?" Gray sat across from Courtney and helped himself to food.

"Heather? That's Issy's mother?" A chill ran through Courtney.

Gray nodded. "Nathan told me."

Abby added, "Yesterday, a woman called Forester Construction, looking for Nathan. It might have been Heather."

Courtney bit her thumbnail. Shouldn't someone have warned her? "Will she come back? I haven't even thought about security in the center."

"Kaden helped with the restaurant security," Abby said. "Ask him."

"Kaden?" Why would he know anything about security? "I guess I can do that."

She hadn't seen Kaden since he'd asked her out. At least they would have something to talk about on their date tonight. Her stomach clenched a little. She didn't know where they were going or how she should dress. Even with the cases of clothes she'd brought to Savannah, nothing ever seemed appropriate.

"Thank you for lunch." Courtney put her dishes

in the dishwasher. "I'm going to check on the day care progress. Anything you want brought over there?"

"No." Abby brushed a hand on her shoulder. It was a gesture Courtney had seen her make dozens of times with her sisters. Never with her. "You're welcome anytime."

Courtney rushed out the door, choking up but refusing to let a tear fall. How could one small touch from a sister-in-law she didn't really like mean so much?

But she *liked* Abby. *Admired* her. She felt dizzy. When had things changed?

Next to a courtyard table, she leaned on her hands, her head dropping as she took deep breaths. She swiped at her eyes. She'd cried more in Savannah than in the last ten years of her life.

No time to dwell on things she didn't understand. Straightening her top over her shorts, she headed across the courtyard. Maybe she could find out where Kaden was taking her tonight. They hadn't set a time and he hadn't followed up. What if he'd changed his mind? What if he'd…

She pressed the spot between her eyebrows. Geez—no other man ever made her worry like this.

When she turned the corner, she spotted Kaden.

He wore a T-shirt and his muscles bulged as he shook concrete from a wheelbarrow. She wasn't attracted to gym rats. But Kaden… *Oh, my.* Her mouth watered. Leaning against the side of the carriage house, she watched. To be truthful, she ogled.

"Hi, Courtney." Bess waved.

Courtney jumped. She hadn't noticed there were other people here. "Hi."

Bess and another man worked the wet concrete around the legs of a small slide. Kaden moved the wheelbarrow over to the second leg. He nodded but kept working and the other man jammed a pole into the liquid mess.

Courtney bit her lip, holding in her disappointment at Kaden's tepid greeting. He was working on a Saturday. She should be noting everything Kaden and Bess had accomplished for the center instead of being worried about his lack of interest.

In addition to the slide, they'd installed a small walkway, a tilted merry-go-round and a tunnel with cut-out windows. She grinned. The kids and she had picked out the bright colors: red, blue and yellow. It had been hard to convince Issy that pink wouldn't work. Issy had been placated, because the girls' bathroom would have a pink door.

Bess pushed off the ground, stretching her back. "I've figured out how to give you a small garden for the kids to plant."

"Great." Courtney ripped her gaze away from Kaden.

"I thought we could attach low planters to the fencing." Bess waved her over to the edge of the playground. "I've got some ideas on what veggies and herbs they could grow."

"I'll take all the help I can get." Courtney had never planted anything. "Can you ensure the beds are low enough so kids can reach them?"

"If we use variable heights—" Bess pushed back her ponytail "—the shorter kids wouldn't have to fight for space with the taller children."

"I like the way you think."

"I've drawn up some ideas." Bess moved back to Kaden and the other worker. "After we anchor the table, let me show you."

"Thanks." Courtney pointed to the entrance to the center. "I want to check out what's happening inside."

Courtney pulled open the new glass door. Hmm, if they were planting, weeding and watering, the kids needed somewhere to wash their hands. They needed an outdoor faucet.

Inside, the space was coming to life. The small reception area was framed in. A door led to a large group area and two classrooms branched off that. Large windows let in the light. Each classroom had a connected quiet area. Some had Sheetrock, some were only framed, but it all looked…hopeful.

The exterior door opened and Kaden walked in. Everything buzzed inside her. Did he feel the change in the air, too?

"Place is starting to look like something," he said.

She smiled. Couldn't help it. "I can't wait."

"Did you see the bathrooms?"

"I haven't gotten that far." She headed through the large group area and down a narrow hall, skirting the handwashing station positioned outside the bathrooms. Her hand clasped her chest. It was really happening. "The toilets are in."

He chuckled, a deep rumbling noise. "I think you're the only woman I know who gets teary-eyed over bathrooms."

"But look." She grabbed his arm. "Everything is kid-size. And bright colors. And perfect."

"You're really into this." His cobalt gaze held hers, as if he was trying to peer inside her head.

She nodded. "I've never had a dream before."

Shock filled his face. "Never?"

She shrugged. Dreaming of the next party didn't count. She wouldn't think about her old life. She wasn't sure she would ever get back to Boston. "What should I wear tonight?"

Kaden's eyebrows snapped together. "Tonight?"

"I thought…" Had she hallucinated it? Her elation at seeing the day care dissipated like smoke up a chimney. "You asked me out. Didn't you?"

"I forgot." He rubbed his head. "With working on the space…"

He forgot?

"It's…okay." She moved to the door as fast as she could without running. She couldn't let him see the hurt. Over her shoulder she called, "Don't worry. No problem."

"Wait!" His boots thumped on the concrete floor. "Courtney."

No way. God, what if she hadn't stopped at the day care? She would have waited like some slumpy girl for a man who wasn't going to pick her up. She'd never been stood up—ever. She turned the corner and made it to the reception area.

His hand closed over hers. "Give me a chance here."

"I need to go…research." Something. Anything.

"I'm sorry." He tugged on her fingers and pressed her back against the closest wall. "I would have remembered and called you."

"Right." He was lying.

"I asked Nathan where he and Cheryl liked to go." Kaden rested his arms on the wall next to her head. "I planned to walk down to River Street. So dress casual."

"Sure. Fine. Okay." She stared at his shirt.

He touched her chin, forcing her to look at him. "I'm sorry."

They hadn't been this close since he'd kissed her. She stared at his lips. Her chest tightened so hard, she struggled to breathe.

He cupped her cheek, stroking his thumb across her bottom lip. Shivers sizzled through her body. "It's pretty rare when I catch you without your shadows."

"I haven't been with the kids all day." Her voice was a whisper.

"They keep me from doing this." He stepped closer, his thighs brushing hers. She had to tilt her head to watch his face descend. He paused. "May I?"

She couldn't form words, so she nodded.

His lips parted and their tongues met and tangled. One arm pulled her away from the wall and banded around her back. His hand caressed her bottom.

Pressed flush against him, she was totally under his control, something she normally hated. Instead, she moaned, her breasts smashed against his chest.

His lips trailed up to her ear and she gasped for breath. He nipped at her neck. "What time?"

She couldn't think. All she could do was feel his hard thigh between her legs. "What?"

He kissed her hard, rolling his hips against her. "What time should I pick you up?"

"S-s-seven." At least she thought that's what came out of her mouth. "I'll meet you in the courtyard."

His last kiss was gentle, but it didn't matter. He'd already knocked her off her feet. She flopped against the wall. Maybe she wasn't ready to date a man like Kaden.

KADEN TUCKED A clean blue polo shirt into his khakis. With the shirt tucked in, he couldn't wear his weapon. He hated that naked feeling.

He shouldn't be leaving the property. Both he

and Nathan had assumed Heather wouldn't return until Monday, but what if she did? If his security system alerted him, the pub was farther away than the fitness center.

The good news was that Issy wasn't at the B and B. The whole Forester family was sailing on Nathan's twin brother Daniel's boat. Kaden could eat and be back before Nathan and his family returned to Fitzgerald House.

And to be going on a date? He'd justified romancing Courtney so that he could stay close to Issy. The fact that Bole had been on the property and Courtney didn't know the full danger made his shoulders itch. Hell, when she'd thought he'd forgotten about their date, she'd run away from him, tears in her eyes. What would she think once he caught Bole and told her the truth of why he was here? Would she still trust him?

Their kiss had kept him on edge all afternoon. Kisses weren't enough. He wanted to spend an evening with her. A *night* with her. He heaved out a sigh. Even though dating her was good for the Bole case, Courtney was a big, big distraction.

He'd take her to dinner. They'd be back on the property in an hour or two, well before Issy returned.

He headed down the steps to the courtyard. A brief rain shower had come through, giving some relief from the heat and humidity. If he'd led a normal life, it would be a nice evening for a date.

His steps quickened across the flagstone paths. He stopped at a table near the Carleton carriage house. Had Courtney wanted to meet in the courtyard because she didn't want her brother to know they were dating? Was she ashamed to date the B and B's handyman?

That was one of the reasons he wanted Courtney to know his real purpose. He wasn't just a handyman, not that there was anything wrong with that career. He was an FBI agent with a mission.

The door of the carriage house opened and Courtney stepped out. He stopped breathing.

Her black curls cascaded down her back. She wore a flimsy see-through red sweater over a black clingy tank top. He wanted to trace all her curves hidden by the sweater. Her black pants only went to her calves.

He was up and moving before she took the last step down. "Hi."

"Hi." She shook back her hair. He'd seen her do it a dozen times, but this time the move took his breath away.

"Are you okay to walk?" Women liked to wear impractical shoes.

She pointed to her toes. "Ballet flats. I can walk forever in these."

"Good." He took her hand and she laced her fingers with his. "Nathan recommended Kevin Barry's pub."

"A pub?"

What had he been thinking? This was a Boston princess. "I guess it's not what you're used to."

"Are you crazy?" She squeezed his fingers. "I live in Boston. Of course I go to pubs."

"I just… I don't know how to compete with the rich men who probably take you to five-star restaurants. Hell, I've never eaten at a five-star restaurant—unless you count Abby's."

"She is a queen of the kitchen."

"Was that sarcasm?" He waited for the light on Bay Street to change. He was pretty sure he knew where the stairs were down to River Street.

She snorted. "It should be. My sister-in-law is just so good at…everything."

"You keep beating us at Quarto. And you're good with children." Didn't she know that? "You're a great storyteller."

She shrugged. "My father doesn't think that's a worthwhile occupation."

"Then he's a fool." He set his hand on her lower back as they crossed the street with the crowd. "Working with children is the most important work there is."

"Then why don't you? Work with children?"

"I've…" He wanted to explain his job and real purpose. "I'd like to do what Granddad did. When I was growing up, he volunteered in sports programs for kids from homes broken apart by drugs."

"Have you volunteered up in Atlanta?" she asked.

They headed down the steps, his hand on her

shoulder. He couldn't confess he was bad with kids, that he couldn't keep them safe. "I haven't had an opportunity."

On the River Street cobblestones, they walked side-by-side. "So you'd like to follow your grandfather's footsteps in more than just construction. Why?" she asked.

"Because of my parents." He didn't expand. That was not a first-date discussion. Not even a third or fourth date one.

Courtney must have caught the finality in his voice. She didn't follow up with more questions. Thank goodness.

"Umm, Abby suggested I talk to you about security for the center," she said.

This he could deal with. He held open the pub door. The hostess seated them at a table facing a small stage. Instead of sitting with his back to the stage, he sat next to her. As they settled into their seats, a server took their drink order. "A Jameson, please."

Courtney ordered a seasonal beer. That was a surprise.

"I have some security ideas," he said after the server left.

The twins who had died had attended an expensive day care with excellent security. The security at the center was probably why they'd been snatched from baseball practice. "We could have key codes at each door. You would have to be diligent in restricting access."

"Do you mean just the front door?"

"No. All doors until you get to the classrooms."

"Parents would have to enter their code and manage kids and bags?"

"Think of it as layers of security."

"That would be cumbersome." She tugged on her ear and silver flashed through her dark curls. "I can see why all doors into the center would need a code or a security card, but we have to think of the parents juggling everything."

Didn't she understand the danger kids faced? "It would be very secure."

"If someone can get in the external door, what does it matter if there are more and more doors?"

He turned so they were face-to-face. "We could have different codes for each door."

"That's crazy. This isn't the CIA. We don't have state secrets." She shook her head and her drive-a-man-crazy curls shifted and settled around her shoulders. "Only one code per family."

What she was saying made sense. "But the kids—"

"Will be safe."

He exhaled. "Does that mean the retinal scan is out and no fingerprint identification?"

She laughed. "All out."

He couldn't keep from smiling back at her. Warmth filled his body. "I'll research different systems."

"Thank you." She tipped her head. "Why do you know so much about security?"

"I…did some jobs in Atlanta."

"I guess I don't know exactly what you do there. Handyman work? Construction?"

Their drinks arrived. A reprieve. He didn't want to lie to Courtney any more than necessary. He held up his glass. "To your success."

"My success. No one's ever said that to me." Her blue eyes were huge. Her lip trembled. She held up her mug. "Thank you."

He liked the idea of being the first person to recognize her strengths. And it kept her from drilling into his career. "What did you do in Boston?"

"Nothing." She shook her head and a curl flirted with her breast. Her finger drew designs in the condensation on her mug. "Shopped. Partied."

"That's all?" That's what he'd thought when they'd first met, but now that he knew her, that life didn't sound like it would be satisfying to Courtney. He blurted out, "Weren't you bored?"

"I wasn't encouraged to do anything else." Her head snapped up and her blue eyes were like laser beams. "But I…"

He waited, but she didn't say anything more. "Yes?"

"I told you before, I volunteered at a library." She stared at her mug. "The weekly reading hour for kids."

Was she embarrassed by that? "And your family

didn't think that was—" What was the word she'd used? "Worthwhile?"

She sipped her beer and set it down with a crack. "I never told them."

"Why not?" Would he ever understand Courtney? "Wouldn't that have softened your father up?"

"It was something I did for *me*." She pressed a hand to her chest. "When I'm reading and see the kids' entranced faces, I can't stop smiling."

And the children had benefited the most. Even if he'd been able to tell Courtney that he was an FBI agent, eventually she'd realize he was a danger to children, while she was a blessing. "I'll bet the kids miss you."

A smile lit her face. "The head of the program took a picture of the kids for me."

She pulled out her phone and scrolled through her messages.

A group of kids held up a poster board that said Miss Courtney, We Miss You.

"That's nice." He hesitated, then asked, "Do you plan to return to Boston?"

"That's what I wanted." She shrugged and her curls bounced around again. "Mother hasn't made any progress with my father. My friends rarely contact me. There's nothing to go back to."

"And you have something here."

She frowned.

"Your day care."

"It's really Abby's, isn't it?" Her shoulders fell. "I'll be employed by Fitzgerald House."

"And that's bad?"

"Abby saw a need and filled it." Courtney circled the rim of her mug with her finger. "I'm a set of hands to accomplish Abby's dreams."

"You're the core, the center of what's happening there." He caught her hands. One was cold from her beer mug. "You're creating the programs. This isn't being a nanny. This is molding young children into good people."

"Then she's made a mistake. I'm not the person to mold young children." She tried to pull away, but he hung on. "I'm the epitome of how *not* to grow up. I've never accomplished anything."

"That will make it easier for you to keep the kids on the right path." He couldn't stand the sadness on her face. With a tug he drew her close and brushed a kiss on her lips. "Don't be so hard on yourself."

His granddad had said those words to him at least once a day for the first year he'd lived with him. Kaden had never believed it. He'd let his brother die.

But Courtney was different. "Josh and Issy adore you."

She stared at him, her forehead furrowed. Normally she would touch the ridge between her arched eyebrows. He hadn't seen her make that gesture in a while. He smoothed out the worry lines with his thumb.

"Are you ready to order?" their server asked.

Courtney asked for fish and chips and he requested the rib eye.

After the server left, Courtney peeked at him from under her thick eyelashes, a promising wicked glance that had him shifting in his chair. "I might share some of my fish if I can taste your rib eye."

"That sounds like a plan." He'd never been big on sharing food because there'd never been anyone to share with growing up. "Did you and Gray share?"

"Mother didn't allow that." She rolled her neck.

"With a boyfriend, then?" Jealousy exploded in his chest. The pain was as sharp as when a pit bull had attacked him and his partner at the first crack house he'd taken down.

"No." She blinked. "Gwen and I always split our meals."

He took a swallow of whiskey and let it burn its way to his stomach. "Will your friend come to visit?"

"No. Gwen used to date Gray." She stared into her beer, and her smile disappeared. "When Gray was working on his warehouse, she and I came to Savannah. That was a disaster. It was probably the beginning of the end of our friendship."

His chest ached for her. When she wasn't playing games, she looked...lost. "You'll make new friends here."

She snorted, then slapped her hand on her mouth. "Sure. Issy and Josh. And the other children."

He tried to catch her eye, but she wouldn't look up. "And me."

"We're friends?" There was that startled, vulnerable look again. "I thought…"

Were they friends? He felt a little guilty. Having to stay close to her didn't mean he needed to date her. Or sleep with her. An image of stripping off the flimsy swimsuit she'd worn on their fishing trip rose in his mind.

"Sure we are." He threaded their fingers together. "What did you think?"

"Most men—" she waved her free hand down her body "—don't look beyond my facade."

"Because you don't let them see anything else." And he'd done the same thing. He brushed a kiss on her cheek. "Don't get me wrong. You're beautiful, but you're so much more than that."

Her eyes shimmered. "Really?"

"Really." She was fragile. He had to get this right. He wouldn't be like the other men in her life. "Tell me what you have planned for the children."

Her hand trembled in his. She stared as if she was trying to discern his truthfulness. Then she talked about her thoughts and plans, even asked his opinion.

Halfway through dinner, a man took a seat on the stool on stage and greeted the audience. Kaden and Courtney stopped talking and enjoyed the music and being with each other. Her smile gleamed with joy.

He wrapped an arm around her, needing to touch her. He didn't want the night to end.

He was getting emotionally involved in this assignment. Hell, it wasn't an assignment anymore—was it?

COURTNEY CURLED A little deeper under Kaden's arm, letting him guide her back to the B and B. "It's a nice night."

"Mmm-hmm." His voice rumbled through his chest.

Was she really more than a pretty face to him, more than a conquest? Could she lower her defenses? Could this thing with her and Kaden be more than the Savannah fling she'd first imagined?

It came down to trust. She'd trusted Kaden with the secret of her library volunteer work. And he'd listened. Maybe she *was* more than a conquest to him.

At dinner, she hadn't worried about who was watching and judging her as the worthless Smythe daughter. No one knew her in Savannah. Sure, she could probably only get preferred seating in restaurants if she dropped Abby's name, but anonymity was freeing.

"I had the best time tonight. Thank you." She waited for Kaden to run his card through the reader on the courtyard gate. She'd been to black-tie parties, openings and her mother's charity dinners, but she'd never relaxed like she had tonight. "The music was a lovely surprise."

"I had fun, too." He held her hand as they moved along the paths.

Would he ask her up to his apartment? She hadn't been interested in a man in so long she didn't know what she wanted him to do.

She'd actually forgotten he was just a handyman. That would never happen at home. She and Gwen had known everyone's social status and net worth.

Kaden walked her to the carriage house door, never saying anything about going back to his place. And she couldn't invite him into Gray's home. Talk about awkward.

"What's going on in here?" He tapped her head.

She swallowed. She couldn't confess she was stressing out about sleeping with him. "Why?"

"You're tense. When we left the pub, you were relaxed. Now?" He squeezed her shoulders. "You're a ball of nerves."

"I don't understand where we're going, what we're doing."

"I don't know, either." He pulled her into his chest, wrapping his hands around her butt and anchoring her to his body. "Let's not overthink this."

Didn't he know she needed to analyze everything? Her family may not acknowledge her IQ, but she was compelled to scrutinize the minutiae of her life. "I don't know if I can do that."

He bent close, brushing his lips against hers. "Try."

Shivers ran straight to her core. He scraped his teeth on the shell of her ear and the shivers turned to lightning that arced through her body. She pressed close, running her hands up his chest and lacing them around his neck.

"How will I keep my hands off you?" he muttered, clutching her tight and fusing their mouths together. His tongue moved in and out, and she met it stroke for stroke. He tasted of whiskey and temptation.

His hand slid under her shirt and up to her breast. *Touch me.*

He chuckled like he'd heard her, cupping her breast and sliding his thumb across her nipple.

Her moan probably woke the guests in both mansions.

"Shush." He covered her mouth with his, pinching her nipple. This time she groaned. Her hands slid to his butt and she hung on as he tormented her breasts.

He ripped his lips away and rested his forehead on hers. His gasps were strong enough to blow her hair off her cheek. Her breaths matched his.

"I'd better let you go before your brother finds us." Kaden's voice sounded rusty.

She mewed a complaint. Right now she wanted to be alone with Kaden. And naked. To have him pull her up the steps, into his apartment, and take her against the wall or door or floor, or on the bed.

He led her up the last steps and brushed a kiss on her forehead. "I hope I see you tomorrow."

"Me, too." She sagged against the door, watching him walk away. Her body was on fire. Was this what the guys who'd kissed her meant when they'd called her a tease? Not fun.

She headed to her room, not wanting to talk to Gray or Abby. Then it hit her. Kaden had whispered, "How will I keep my hands off you?"

She'd obviously given him the green light. Why would he need to do that?

CHAPTER NINE

KADEN TUCKED IN the clean sheets and replaced the comforter. He dusted the bureau with a dirty towel and tossed it into his laundry pile. He was ready to shut off his computer, but pulled up the camera that covered the Carleton House courtyard.

Courtney sat at a shaded table. She worked between a laptop and her notebook where she scribbled her day care ideas.

Her sundress was the same color as her Caribbean blue eyes and left her shoulders bare. He could give the straps one sharp tug and find only Courtney underneath.

In the living area, he picked up the newspaper and dropped it in his recycling bin. Then he washed his lunch plate and glass. Finally, he locked his weapon on the top shelf of the closet.

This was as clean as he could get the apartment. No skivvies decorated the floor and a fresh box of condoms occupied the nightstand.

He should avoid Courtney. Around her, he forgot why he was in Savannah. Not just for his granddad, but to capture Heather.

But he couldn't stay away.

He shut down his computer and headed to the courtyard. Nathan, Cheryl and the kids would be away from the apartment all day. First they planned to walk through their new house, then make paint decisions. For dinner, they were heading to Nathan's parents' home. With both Nathan and Daniel there, Issy would be safe. If Heather showed up, Nathan would delay her and call him.

He could spend the evening with Courtney.

She glanced up as he moved toward the table. Her smile beamed. "How's your day going?"

Better now. He took a chair. "Good. Did some paperwork." And he'd checked in with Roger.

She frowned. "You have paperwork?"

Way to blow his cover. He'd completed his weekly task force report. "You know, paying bills."

She still frowned.

"Don't you have bills that need paying?" he asked.

She chewed her lip. "My father does that."

"Honey, you've led a sheltered life."

She shut the laptop a little harder than necessary. "I know."

"Sorry." He grabbed her hand. "I wasn't making fun of you."

"It's just, everyone is so…industrious down here. Sometimes I feel like an idiot."

"You're not." He twirled the ring on her finger. "Do you have dinner plans?"

"I'm not very hungry." She shrugged. "I was going to eat B and B appetizers and call it dinner."

"What about eating with me?"

"You want to go out again?"

He shook his head. He'd spent most of the night just replaying their kisses. "I'm thinking of getting delivery. Pizza. Chinese. Whatever."

"What do you want?" she asked.

"You." His voice was a low growl.

"Oh." She blinked, her blue eyes growing even larger. "Oh."

He'd lost his cool. "Are you okay with that?"

"I couldn't sleep last night." She gathered her notebook and the computer, hugging it to her chest.

"I couldn't sleep, either," he choked out. Damn, he wanted to be her notebook.

She chewed her lip.

Was she going to run? She should. Maybe it was worrying about his granddad, or working under-cover, or just twiddling his thumbs waiting for Bole to show up, but he felt like he was dangling over a cliff.

"Let me just…" She held up her things, then raced into the carriage house through a sliding door on the side of the building.

He watched the door, his fingers rattling against the glass tabletop. He'd been too intense and scared her away. What was he thinking? They barely lived on the same planet. He came from drug dealers. She was all money and sophistication. He'd never dated a woman like her.

He stared at the door she'd escaped into, willing it to open. Damn it. He stood, ready to go knock on the glass.

She exited through the main door.

Relief flowed through him like the swish of a basketball through the basket, and hitting only net.

"You look worried," she said. "Did something happen with your grandfather?"

"I was watching that door." He pointed at the slider. "I thought you were brushing me off."

She laughed. It would have been irritating if it wasn't so musical. She linked their arms and tugged him along the path. "I needed to leave a note for Gray saying I had dinner plans. And I couldn't go out the sliding door, because it doesn't lock from the outside."

"You could have said something," he grumbled.

"I figured you understood what I meant when I said I hadn't slept last night." She stopped and stared into his eyes. "I was thinking of you. Of wanting to be with you. Naked."

"Okay." His breath whooshed out. "Same page."

He cupped her elbow and hustled her to the carriage house.

"You really were worried." There was that laugh again. Something she hadn't done much of when he'd first met her.

He swiped his card. "Not anymore."

Climbing the steps took forever. Somehow the hall had grown as long as a football field. He almost sprinted to unlock his apartment.

Courtney walked in as he held the door. "This is just like Cheryl and Nathan's place, but reversed."

He pushed the door shut, grabbed her hand and spun her around, backing her up against the wood.

"This is what I wanted to do last night." There was an unfamiliar growl in his voice.

Courtney's mouth dropped open.

He covered it with his. Filled it with his tongue.

She moaned, the sound vibrating their lips. Her fingers clutched and crept under his shirt. She smelled like dark exotic flowers and tasted of lemons.

He planned to savor her.

Courtney's leg wrapped around his calf. He reached down and tucked it higher. Then rolled his groin against her center. Heat poured off their coupled bodies.

His fingers worked the knot of her dress free. She arched her neck, her head thumping on the wooden door. The fabric slipped away from her breasts.

He stared. Her pink nipples tightened into sharp tips.

"Kaden," she choked out, her arm covering all her lovely pale skin.

"Don't be embarrassed."

"I just… I haven't had a Pilates class since Boston." She clutched the fabric over her stomach.

"You don't need a class like that to keep you in shape. You're beautiful."

She stiffened and wouldn't let him tug her arm away.

Commenting on her beauty was the wrong thing to say. Had the FBI's psychological classes been wasted on him?

She'd told him no one saw beyond her facade. Her father saw her as an ornament.

"I see you, Courtney." He touched her heart. "Inside, where you're beautiful."

"Thank you," she whispered.

Courtney wasn't the kind of woman you banged against a door before zipping up and going on with your life. He eased away, taking her hand, and led her down the hall. "Come with me."

She clutched the top of her dress to her breasts. As they passed Issy's old bedroom, she stopped, taking in the princess kingdom mural. "Wow. That's incredible."

"If you like that, you'll love the bed I'm sleeping in."

"Four-poster. I do like it." She toed off her sandals, then stood in the center of the room, her bottom lip caught between her teeth. Panic flitted across her face.

He took her shoulders in his hands. "Are you sure you want this?"

Her blue eyes were bottomless. Her breath came out in little puffs, fluttering against his neck. "Y-yes. I—I don't do this… Not often."

"Do?" What was she talking about? Then it dawned on him. His eyebrows shot up. "You don't sleep around?"

She shrugged, her lip caught between her teeth. "It's just… I was never that interested before."

Was this an innocent act she used to drive men wild? Sometimes he didn't understand Courtney. But this seemed real. And she'd picked him. Damn.

"We'll go slowly." He pulled her hands away from the top part of her dress. "It's been a while for me, too."

"You? But you're beautiful." She helped him ease the fabric down over her lovely breasts.

He winced. "That's not what you tell a man."

"Okay. Handsome. Strong. You know what I mean." She tugged on the bottom of his shirt. "I'd like to keep the nakedness…even."

"My pleasure." He tugged his shirt over his head. Leaning in, he brushed his chest against her breasts. "Heaven."

She ran the heels of her hands up each side of his chest. He shivered. Her thumbs lingered on his nipples, brushing back and forth until they formed small, hard nubs. Then she pinched them.

His breath heaved out. He wanted to throw her on the bed and bury his body inside hers, but he'd promised to go slow. Backing her against the bedpost, he pulled up her hands and wrapped them around the wood above her head. Easing her dress down, he kissed each delicious inch of exposed skin. Then he dropped to his knees as he slipped off her dress.

Her peach-colored thong was like a red cape flashed in front of a bull.

He dropped kisses on her hips, sliding his hands around and cupping each luscious cheek. His tongue sought out the small indentation of her bellybutton.

Courtney's eyes were half-closed, her head flung back. With her back arched and her hips thrust forward, she was an erotic dream he would never forget.

Kaden kneaded her ass and her feet slid apart. Planting kisses on the inside of her thighs, he worked his way up and inhaled her essence. Heat poured off her, warming his lips as he pressed a kiss on her silk-covered center.

Courtney moaned.

He did it again, eliciting another groan. Slipping a finger under the silk, he stroked. Finally, he pushed away the last barrier between her flesh and his mouth. His hand caressed the full length of each silky leg as he lifted each foot and tossed her clothes aside.

"Kaden," she whimpered.

He held her hips, helping her rock a little with each slide of his tongue. His erection jammed against his zipper, but he ignored the sweet pain.

"Please." She pulled on his hair. "I don't want to come without you."

Courtney hid generosity behind her facade. She had so many layers. He wanted to peel each one back, like the clothes he'd stripped away, and find the real Courtney Smythe.

HAD SHE SCREWED UP? Courtney wrapped her arms around her stomach, suddenly cold without Kaden's touch. He stood, unzipping his shorts.

She should help him, be the vixen everyone expected her to be in the bedroom. Instead, she sank onto the bed and curled her arms around her chest.

"What's wrong?" Kaden, still wearing his shorts, sat next to her.

She was naked.

Why couldn't she reach out and touch his erection? She wanted to. She wanted to be the woman she pretended to be. The sexy, confident woman that men desired.

"I'm fine," she lied.

He stared into her eyes. Lacing their hands together, he kissed one temple, then the next. Then his lips cruised her face and neck, and somehow she was on her back and his mouth was on her breast. "Oh—oh."

He chuckled. "I think you said that before."

She found some strength and pushed him so he was lying on his back. "My turn, okay?"

"Not just okay." His hands tightened on her hips. "Fun. Wonderful."

Wonderful. Her body might have been hot from his touch and his kisses. But the way he said *wonderful* warmed her soul.

She kissed him, easing her body down so they were skin-to-skin. Her hands roved his arms and chest, exploring the muscles she'd ogled for so many days.

But he wasn't naked. She slipped his shorts down his legs. When she brushed against his erection, he groaned.

"I want you as crazy as I feel," she murmured.

She kissed her way down his abs. *Num.* Then took a deep breath and cupped him, drawing out another groan.

"Stop," he grunted.

Ignoring his plea, she tugged on the elastic of his underwear and skimmed it down his legs. He sprang free. Fascinated, she stared.

"Come back here." Kaden sat up and kicked off his underwear, stopping her when she started to lower her head. "Nope. It's been too long for me." He pulled her until they were side-by-side on the bed. "I don't want to embarrass myself."

He brushed a kiss on her lips and she leaned into his heat. Everything in her body went liquid and churned with energy. She wanted to melt around him, over him.

"Do you have protection?" she gasped.

He shifted and the drawer squealed as he pulled out a condom. "Would you?"

Her hands shook as she ripped open the packet. Why couldn't she fake her way through this? She tried to stroke it on him, but the trembling got worse.

"Hey, hey." He took over. "Do I scare you?"

She sat on her haunches, her head drooping. "I'm just… Don't expect much."

"What I expect is we'll give each other pleasure." He brushed a kiss on her forehead. "That's all."

"Pleasure." How could he always say just the right thing? "You're wicked smart."

"I am." He grinned.

He laid her on the bed and settled between her legs.

She inhaled as he entered her. Would it hurt? But this was Kaden. Each inch he stopped and pulled back, letting her adjust.

"Please," she gasped, trying to pull him deeper.

He slid home and waited.

She lifted her hips, willing him to move. "You're torturing me."

He released a strained chuckle. But he stroked in and out, setting off waves of heat and longing. It wasn't enough.

She shifted and he took the hint and rolled over, taking her with him.

"Is this what you want?" he gasped.

"Oh, yes. Yes." She placed her hands next to his head and worked her hips in tight circles. There. There was the spot. She wanted this—being with Kaden—to be perfect.

"I like this view." He grinned and she smiled back.

Everything inside her quivered. His hands

clamped on her hips as he rose beneath her, grinding into her and stretching her legs wider than she thought possible. His smile morphed into clenched teeth. "Courtney."

She was almost there. And the world flipped so she was underneath him. He drove into her. She locked her ankles around his thighs and hung on as he thrust into her again and again.

Stars flashed behind her eyes.

"So good," he groaned. His teeth were gritted, his expression fierce as he found his own completion. "So good."

He collapsed on her. It took all her energy to stroke his damp back.

After their breathing leveled to gale force winds, he kissed her. Then, rolling on his side, they lay face-to-face. "Amazing."

Her gasps ruffled his hair. "Amazing."

They both gulped air. The frantic beat of her heart slowed. And lethargy filled her body. She couldn't keep her eyes open.

He kissed her nose. The mattress moved and Kaden took his heat away, but pulled up the comforter. "You never did tell me whether you wanted pizza or Chinese."

She rolled to her back and laughed. "Your choice."

"WHY ARE YOU SMILING so much?" Josh asked Courtney while she supervised the kids' snack.

"It's a good day." She'd heard people hated Mondays, hated going to work. If everyone had had her kind of Sunday, they'd still be smiling, too.

Eating Chinese had been fun, because Kaden had never used chopsticks. She'd tried to teach him, but ended up feeding him most of the food. In bed. Between making love. The only sad part was after dinner, he'd walked her home.

"You're doing it again." Josh rolled his eyes. "My mom gets that face sometimes. After Papa kisses her."

She chuckled. Josh's papa probably had done more than kiss Cheryl. Courtney ruffled his streaky blond hair. "Finish up. It's a beautiful day, and I'm in the mood to have art time in the court-yard. What do you say?"

Issy and Josh nodded.

Since she'd been studying the child care regulations, she was more aware of getting the kids outside and keeping them active. This week she was working on schedules, testing what held their interest and what didn't.

But first they needed to clean up. Issy hummed a cleanup song and Josh sang the words.

The classrooms needed sound systems. Especially if there was a cleanup song.

She was going to make her center a success. On her day off next week, she planned to visit Issy and Josh's previous day care and spend the morning with the director.

"Do we have everything?" she asked the kids, slathering sunscreen on Issy's shoulders.

"Yeah," Josh said. Issy nodded and they shrugged on their backpacks.

With her first paycheck from the Foresters, she'd bought a big tote, even though she'd been in desperate need of a facial. It wasn't a couture bag, but it did the trick. She double-checked that they had water and additional art supplies. "Let's go."

After locking the apartment door, they headed down the steps. "What a beautiful day."

"You said that already." Josh rolled his eyes.

Issy pointed at a butterfly flitting between the flowers.

"Maybe you want to draw a picture of a butterfly?" Courtney asked.

Issy grinned.

Courtney had spent a lot of time in the courtyard, but she'd never noticed how pretty everything was. Bess's garden sparkled. Red and purple flowers brightened small corners and vines covered in yellow flowers spilled from dark blue pots. She wanted to learn all the names so she could teach the children.

They headed to the empty Carleton House patio.

Would Kaden be interested in taking a walk tonight? She wanted to hold his hand and really see Savannah. She wanted to kiss him as the streetlights blinked on.

As they settled at the table, she looked at her phone. "We can spend forty minutes here."

Josh and Issy pulled out their sketch pads.

"I went with Papa and checked out the new play equipment. It's cool," Josh said.

"Thank you for helping pick the colors," Courtney said.

"Can Papa and I paint a mural?" Josh scrunched up his face. "Not that princess stuff, but something else."

"I like the idea of a mural." Courtney made a note in her almost full notebook. Maybe she could start a tradition of adding handprints of all the children to the wall. She could include notes on something special about each child.

Issy drew what Courtney thought were flowers in a pot. Josh did a sketch of the Carleton carriage house.

The alarm on her phone buzzed. Forty minutes were up. "Once we pick up, I thought we could check out the new books that arrived today. Josh, you can practice your reading."

"I want to pick the book." He shoved his sketch pad into his backpack.

They could grab a book and work on reading in the play area.

As they walked toward the frog fountain, Josh tugged on her hand. "Can we make a wish?"

She shook her head. "I don't think Bess wants coins in the fountain."

"I want to wish for a puppy," he said.

"I know." Courtney set her hand on his shoulder. "Next time we go by Bledsoe fountain we'll make wishes."

Her wish would be spending more private time with Kaden.

Josh kicked a pebble in the path. "I just want a puppy."

"Patience is a virtue." Something her mother had always said.

"Come on, let's go to the day care." Maybe Kaden would be working. Her smile bloomed again.

KADEN LOADED THE trolley with the final stack of chairs from the Sunday event held in the Fitzgerald House ballroom. Thank goodness, neither he nor Courtney had needed to work yesterday. He grinned. Sunday had been…incredible. He wanted to make love to Courtney again tonight. And every night.

His phone alerted him that Courtney and the kids were moving from the Carleton House patio back to Fitzgerald House.

Since he was working alone in the ballroom, he called Roger.

"Any word on getting some backup down here?" Kaden asked.

"Give me another day," Roger grumbled.

His neck itched. "Then let me tell Courtney about the possible threat."

"I thought you were sticking close to the nanny and the kids."

He'd been *very* close to Courtney Sunday. But that wasn't enough. The alert sounded again. Had to be Courtney and the kids.

"If Bole grabs Issy, we'll have lost our advantage," Kaden said. And their lure.

He waited. He'd learned to let Roger think.

"Fine," Roger said. "I'll get some help down there. Give me a day or two."

"Thanks." After hanging up, Kaden finished closing up the tables.

The facial recognition alert went off again. Now where was Courtney taking the kids?

He flipped over to the cameras. Shit. Bole was in the parking lot.

He jammed his phone in his pocket. Pulling his gun, he streaked out the door.

"Bella? Bella!" A woman called.

Bella? Courtney didn't see anyone in the courtyard. Maybe they were filming a sequel to the *Twilight* saga in Savannah. She giggled. Nothing would wreck today's good mood. "Come on, kids, let's pick out our books."

Issy tucked herself between Courtney's legs, trembling.

Courtney stroked her hair. "What's wrong, sweetie?"

Issy bit her lips and didn't answer.

"Bella. Come here." The woman's voice carried through the courtyard. "Now!"

Issy whimpered.

"What's wrong?" Courtney put her hand on Issy's head and then turned to look at whoever was calling for this Bella.

A redheaded woman stormed down the path from over by the parking lot. Courtney frowned. She didn't know many people in Savannah, but the woman looked familiar.

"Bella. Get over here." The woman pointed to Issy. "We're leaving. Right now."

Issy's whimpers escalated into sobs. Josh put his arms around his sister.

"Who are you?" Courtney put herself between this crazy woman and the children.

"Bella's mom. Heather." She closed the distance between them and reached for Issy. "I've come for her."

Courtney pushed Issy closer to the fountain. Issy's mother? That's why she looked familiar. She'd changed her hair color to bright red. It made her skin look sallow.

"I'm afraid you'll have to talk to Nathan." Heather would not take Issy.

"Don't tell me what I can and can't do with my own daughter." Heather grabbed again.

Courtney slid the kids along the fountain, closer to the apartment steps, batting at Heather's grasping hands.

If she went to the apartment, no one was there. The kids would be safer in Fitzgerald House, but Heather blocked the way between them and the door.

"I want my kid." Heather reached for Issy.

The courtyard was empty. Where was everyone? For once, no crew worked on the restaurant.

"Abby! Kaden! Cheryl!" Courtney yelled. She stretched out her arms to keep Heather from Issy. "Help!"

"Shut up. She's my daughter." Heather shoved Courtney's shoulder. "I'm taking her. Now."

"No." Courtney's heart pounded in her ears. She jabbed her elbow into Heather's side, making her stumble.

Issy sobbed. Couldn't anyone hear them? Courtney had to hold off Heather. "Josh, Issy, go to Abby."

"I want my daughter." Heather swung her purse and caught Courtney in the chest.

Courtney staggered. Pain surged through her. "Run to Abby. Now!"

She drove the kids around the back of the fountain, then swung her tote at Heather's head. The bag ripped, and sunscreen and crayons spilled out.

Heather howled and rammed her fist into Courtney's face.

White lights flashed. Blinding pain splintered Courtney's head. She flailed and caught Heather in the stomach. They crashed to the ground. Twisting, she threw her body on top of Heather. "Help!"

"Courtney!" Kaden called from somewhere above them.

Thank God.

Heather bucked, rolling and punching. Courtney's head smashed into the fountain. Stars clouded her vision.

"Stop! Leave her alone," Kaden called from the terrace steps.

"Kaden," Courtney squeaked. "Help!"

Heather punched her in the shoulder and scrambled to her feet, kicking her in the belly.

Waves of agony washed over her. She clutched her stomach, curling into a ball.

"Stop!" Footsteps hammered down the steps.

"Bitch." Heather kicked her again. Then ran.

Nausea surged like a tidal wave. She couldn't succumb. The kids needed her.

"Issy, Josh." She tried to sit, but her head swam. She collapsed onto the stone path, her head throbbing. When she touched her cheek, blood covered her fingers.

"Courtney. God. Are you okay?" Kaden knelt next to her. He held a gun in his hand. A gun?

"The kids," she gasped through the agony. "Make sure...safe. Abby. Kitchen."

"Where is she? Where's Bole?" he asked.

Courtney pointed. "Ran. Please. Check the kids."

He scanned the courtyard. "I'll be right back."

She closed her eyes. Nothing made sense. Why did Kaden have a gun? But the hammers in her head shut down her thinking. She had to concentrate just to breathe.

Sirens sounded in the distance. For her or Heather?

Abby knelt next to her, clutching her hand. "Oh, no."

"Kids?" Courtney choked out on a cough.

"Safe." Abby brushed her hair back.

Courtney moaned.

"I'm sorry." Instead of touching her head, Abby squeezed her shoulder. "Kaden's calling 911."

Kaden. Gun.

Her stomach churned and Abby helped her turn on her side as she threw up. Then her sister-in-law eased her away from the mess.

"S-s-sorry," Courtney sobbed.

"Don't be." Abby set Courtney's head on her lap and pressed a towel against her face. "Rest."

Courtney closed her eyes against the glaring sun. She couldn't stop shaking.

"Gray, get back to the B and B. Right now. Courtney's hurt." Abby sounded scared.

Courtney kept her eyes closed. It hurt too much to open them. Maybe if she slept, the pain would disappear.

There was a rattle of metal. Abby leaned close. "The paramedics are here."

She was cold. How could she be cold in sweltering Savannah?

"Ma'am, can you tell us your name?" a woman asked. Another woman knelt next to her arm and touched her face.

"Umm?" Her teeth chattered.

"Your name."

"Courtney. Smythe."

She endured their pushing and prodding. Groaned when they strapped her on a board. Couldn't they move her away from where she'd thrown up?

Running steps pounded on the paths.

"Courtney!" Gray called.

"I'm 'kay."

"Your face." Terror filled his voice.

"Hit. Fountain." She flopped her hand up and down.

Gray caught it and held on. "I'll come with her to the hospital. I'm her brother."

Conversation swirled around her, but her world had narrowed to the wrenching pain in her head and chest.

More boots pounded up to the fountain.

"Where's Issy? Josh?" Nathan cried.

"In the kitchen with Cheryl," Abby said.

Kaden's voice cut through the chaos. "How is she?"

"Where were you?" Nathan growled. "You were here to protect everyone!"

She opened her eyes, squinting against the light.

Nathan shoved Kaden, whose hands shot into the air in surrender.

"I ran as fast as I could," Kaden said.

"It wasn't good enough," Nathan snapped back.

Nathan shouldn't be pushing Kaden. He had a gun. Why did a handyman need a gun? She frowned, setting off explosions in her head. Tears poured from her eyes.

"Ready to transport," someone called out.

"I need to talk to the witness," Kaden said.

"Witness?" Now Gray was snarling. "That's my sister. You'll have to come to the hospital. Or better yet, wait until she's recovered."

Witness? Guns? Courtney closed her eyes. She didn't understand anything.

KADEN PACED OUTSIDE Courtney's room. Nathan had been right. He hadn't kept Courtney safe. He hadn't captured Bole. He'd failed.

If he'd paid attention to the first alert, Courtney might not be in the hospital. From the third floor terrace he'd watched Heather shove Courtney into the fountain. His heart had stopped. He'd been too far away. He'd yelled, hoping to distract Heather. By the time he'd run down the three flights, blood had poured from Courtney's forehead and cheek. He should have chased Heather; instead he'd rushed to Courtney's side.

They'd had a perfect night together and now she was in the hospital. How much more could he screw up?

A nurse emerged from behind her curtain.

"May I?" he asked, flashing his badge.

The woman's eyebrows rose, but she nodded. "You'll have to leave when the surgeon arrives."

Surgeon? Oh, God. He shoved through the curtain.

Gray blocked his view of Courtney. He turned his head and frowned. "What are you doing here?"

Kaden moved next to Courtney's bed.

She was too pale. Bandages covered half of her face. Blood matted her beautiful hair and streaked her chin. He wanted to clean her up and take her hand, but Gray's animosity and the fact that he needed to question Courtney held him back.

"I'm with the FBI. I need to ask Courtney some questions." He locked his hands behind his back to keep from reaching for her.

Gray's mouth dropped open. "FBI?"

He nodded.

Courtney closed her eyes.

"How are you?" Kaden asked her.

Courtney started to wag her head, but winced. "Fine."

"She's not fine," Gray interrupted. "She needs stitches."

"The nurse mentioned a surgeon," Kaden said.

"I'm not letting a med student put stitches in my sister's face," Gray snapped at him. "I've requested a plastic surgeon."

"Gray. Stop." Courtney's speech slurred.

Gray took his sister's hand. "I'm just worried about you, brat."

Was it more serious than the slice on her face? Did she have a head injury? "I need to ask you a few questions about Heather Bole." He looked at Gray. "In private."

"I'll stay with my sister."

"It's okay, Gray." She squeezed his hand.

Gray glared but left the room.

Didn't Gray know Kaden agreed with him? It was his fault Courtney was hurt. People around him got hurt. He'd thought it was only children. Now he was afraid it was anyone he cared about.

She slowly tilted her head toward him. Pain-filled blue eyes drilled into his.

"FBI." Her eyes narrowed, as if she was trying to remember something. "Did you have a gun?"

"Yes." He touched the furrow between her eyebrows. He couldn't stop himself. Then he took her hand when he really wanted to kiss her. "I've been working undercover at the B and B, hoping Heather would show up. We assumed she'd come back for Issy."

"Undercover. You needed to stay close to Issy." Her words were flat, nothing like the energy that had filled her voice when they'd made love. She must really be hurting.

"Since I was down with my granddad, it made sense." He touched her shoulder. "Are you really all right?"

Her eyes fluttered shut. "Fine."

"Can you tell me what Heather Bole said to you?"

She took a deep, shuddering breath. "She insisted that Issy, but she called her Bella, come with her."

"That's it? Did she say anything else?" It was too much to expect that Heather had blurted out where she was staying. "Tell me everything you can remember."

Courtney inhaled, grimacing as she did. Then she walked him through her brief encounter with Heather Bole. It didn't take long.

She asked, "Are Issy and Josh safe?"

"Yes. Because of you." He hadn't been able to keep Courtney safe. "You're a hero."

She rolled her eyes. Then her face crumpled.

He hurt along with her.

"How are the kids?" she asked.

"They were with Nathan and Cheryl when I left for the hospital."

"Why does the FBI want Issy's mother?"

"Murder. Running drugs."

"And you couldn't tell me you worked for the FBI?" She closed her eyes, dismissing him.

"When I got the alert that Bole was on the property, I was on the phone with my superior. Getting approval to tell you." It sounded weak.

"How convenient." Courtney didn't even open her eyes.

"I'm so, so sorry." He took her hand but she tugged it away. It was like a bullet to his chest.

"Why are you sorry?" Her gaze zeroed in on his.

"I was there to catch Bole and keep Issy safe."

"Did you catch her?"

"No." Agony filled the one word. "And you were hurt."

He'd failed. Courtney was injured. When he'd left the B and B, Issy had still been whimpering.

His phone buzzed. Roger. "I have to take this."

He backed out of the room. Gray scowled at him from whatever phone conversation he was having. Without a word, Gray headed back into Courtney's room. "Mom and Dad are in the air."

Kaden let his phone ring. He waited outside the open door, eavesdropping.

"I don't want them here." Was Courtney crying?

"There's no way you could keep them away."

"I don't want them to see me like this."

Kaden finally answered his phone. "Yes?"

"I got your message. What went wrong?" Roger asked.

"When I was on the phone with you, I got an alert that Bole was at the B and B. By the time I got to where she was, she'd run." And because Courtney was hurt, he hadn't given chase. There had been too much blood. He hadn't been able to leave her.

"I thought you were sticking close to the nanny and the kids?" Roger's voice was an angry growl over the phone.

"I *am*." He sagged against the wall. "But I can't Velcro myself to them."

"You blew our best shot at catching her."

"Bole hurt Courtney."

"Who? The nanny?"

"Yes. She should have known about the threat earlier." If Courtney had been better prepared, she might not be lying in a hospital bed.

"I thought we'd agreed you could tell her."

"Not soon enough. Courtney was injured before I could talk to her." Finally telling her the truth should have eased the weight on his shoulders, but it hadn't.

"Does Heather know you're a Fed?"

He replayed the few words he'd yelled. "No."

"Maybe she'll be back." Roger tapped away on his desk. "We'll keep you there for another week or two."

Another two weeks?

Courtney being hurt was unforgivable. And it was his fault.

"You need to replace me," Kaden said. "I failed."

KADEN WORKED FOR the FBI. He'd lied. To her.

Courtney longed to curl into a ball, but her face and head hurt if she moved. She closed her eyes, blocking out everything, including her brother and the knowledge that Kaden was right outside her room talking. About her.

Kaden had just said he'd been sticking close to

her *just* to get to Issy's mother. Was he making sure she could hear that she'd meant nothing to him? She'd been part of his job.

Nausea rolled through her stomach.

Velcro. He'd complained he couldn't Velcro himself to her and the kids. She'd trusted him, trusted that he'd seen through her facade.

She hurt. And it wasn't just her face and head and body. Whatever she and Kaden had shared had been a lie. Tears burned her eyes. He'd only been with her to stay close to Issy.

Had he slept with her because of his *job*?

Kaden's voice droned. Was he giving her a score for her performance in bed to his FBI cronies? This was worse than just being a pretty ornament. He'd used her. He'd betrayed her.

She didn't have the energy to wipe the tear that sneaked down her cheek.

"Are you okay?" Worry filled Gray's voice.

"Fine." But her voice cracked. Everything cracked.

"Ahh, honey. Your face will be perfect. Don't worry. I checked out the surgeon. He's one of the best in the state."

Tears flooded down her face. Her brother thought that's what she was worried about?

Gray rubbed her shoulder. "Do you need something for the pain? I could check with the nurse."

"I'm f…"

He touched her shoulder. "I know you're fine.

Let me check whether they can give you something so you stay fine."

Gray headed out the door. The solitude was a relief.

She closed her eyes and sank under the weight of Kaden's betrayal. She'd been so stupid. Footsteps echoed in the room and a hint of Kaden's piney scent wrapped around her. Even though the light drilled holes behind her eyes, she couldn't keep from staring at the doorway.

Kaden. Her heart throbbed at the sight of him.

"I'm so sorry." Kaden brushed a kiss on her forehead, and another flood of tears threatened to fall. "Don't cry. It kills me to see you cry."

She needed to be strong. "You don't have to pretend anymore. I heard your conversation. You were just hanging around me to stay close to Issy."

The chair squealed on the linoleum as he pulled it closer to the bed. "Courtney…"

"No." She had to keep going. Had to regain control, something she'd given up the moment she'd kissed him.

Her hands shook, so she clenched them into fists. "You don't have to pretend. Your secret is out. I understand. No more lies. I was suspicious about why you'd been…friendlier after I started to take care of the kids. Now I know."

"That's not true." He tried to take her hand and she tucked it under the sheet. "I never wanted to deceive you."

"Good news—you can stop now." She tried to smile, but pain blasted through her face. "No more having to sleep with the nanny to stay close to the kids."

"That's not what happened." He squeezed her knee.

She shook her head. "We're done."

"What?" He frowned. "No."

"Last night won't happen again." She forced the words through the wall of pain in her chest.

He clutched her arm. "Don't do this."

Don't do this? He'd lied to her. Had anything been real? "Tell me the truth."

"Yes," he answered. "If I can."

"Did you start flirting with me because I was taking care of Issy?" Even the question ripped into her like broken glass, shredding apart her heart. "The truth."

"Maybe. At first, but…" He couldn't finish his sentence. "Courtney."

"The times you ran into us going to the library or Bess's greenhouse or into the squares? They weren't a coincidence, were they?"

He swallowed. "No."

"How?"

He didn't answer for a moment, then choked out, "I installed a camera system throughout the B and B. It alerted me wherever you went."

"You spied on me?"

"I… It's not like it sounds. We hoped Bole would come for her daughter."

"But you kept track of me?" She shivered.

"I kept an eye out for Bole…and you and Issy."

Each answer hurt more than the wounds Heather had caused. "It's why you took us fishing."

"Yes." He exhaled. "I couldn't have you run into Heather on your own."

She stared at him. "But I did."

"I'm so sorry." His forehead was a mass of wrinkles. His voice was deep and gravelly. "I've asked my superior to replace me."

Replace him. His words had edges as sharp as Abby's knives. That's what she wanted, right? Kaden gone.

"I'm not sleeping with a new agent," she whispered.

"Don't," he gasped. "It wasn't like that."

Oh, God, it hurt. Everything had been because of this Heather Bole. Kaden had used her. Used Issy. "Please leave."

"Courtney. Everything changed. You *mean* something to me." He scooted the chair closer and clutched her hand through the sheet. "Give me a chance."

"You used me." Each word boomed in her head, banging like hammer strikes. She wasn't worth loving. He'd said all the right things, but nothing had been real.

He jerked back. "I had to. I'm trying to capture

someone who doesn't deserve to be free. Doesn't deserve to have a child in her..." He trailed off.

"You can justify all you want. You *used* me."

"It was for a good cause."

She couldn't do this anymore. She wanted to mean more to Kaden than his job. Apparently that wasn't going to happen. "Leave."

He stood. "I only wanted to get Bole off the street."

"Well, you failed." Even though she knew it would hurt, she rolled over and closed her eyes.

The door creaked. Tears slid down her sore cheek, adding salt to the wound. He'd done what she'd asked. He'd left her. She could only hope now that his cover was blown, he would leave Fitzgerald House. After today, she deserved some good luck.

Gray returned. So did the nurse. Apparently the surgeon was doing something important, like reconstructing a face from an accident. Her little cut didn't matter.

She lost track of time, drifting in and out of the twilight of sleep. Sometimes Gray was sitting next to the bed, sometimes he was gone.

"Where is she? Gray, where's Courtney?" Mother said from outside the partially open door.

Why had Gray called the parental units? She'd been a burden to them in Boston. They didn't seem to miss her now. Why would they come to Savannah?

She kept her eyes closed, wanting to disappear.

But footsteps rushed into the room and stopped by the bed.

"Oh, Courtney." Her mother grabbed her hand, jarring her body.

She couldn't hold back her whimper.

"I'm sorry." Mother patted her hand. "Your face. Look at your face."

Courtney hadn't looked. Based on her mother's distress, she might never look again. Guess she wasn't going to be a pretty little ornament anymore. Panic tried to bubble up in her chest, but between the pain and Kaden's betrayal, being pretty didn't matter anymore.

"I've talked to the best plastic surgeon in Boston." Her father pushed his way next to her bedside. "We'll arrange an ambulance to get her to the airport. The doctor will repair her face as soon as we land in Boston."

"What?" Courtney cried.

"We're taking you home." Father's eyes narrowed as he looked at the bandages covering her forehead and cheek. "Gray says it's bad. We'll want to minimize the scarring."

Couldn't let your ornament tarnish, right? "Gray's already contacted a surgeon. We're waiting for him to complete a surgery."

"You've been here for hours. And this is your face. Your beautiful face." Father touched her hand. "I'm bringing you home."

This was exactly what she'd wanted. Her father wanted her to come home. She should feel…elated.

But the thought of going home, of being the person she'd been back in Boston, wasn't what she wanted anymore. She didn't belong. She wasn't sure where she belonged.

Who would run her day care? She'd done all the work. She'd made all the plans. This was her responsibility. "I'm not leaving Savannah."

Father frowned. "You've been begging your mother to let you come home. Here's your chance."

She scrambled for reasons not to do this. "But— but I drove here."

He waved away her objection. "I'll hire someone to drive your car home."

"I can't leave the children."

"Babysitters are a dime a dozen."

Everything in her body stilled. She gritted her teeth. Mistake. Pain pummeled her head. "I'm opening a day care. I can't leave."

"You will leave," her father insisted. "Being a babysitter isn't rocket science."

"It may not be. But it's important." She kept her voice low and said, "No."

Gray moved to the head of the bed. Whose side would he take? Would he want to get rid of her so bad that he'd kick her out of his home?

If he did, she'd find an apartment.

"People are relying on Courtney," Gray said.

Courtney nodded and paid for the action with a wave of pain. Tears filled her eyes.

"She's not safe here," Mother said. "What if this awful woman comes back?"

Gray touched Courtney's shoulder. "I'll make sure she's safe."

"I know about the danger now," she said. "I won't be vulnerable again."

"But your face." Tears streaked Mother's mascara. "We have to make sure there's no scar."

Mother never lost her composure. If the apocalypse occurred, she'd keep her small island of sanity through sheer will. A possible facial scar was what it took to make her mother fall apart?

Everyone talked about Courtney like she didn't have a say in what was going to happen. Apparently a scar on her face was the last straw. "I'm not leaving Savannah."

Her father started to open his mouth, but Gray interrupted, "Father, why don't you meet the surgeon?"

Her parents lapsed into silence. Courtney closed her eyes. If her face scarred and she no longer had her looks, what else did she have? No wonder her parents were freaking out. She was nothing without her beauty.

But she wasn't leaving Savannah.

KADEN STARED AT Courtney's hospital room door. He wasn't welcome across the threshold, but he couldn't leave. He had to apologize—one more time.

Courtney thought he'd only been with her because of Heather. Everything she'd accused him of had been true. He hadn't wanted to be close to her until she started taking care of the kids. He'd joined their outings so they didn't run into Heather when they were alone.

He paced. Staying close to Courtney and Issy had been by design. Sleeping with her had not. He'd slept with her because he couldn't stay away. He wanted to be as close to her as he could be.

She'd pushed him away because he couldn't lie. He didn't deserve her forgiveness. He'd been responsible. He'd failed to keep her safe.

Gray walked out of the room.

"How is she?" Kaden asked.

"Fighting with my parents. They want to take her back to Boston."

Boston. That's all she'd wanted. "When do they leave?"

"She said no. She has a responsibility to the kids." Gray went to the elevator and jammed his finger on the button.

Kaden followed. "So she's staying?" Hope infused his voice.

"That's what she says. Father and Mother are still arguing, but Courtney just pretends to sleep." Gray pushed on his temples. "Maybe she'd be better off going home. Maybe Boston is safer."

But Kaden lived in Georgia. Not that that would matter to Courtney. She'd booted him from her life.

If she moved back to Boston, he wouldn't get the chance to convince her he hadn't been using her.

"As long as you're hanging around, can you help carry coffee?" Gray asked.

"Sure." Kaden followed Gray to the cafeteria and helped him pick up coffee and tea and carry it to Courtney's room. Hopefully she wouldn't kick him out if he was carrying hot liquids.

When they entered her room, Courtney's eyes were closed. Her parents stared at her from opposite sides of the bed.

"Here you go, brat." Gray nudged her foot. When she opened her eyes, he handed her a cup of tea.

She was too alert to have actually been sleeping. She glared at Kaden while dipping her tea bag up and down in the hot water.

"Mother." Gray pointed at the coffee Kaden held and he handed the cup to her.

"This is Kaden Farrell," Gray said. "Our parents, Olivia and Wallace Smythe."

"Sorry to meet under these circumstances," Kaden said.

"He's FBI." Courtney sniffed. "Are you here to interrogate me again?"

"Interrogate?" her mother exclaimed.

"No." He stared into Courtney's pain-racked eyes. "I'm worried about you."

"Right." She harrumphed. "You're worried about the innocent bystander getting hit?" She pointed at her bandages. "Been there, done that. Maybe I'll print up T-shirts."

All the Smythes glowered at him.

"I'd just gotten authorization to tell you who I was." He kept his voice low when he wanted to shout. He had to get her to understand. "There were…circumstances."

"If I'd known Issy was in danger, I would have taken more precautions," Courtney snapped. "She was terrified."

"It was politics." His excuse was weak. He'd underestimated Bole. And worse, he'd underestimated Courtney, just like everyone else in her life did.

Roger needed to pull him from this assignment.

"And was it political when you asked me on a date without telling me why you were really at the B and B?"

"What?" Gray snarled. "He was dating you?"

"Not anymore." Courtney waved, but her brother looked capable of taking Kaden's head off.

Her statement was another shot to the chest. Kaden couldn't keep the exasperation from his voice. "I was undercover."

"Yet you still asked me out."

The Smythe men watched their conversation like a tennis match, crossing their arms and staring at him.

"I'm sorry." He held out his hands to her.

She rolled her eyes. Pain streaked across her face. "Why don't you leave and find this monster of a mother. You're not doing any good here."

"That's an excellent idea," Gray said.

Kaden nodded. Trying to explain hadn't changed anything. Courtney wasn't going to forgive him.

He left the room, but headed straight for the waiting area. Until the plastic surgeon took care of her, he wouldn't leave.

COURTNEY CHOKED DOWN her breakfast. The hospital food did not live up to Abby's.

"I don't know how to thank you," Nathan said for the third time since arriving at the hospital.

"Anyone would do what I did." Courtney pushed away the tray.

"I don't believe that." Nathan smiled.

After two hours of getting stitches, Courtney's father had insisted the hospital keep her overnight. At least she'd convinced her family she didn't need anyone staying in her room. "How did Issy sleep?"

Nathan closed his eyes and swallowed. "Not well. She had two nightmares."

"I'm so sorry." She touched the get-well cards Josh and Issy had drawn for her. Nathan had also brought a small duffel with the clothes Gray and Abby had packed for her.

Nathan shook his head. "She's worried you'll die."

"Oh, God." She sat up, making her stomach ache. "Once I get home, can she come over and see that I'm all right? I can't wait to give them hugs."

"That might help," Nathan said.

A nurse knocked and entered her room. "I have your discharge papers and instructions."

"I'd better go. Gray will be here soon." Nathan gave her a hug. "Thank you for keeping the kids safe. We owe you so much."

Courtney listened to the nurse's instructions and then took the bag of ointments and pads she handed her. "Thank you."

She headed into the bathroom one more time. Leaning on the sink, she stared in the mirror. The bandages covered her forehead down to her cheek. The doctor had been optimistic that the scar wouldn't be noticeable. Her family was *ecstatic*.

At least her eye was undamaged. She hoped any scar wouldn't frighten the children. That would be terrible. She straightened her shoulders and touched the furrows on her brow.

Her mouth dropped open. What she looked like didn't matter. The scar, if there was one, didn't matter. Heather had freed her from that worry. From now on, the kids were all that mattered.

"Courtney, are you in the bathroom?" Gray called.

Taking a deep breath, she looked at the new her. She could do this. "I'll be right out."

In the room, Gray smiled. "The mummy look is good on you."

"You're a laugh a minute." She picked up the bag of wound care supplies, the cards and her prescriptions. "I'm ready."

Gray kept a hand on her elbow and she was shaky enough to appreciate the help.

"Maybe you want a wheelchair," he said.

"The only reason I spent the night was because Father hounded the staff. I want to walk out on my own."

"We'll walk out together."

She shuffled down the hall, her bruised stomach protesting. At least Heather hadn't broken any ribs. They crossed in front of a waiting room.

Kaden's large body was scrunched into a chair. His eyes were closed and his head rested on the chair back.

She whispered, "Did he sleep here last night?"

"It looks like it." Gray walked into the room and tapped Kaden's foot with his own. "Farrell?"

Kaden jerked awake, reaching behind his back.

"Kaden!" she said loudly. Did he have a gun in the hospital?

"You're up?" Gravel filled Kaden's voice.

"I'm leaving," she said.

His face went pale. "You're leaving Savannah?"

"The hospital."

Relief flooded Kaden's face.

"Gray, can you give us a minute?" she asked.

"I'll bring the car around." He scowled at Kaden. "Can you get her to the entrance? Safely?"

"Of course." After Gray left, Kaden put an arm around her waist.

She didn't want him to touch her—ever. It hurt too much. But so did walking. "Why are you still here?"

"I couldn't leave when you were hurt." His blue eyes pleaded with her.

His words were as painful as the stitches in her cheek, but they pierced her heart, not her flesh. "With your cover blown, I assumed you'd head back to Atlanta. If that's really where you live."

"I really live in Atlanta." He tightened his hold on her. "My cover wasn't blown."

Her frown set off pounding behind her eyes. "But…"

Hadn't she learned he was FBI in the courtyard? "Didn't you have a gun when—when all this happened?"

"Bole didn't see it. For all she knows, I was a guest who stumbled on her beating you up. She doesn't know I'm FBI."

"So the FBI will continue to use Issy as bait." She spat the last word out like it was the bitterest food she'd ever tasted.

"I thought I could get there in time." His shoulders drooped. "I should have known better."

They moved outside to a bench. She sank onto the surface and tipped her face to the sun. The warmth felt good.

He sat next to her. "I'm sorry I couldn't keep you safe. I wish you could forgive me."

He was clueless. "I don't expect you to keep me safe."

"I did. I do." He took her hand. "Can you give me another chance?"

"You *used* Issy and me for your job. Used us." Why couldn't he understand? He'd pretended to see the real her. "If you'd told me what was going on, you would not have needed to sleep with me."

"I didn't sleep with you because of my job." His jaw clenched. "My being with you was…for me."

He would never convince her he hadn't gotten close to her because of his job. "We'll have to agree to disagree."

"Courtney—"

"No." She held up a hand. "I'm not arguing with you."

"What will you do now?" He reached out to touch her cheek, but she shifted away. His hand dropped to his lap with a smack. "Will you head back to Boston?"

"I'm not going back to Boston." It was time to take control of her life, and that life wouldn't include Kaden. "I have children to take care of. I have a day care to run."

And she would keep Issy safe.

She would be smart, vigilant. This was her job. And unlike Kaden, she wouldn't screw it up.

CHAPTER TEN

COURTNEY STARED IN the mirror. A raw red slash spanned from her forehead to her cheek. She didn't recognize her face anymore. It was individual features: eyes, nose, mouth, hair and the red scar. Should she be crying about her injury? If her face had defined her before, now it was her badge, guiding her toward a new life of courage.

The stitches were out. The doctor was pleased with his work and her progress. She massaged in the creams the surgeon's assistant had insisted would minimize the scarring, watching the clock to ensure she met her daily massage goal. But she didn't care about having a scar. It was one more indication that she wasn't the old Courtney. She was new and improved.

It had been a week since she'd fought with Heather. No one had spotted Issy's mother since then. For a blissful seven days, Courtney hadn't seen Kaden. He was still hanging around the B and B. He'd sent flowers with another worthless apology. But she hadn't laid eyes on him.

For the last week, the Fitzgeralds, their spouses and significant others, along with Cheryl and Nathan, had taken care of the kids. Today she would finally have Josh and Issy all day. She was glad

Josh had a day off school. They planned to spend the morning in the new facilities.

She'd had plenty of time while resting and healing to create daily schedules. She and Abby, with Cheryl's input, had hired an experienced assistant for the day care. Courtney was happy to have Martha's help. And Martha loved her plans.

She walked out of her bedroom and into the carriage house kitchen. Mother sat at the island with a cup of coffee and her iPad. Probably reading the *Boston Herald*. A Savannah paper wasn't good enough.

Mother's gaze zeroed in on her scar. Her chest shook as she exhaled. "You shouldn't be working while you..." Her hand waved at her face. "You don't want an infection and children are germ factories."

"The doctor was happy with the way I was healing. He said it's fine to work." Courtney headed to the coffeemaker. "I need to get back to my job."

"But your father said you could come home." Mother set a hand on Courtney's arm as she boosted herself up onto a stool. "I thought that's what you wanted."

"I thought I did, too." She sipped her coffee. "Not anymore."

Weeks ago, she would have been on the family plane. Now she had something to prove. She had a business to create. "Maybe my work isn't a multimillion-dollar real-estate empire like Gray's, but what I do is important."

"Babysitting?" her mother asked.

"It's more than babysitting," Courtney explained. "I impact children's lives. If I can make one child feel worthwhile, I'll make a difference."

"You don't need to work." Mother's lips pinched together.

"I *want* to work, to be useful." Maybe if Courtney had had a teacher who'd understood that she'd felt worthless, she would have found her passion sooner.

"Come back to Boston and do something...useful. Take over some of my charity work."

"You do great work." She linked her hand with her mother's. "But I need to be more...ground-level. Individual."

Mother squeezed her fingers, holding her gaze. "What is it about this place that changes my children? First Gray. Now you? Is it Savannah or the Fitzgeralds?"

"I don't know. Father started the change by forcing me to face my...shiftless life." Courtney finished her coffee. "Back in Boston I used to run a reading hour in one of the libraries. I never told anyone."

Except Kaden. Before she'd discovered he was only with her because of Heather Bole. Obviously, she was a terrible judge of character.

Mother blinked. "You did?"

"I love children." She slipped off the stool. "I also make up stories."

Mother's blue eyes filled with tears. "I didn't know."

"I didn't tell you." She pulled her mother into a hug. "I love you. Have a safe flight home."

"If you need anything, call. Or I'll send the plane to bring you home." Mother brushed back the hair from the side of her face with the scar. "I hate the idea that your beautiful face might scar."

"My looks don't define me." Not anymore. "I'll be fine."

After hugging her mother one last time, she headed to the Foresters' apartment. She and the kids would have breakfast in Fitzgerald House. When the center officially opened, they would eat in the day care, with food provided by the B and B. Knowing Abby and Cheryl, she would have the best-fed kids in the area.

She knocked on the door and then let herself in with the key. Walking into their home didn't feel awkward anymore.

"I'm in the kitchen," Cheryl yelled.

"Miss Courtney." Issy ran over and wrapped her arms around her knees.

"Hey." She knelt and gave Issy a hug. She wasn't supposed to pick up anything heavy for a while.

Issy pointed at her face, and whispered, "Hurt?"

"Not too bad." Now that the stitches were out, there wasn't any tugging. "Where's Josh?"

She pointed toward the bathroom.

Courtney took Issy's hand and they headed to the kitchen.

Cheryl looked up from unloading the dishwasher. "It seems strange not to be feeding the kids breakfast."

"Hopefully, that will make your day easier." Courtney appreciated that Cheryl didn't stare at her face. "How's everything going?"

Cheryl sighed. "Issy, will you knock on the bathroom door and tell Josh that Miss Courtney is here?"

Issy ran down the hall.

Cheryl took a seat at the kitchen table. "She had more nightmares last night."

"I'll see if she'll take a nap today."

"At least she's still talking." Cheryl pressed a hand to her chest. "But she's afraid to leave the apartment."

"Is Heather still in Savannah?" Had Kaden said anything to the Foresters?

"Kaden doesn't know." Cheryl twisted her fingers together. "He'll stick close to the day care. And eat his meals with you and the kids."

Great. Not. "Thanks for the warning."

Cheryl frowned.

No one had known about her and Kaden. Just another reason to believe his feelings for her weren't real.

"Nathan's working at the restaurant all week," Cheryl said. "He'll be close, too."

"Did you know Kaden was with the FBI?"

"Yes." Cheryl paced to the stove and pulled off the towel hanging on the handle. She refolded it so the edges were perfect. Then she straightened a cruet and large salt and pepper mills sitting on the counter. "I wish I could have told you. Kaden was the one who suggested you become the kids' nanny."

"He did?" She smiled. Then stopped.

It wasn't because Kaden had understood her. He'd wanted the kids to stay at the B and B. The hits just kept on coming. "I understand he's asked to be replaced."

"Nathan didn't say anything." Cheryl's hand pressed against her chest. "Why?"

"Because he failed?"

"But I…trust him with Issy and Josh. So does Nathan." Cheryl bit her lip. "Do you?"

Not with my heart. Could she trust him to keep the children safe? "I don't know."

Josh and Issy ran into the kitchen.

"Let's go get breakfast." Courtney pushed away from the table.

"I'll be there in a few minutes," Cheryl said. "I want to throw the wash into the dryer."

Courtney held Issy's hands as they headed across the courtyard.

Josh ran ahead, peering around the palm trees and fountain. "I'll check and see if your mom is trying to steal you."

Courtney's chest ached for Issy. "Don't leave my sight," she called to Josh.

Issy twisted her head, looking around, her lip caught between her teeth.

"What do you think we'll have for breakfast?" Courtney asked, trying to distract her.

"Pancakes?" The little girl's eyes lit up.

"Maybe." Although she was hungry for Abby's muffins.

When they crossed by the frog fountain, the little girl's fingers gripped her hand.

"She's not here," Josh yelled.

Issy relaxed.

Courtney held the door and they moved inside.

"Hey, guys." Abby looked over from her big griddle. The bacon she flipped sizzled. "Let me get this onto a platter."

Now Courtney wanted bacon. She was going to be two feet wide if her appetite didn't slow down. Maybe it was her skin trying to heal. Did bacon have healing powers?

She poured the kids juice, served them fruit and got them seated. Then Abby brought over a basket of warm muffins.

"Anyone want cream cheese or butter on their muffins?" Courtney asked.

"I like butter." Josh eyed the bowl and grabbed the biggest muffin.

Courtney helped him spread his butter. Then

she helped Issy, who pointed to the cream cheese. "Like you."

"I love cream cheese on my muffin."

"When are the new kids coming to day care with us?" Josh asked.

"Don't talk with your mouth full." Courtney grimaced a little at her mother's words coming out of her mouth. But she had to help them learn their manners. "Daria's coming on Thursday. Theresa on Monday."

"I'll still be the oldest."

How did he know that? "Have you met Theresa?"

He nodded and swallowed. "At the Fitzgerald House picnic. End of last summer." He turned to Abby. "Will there be another picnic?"

"Labor Day weekend." Abby dropped off a plate with bacon and sausages. She set her hand on Josh's shoulder. "And the staff will be testing the food from the restaurant."

"I want to win all the games." Josh snatched a piece of bacon.

"Josh," Courtney warned.

He rolled his eyes. "May I have a piece of bacon, please?"

"Yes." She helped Issy select a sausage. When she finally had a chance to bite into her muffin, she moaned. "What is this? Apricot?"

"Yes," Abby said. "New recipe. What do you think?"

"Heavenly." She took another bite.

Abby grinned. "I'm glad." She touched Court-ney's arm. "How are you feeling?"

"Pretty good." She didn't want to say anything negative with the kids around. "Excited to get into the center today."

"Marion and the cleaning crew were over there for the last two days. Thanks for sending her the information on cleaning. It was really helpful."

"Since I couldn't do anything but sit, I did re-search." It was strange to be talking business with Abby. In a really cool kind of way. "The kids and I are unpacking and organizing today."

"Kaden will do all the lifting." Abby pointed at Courtney's cheek. "I don't want you to set back your recovery."

Kaden. The muffin she'd swallowed made a lump in her stomach. She didn't want him hang-ing around all day.

"I'm strong. I can lift stuff." Josh bounced a little in his chair. "Maybe we can play Quarto."

"Maybe." And beating Kaden at the game might be the perfect salve to her ego. He thought he was so smart that he could keep up a lie and fool her into believing she mattered to him? He was no dif-ferent than all the men who hadn't seen beyond her face and body. She'd show him strategy was her game.

Cheryl came in just as Courtney was getting the kids out of the door. She kissed her kids. "Have a good morning. I'll see you at lunch."

As they headed to the day care, Josh scouted the jungle of courtyard plants. Bess had designed the space with too many hidden alcoves. Issy's mother could be hiding anywhere. Kaden's spy cameras had better be working.

To Issy she said, "Let's see how fast we can walk."

Issy nodded, moving her feet a little faster.

Since her last visit, a six-foot-high wooden fence had been built around the play area. The gate had a keypad lock.

Was all this security for Issy? She tried her code and the gate clicked open. The fence would keep the noise down for any guests in the courtyard. And they wouldn't be able to wander in.

Josh slipped through the opening. To his sister, he said, "You're safe."

Courtney smiled as she keyed in her code to the door into the center. Inside, her smile slipped away.

Kaden stood among the boxes filling the entry. His arms, folded across his chest, emphasized the muscles she'd examined intimately the night of her foolishness. His long legs were spread like he was balancing on a ship deck during a storm.

"Hello." He gave Josh a fist bump and turned to Issy. "Good morning."

"Morning." Issy tucked her head next to Courtney's knee.

Kaden came close—too close. He stared at her face, but his gaze didn't linger on her scar; it moved to her lips and then back up to her eyes. "How are you?"

"Ready to work." His darn piney scent made her salivate.

She didn't want to get into a heart-to-heart discussion. Or listen to him apologize again. She didn't want him around at all. But since he was here, she would use his muscles. "Let's start on the furniture."

He pulled out a box cutter and sliced through packing tape.

She grabbed a pair of scissors out of her bag.

"I break down boxes for my papa at our work sites," Josh said. "I'll help Mr. Kaden."

"Issy, you're with me," Courtney said.

They stripped away plastic and tape. Issy was big enough to drag the small chairs into the classrooms. Courtney kept her back to Kaden as he and Josh assembled the tables.

But every time she looked around, Kaden was staring at her.

"Where do you want these?" he asked.

"The taller tables go in room two. The shorter ones in room one." She didn't look up after giving him the directions. "The really large table will go in the activity room."

Kaden and Josh carried the tables into the correct rooms.

Would she really have enough students to fill

the day care? It didn't matter. *Plan for success*, Gray had said.

She and Issy knelt next to a box. "Let's open the books."

While Kaden and Josh put together bookcases in the classrooms, she and Issy organized books by age group. Then Josh carried them into the correct rooms.

"Why don't we bring the boxes into the room?" Kaden asked. "Then you only have to make half the number of trips."

"I guess that makes sense." Although she liked having a room separate her from Kaden.

He stacked two boxes and carried them into one of the rooms. Then came back for another load.

Courtney moved into a classroom and took a seat in one of the small chairs. "Thank you."

It took a little longer to get the books unpacked, because the kids oohed and ahhed over each new story.

"Can I read one?" Josh asked.

"Sure." She touched Issy's shoulder. "Do you want Josh to read to you or do you want to keep helping?"

She pointed at Josh.

"Use your words." She wouldn't let Issy backslide because of Heather.

"Josh," Issy whispered.

"Hang on." She found the right box. "Kaden, can you open this one?"

"Sure."

Inside were beanbag chairs. Kaden fluffed up a bright blue chair and Josh grabbed it. "Cool."

He dragged it next to the window. "Come on, Issy."

Kaden pulled out three more chairs. "Two in each room?"

"Yes. One blue and one yellow." She wanted everything bright and cheerful.

She went back to sorting books.

When Kaden approached her, he took another small chair and sat. What was the weight limitation on the chairs?

Kaden set a hand on her thigh. "How are you really feeling?"

She jerked her legs out of reach and his hand slipped off. "I'm—" She would have said *fine*, but he shook his head.

"Sore." She shrugged. "Tender."

"I wish I'd gotten to you faster. I hate that Issy is so afraid. And that Josh needs to protect his little sister." He held up his hands. "I hate that you were hurt."

"This wasn't your fault." She pointed to her cheek and lowered her voice. "This was Heather's fault. You're responsible for not keeping me informed."

"I know, but I still feel responsible for your injuries." He reached for her hand.

She didn't want his touch. He'd used her, controlled her, lied to her. "I thought you were being replaced."

Kaden snatched his hand away.

"I've asked. Roger, my superior, hasn't sent anyone yet." He stood and sliced through the packing tape on another box. In a low voice that didn't carry over to where the kids sat, he said, "I didn't sleep with you because of my job."

She swallowed, unable to respond.

"I wish I could...make it up to you. I—"

"Do you know how you can make this up to me?" she interrupted.

"What?" He stumbled closer and took her hands. "Tell me."

"Teach me to defend myself."

KADEN'S MOUTH DROPPED OPEN. Courtney wanted him to teach her self-defense?

"I've had years of training." He'd never taught anyone. Sure, he'd helped Quantico classmates when they were having trouble with moves, but... "I don't think this is a good idea."

"I don't believe that. There are self-defense classes all over. I thought it would be easier if you taught me."

Cheryl bustled in with a basket. "Lunch is here."

He wasn't going to say anything with Cheryl listening, but he couldn't keep his mouth shut. "I wouldn't want you to get too confident. That happens sometimes. People get a few moves and then get cocky and hurt."

"What are you two discussing?" Cheryl set the basket on the table where he and Courtney were sitting.

"I want Kaden to teach me self-defense." She glanced over at the kids. They were engrossed in their book, ignoring the adults. "In case she comes back."

"What a great idea!" Cheryl placed a hand on his arm. "I want in, too."

"What?" He didn't want to do this.

"What if Issy and I are alone?" Cheryl kept her voice low. "She may not be my biological daughter, but I love her. She's mine. I won't let anything happen to her."

Courtney stood and linked her arm with Cheryl. "Please, Kaden."

Didn't Courtney understand that he would have to touch her to teach her? Was she trying to kill him? "We'd need a—a gym."

Courtney pointed to the activity room covered in soft gym flooring.

"Please," Courtney whispered again. It was the same voice she'd used when she'd begged him to sink into her while they'd made love.

He hadn't ignored her then. He couldn't now.

Heaving a sigh, he shook his head. "We'll start after your doctor clears you for strenuous exercise."

"I didn't even think about that." Courtney held her hand near her face. "All right."

How long a reprieve did he have? Could he catch Bole before Courtney healed? Or maybe Roger would send down his replacement. No matter what happened, teaching Courtney self-defense would be torture.

"I'M NOT SURE what I should teach them," Kaden complained to his grandfather as they played chess a week later.

His granddad moved his bishop. "You'll come up with a plan."

Kaden frowned at the board. Shoot. He was losing. Again. He stared and stared. Then finally tipped over his king. "You got me."

"You're letting your worry for Issy distract you." Granddad stuffed the chess pieces back in the box.

Granddad was only half-right. He was worried about Issy, but his stress was because of Courtney. He wanted to convince her that what they had together—present tense—was real. It wasn't about his job. It was about her.

"Abby stopped by yesterday," Granddad said. "When I'm released, she wants me to stay in Carleton House."

Kaden caught his grandfather's hand. "I'm glad."

Since Roger still hadn't sent another agent, Kaden had worried about taking care of his granddad *and* keeping watch for Heather if Nigel moved back to Tybee.

Maybe after the incident with Courtney, Heather would never return. He didn't want Courtney, Issy, or any of the Fitzgeralds or Foresters hurt because of Bole. He wanted to capture that scum of a mother and shut down her drug ring.

But Roger had promised to replace him.

"I won't be treated like an invalid," Granddad grumbled.

"How about an honored guest and friend?" Kaden asked.

"That would be fine." Nigel waved his hand at the plants and flowers and boxes of food. "I'll take a bit of what the Fitzgeralds and friends have left for me, but I want to share with people who don't have family here like I do. I'll want you to deliver them the day I leave."

"I will." His granddad had the biggest heart around.

Kaden set the chessboard and pieces in a drawer. "You know you're going to get out of here in time for the Fitzgeralds' annual picnic."

"Good planning on my part." Granddad's head sank into his pillows and his eyes closed. "You'd better get to your self-defense class. Take care of my ladies."

"I will." He brushed a kiss on his grandfather's forehead. "I love you."

His granddad touched his chest and whispered, "I love you more."

Kaden waved to the receptionist and hurried to his car. Love filled in some of the gaps in his heart. How much longer would he have his granddad? There might be more action on the drug front in Atlanta, but maybe he needed to request a transfer to Savannah. Then he could be here with Granddad...and Courtney.

He had to convince Courtney that although he'd *started* hanging out with her because of his job, after getting to know her, everything had changed. He cared about her. She was finding her way to an honorable life just like his granddad had. He wanted to be around to watch her flourish. Over the last week, he'd missed hearing about her successes and setbacks. Missed touching her. Missed *her.*

His chest ached. Had he fallen in love with Courtney?

How would he know? He'd never loved anyone but his brother and Granddad. Maybe his mom and dad, but that love had died. This need to see Courtney, to have her smile at him, was more than friendship.

Love.

Reeling at the thought, he headed to the B and B. What could he offer someone like Courtney? She'd had the best in life. His job, his need to get drug dealers off the street, was everything to him. But not being able to watch a smile dawn across her face made him ache.

Damn. His mouth dropped open. If he had to choose between getting Courtney back and his job, he would choose her.

He'd planned to arrive before his students, but when he keyed in his code, he heard voices, female voices. More than two.

From the doorway, his gaze tracked directly to Courtney as if he was a compass and she was his due north. His heart pounded a little faster and his body ached.

She wore yoga pants and a clingy top. Her exercise clothes weren't seductive, but they showcased her body. A body he longed to touch again. Surgical tape crisscrossed her cut.

Cheryl and the Fitzgerald sisters were also dressed in exercise clothes. Issy and Josh played at a table nearby. Gray and Liam installed cubicles along one wall with the two Forester brothers.

"Here's Kaden." Courtney was all business, not meeting his gaze. She clapped her hands. "Let's get started."

"I thought it was going to be you and Cheryl?" Had dumber words ever come out of his mouth?

Dolley waved her hand to encompass the group—her sisters, Cheryl and the men. "All of us."

"Okay." He grabbed the mats he'd picked up this afternoon. They wouldn't be enough, but they might cushion some of their falls. "I didn't plan for—" he counted "—nine of you. We'll have to take turns."

They lined up on the opposite side of the mats from him. Courtney made fists, her face scrunched up like she was ready to box.

He widened his stance and asked, "What's a person's best self-defense?"

Answers rang out. "Running!"

"A gun?"

"Kick them in the groin."

He shook his head and held up his hand. "Prevention, people."

"Why didn't I think of that," Courtney muttered.

"Because you're all thinking of attack. First you need to know what's going on around you." He pointed to his eyes and his ears. "These are your best tools to keep you safe. Be aware of your surroundings. At night, stay where it's lit." He dug into his pocket. "Thread your keys through your fingers."

He kept going, sure he was repeating things they knew. "Pay attention when the hair crawls up the back of your neck. Someone might be watching."

"Should I make the lighting brighter in the courtyard?" Bess asked.

He glanced out. "I don't think you need to do that. The walkways between the two houses are bright. That's good."

"Let me know if you change your mind," Bess said. "Or have suggestions."

"I will. I hope you never have to use any of this advice." He talked about getting loud. About pushing. Then walked through the vulnerable parts of the body. "Sandra Bullock had it right in her movie. *SING*."

"We're supposed to sing a feckin' song?" Liam asked.

"No." Dolley gave him a friendly elbow.

All the women had apparently watched the movie. They chanted together. "Solar plexus, instep, nose, groin."

Everyone laughed. Courtney's laugh sparkled above the rest. The other men hugged their mates. Kaden shifted on the balls of his feet, wanting to wrap his arms around Courtney.

Not going to happen. He'd ruined their chance of being together.

Kaden clapped his hands. "It's time to work on how to react if someone attacks you."

Before he could ask, the couples had paired up, leaving Courtney by herself.

He inhaled. "Courtney, can I use you to demonstrate?"

She didn't look him in the eye. "Sure."

Demonstrating attacks and defenses and touching Courtney was torture. It was as close as he'd been since they'd slept together. And a lot less satisfying.

He put Courtney in a choke hold. "Get your

hands up around your neck before someone can strangle you."

She jammed her hands up and poked his chin. "Good."

Her dark, sinful scent filled his nose. Damn, he'd missed the smell of her hair and the feel of her silky skin under his fingers. Her curls tucked into a ponytail brushed against his skin, driving him crazy.

He described how they could break different holds, then demonstrated on Courtney.

As everyone worked, he attacked by grabbing her shoulders. She swung her arm around, then kept spinning like he'd taught her. And clocked him with her elbow.

He went down. Hard. The room wobbled.

"Kaden!" She knelt, her hand stroking his chin. "Are you okay?"

The room went silent. He lied on the mat, letting Courtney touch his face.

"I'm so sorry." She leaned over him, touching his arms and chest.

It was wrong, but damn it, he couldn't take his eyes off her cleavage bobbing near his chest.

Footsteps sounded next to his head. He closed his eyes and caught her roaming hands. "I'm good. Nice work."

To prove he was fine, he stood and pulled her up with him. He held her hand a few moments longer than necessary. What was worse? Being clocked by the woman he loved or having her break his heart?

"I think we can call it a night," he said.

The adults laughed.

"I've got treats in the kitchen," Abby said.

"And Jameson or beer?" Liam asked.

"Am I Abby Fitzgerald?" She grinned.

"Smythe," Gray added under his breath.

They laughed again, but there was another sound.

Whimpering came from where the kids were sitting. He and Courtney jerked around. Issy rocked back and forth, her head tucked between her knees.

They rushed over.

"Honey, what's wrong?" Courtney knelt and rubbed her back.

Kaden tipped up Issy's chin. "Did you see what Miss Courtney did? To me?"

Issy nodded. Tears clung to her eyelashes. "Did she shoot you?"

"Oh, God," Courtney whispered.

"No. She hit me with her elbow, but I'm okay." He took her hand and patted it on his chest. "She's learning how to protect you."

Her blond eyebrows smashed together in a frown. "Me?"

Courtney nodded. "Kaden is teaching us how to defend ourselves. To defend you."

"From Mommy?" Issy's voice was a soft whisper.

Nathan and Cheryl rushed over and touched her shoulders. Josh took her hand.

"Yes, short stuff." Nathan's voice cracked. He

picked up Issy and nestled her into his chest. Cheryl hugged the two of them and Josh kept his hand on his sister's leg. They were a unit.

Kaden and Courtney slipped away, letting the family take over.

Heading out the door, the rest of the adults followed. He and Courtney straightened up the room.

What a heavy burden Nathan and Cheryl carried, keeping Issy and Josh safe. How did they do it day in and day out?

Courtney set her hand on his back. "What's wrong?"

He slid away and folded up the mats. "What do you mean?"

"I saw your face as you watched Nathan, Cheryl and the kids. It went…blank. Like someone died. Full of—of despair."

"Someone could have died." Didn't she understand? He took her shoulders. "You. You could have died. Heather could have had a gun. You could have been shot."

He wrapped his arms around her, needing to touch her.

It was like hugging a boulder. Until she softened and hugged him back. She carefully rested her forehead on his chest. "She didn't have a gun. She didn't hurt me. I'm fine."

"But she did hurt you." He pulled away and touched her cheek. "I shouldn't have let this happen."

"Maybe it will keep people from looking at just my face." Bitterness filled Courtney's voice.

"You will always be beautiful to me," he whispered.

They were so close. Her gaze dropped to his mouth and lingered like a soft kiss.

He brushed his lips on hers. When her mouth opened, he took it as an invitation. He had to kiss her again. Touch her again. He couldn't go a lifetime without her taste being part of his day.

He stroked his tongue against hers, keeping it gentle. He brushed kisses on her uninjured cheek and eye. "I missed you, missed this."

She hummed, just like when they'd made love.

Needing her to understand, he placed his hand over her heart. "Your beauty comes from here. Not your face."

She swayed and her face went pale.

"Are you all right?" He guided her to one of the small chairs and set her in it. "What's wrong?"

"I need to…rest." She rested her good cheek in one of her hands. "I should get back to Gray's place."

"You did too much." He stroked her hair. "Let me finish picking up. Then I'll take you back."

She nodded.

He made quick work of tucking away the mats and moving tables and chairs back into place. Then he scooped Courtney into his arms.

She smacked his arm. "Don't carry me."

"You're exhausted. You're still recovering from a trauma." And he needed to hold her.

She didn't fight. Just set her head on his chest, defeated.

The trip across the courtyard was too short. A couple sitting outside the Carleton House library sighed loud enough for him and Courtney to hear them. The couple didn't know this was a mockery of romance. Sure, he wanted to sweep Courtney off her feet, but she was too blasted tired to complain that he was carrying her.

"I'll see you tomorrow." He set her down on the top step of the porch and leaned in to kiss her goodnight.

Courtney placed a hand on his chest. "Stop. Our kiss in the center was wrong. It won't happen again."

"But we both wanted it." Didn't they? He hadn't forced her, had he?

"It doesn't change what happened." She spun and disappeared into the carriage house.

And his heart broke into a few more pieces.

COURTNEY GOT READY for bed, avoiding the mirror. *You will always be beautiful to me.* Was Kaden using her again?

He'd put his hand on her heart and kissed her so tenderly, she'd wanted to curl into his arms and spend a lifetime there.

No one had ever seen beneath her face. Not her parents or her supposed friends.

Why Kaden? The man who'd gotten close to her for his job. Why did he have to be the one to see through the facade?

Was he exploiting her vulnerabilities so he could stay close to her and Issy? He'd done so before. Why would he change now?

Still ignoring her reflection, she headed into the bedroom and stared out the sliding glass door at the Fitzgerald carriage house. Kaden's apartment was on the opposite side of the building. Was he still awake?

She should be moving on. That had never been a problem before. But when Kaden was near, she wanted to jump into his arms, tell him about her day and funny stories about the kids. After she'd smashed her elbow into his chin, she'd longed to kiss his injury better. Her fickle heart refused to believe what she and Kaden had shared had been fake.

At least she'd come to her senses as he'd carried her back to the carriage house. She'd have to make sure they didn't get too close. Because if they did, she'd want to get closer.

Swallowing back the tears that threatened to fall anytime she thought about Kaden, she sank into a chair. If she tried to sleep, she'd dream about him. And wake up aching.

Her chest tightened. She drew in a sharp breath.

Had she finally fallen in love? No! She couldn't have. Not with Kaden.

But the pieces fit. The way her body wanted to be near his. The way she couldn't stop looking in his eyes. The need to touch him, even after he'd betrayed her.

She wrapped her arms around her legs and rested her chin on her knees. She'd known she was smart, even if her family or friends didn't acknowledge her intelligence. But falling in love with Kaden was stupid.

She would ignore it. Ignore him.

She refused to be in love with a man she couldn't trust.

CHAPTER ELEVEN

KADEN POURED HIS morning coffee and ran the license plates of the cars in the parking lot and those parked near the B and B. It was routine now. Wake up. Scan the surveillance cameras. Enter the plates and wait for the results. He had to smile when the camera scanned the new sign: Fitzgerald House Day Care—Now Open.

He was so damn proud of Courtney for pulling this off.

For the first time a name jumped out at him. *Salvez*. He sloshed coffee on his hand. Sucking on his singed fingers, he skimmed the license plate information. Not Hector Salvez, Heather Bole's new partner. It was a Michael. Kaden didn't believe in coincidence. He called Roger.

"What's up?" Roger asked.

"I've got a plate registered to a Michael Salvez. Black Land Rover."

"Michael, not Hector?"

"Yeah. Can you find out if there's a link between Michael and Hector?"

Today would be the worst day to have Heather show up. He was picking up Granddad at eleven and moving him to Carleton House. "There's a party at the B and B today. It'll be a mob scene. I want backup."

"Your replacement's on his way," Roger said. "He should be there by noon. You can back him up."

Kaden jerked, spilling the rest of his coffee. "Who's replacing me?"

"Boyd volunteered."

Of course Boyd had volunteered. He had the hots for Courtney. "Boyd…" Kaden started to protest, but he *had* requested a replacement. This was what he wanted. What Courtney deserved.

He would warn Boyd away from Courtney. Or maim him if he touched her.

"Get Boyd up to speed and you can spend the rest of your time in Savannah helping your grandfather," Roger said.

Kaden rubbed his neck. He would be off the case. He could fulfill his granddad's wish and take him home.

And never see Courtney again.

He spread peanut butter on a piece of toast and called it breakfast. Time to head down and pull tables and chairs for the party. Abby and her crew could set up while he picked up Granddad.

He'd just rolled out the first trolley, when Courtney came up next to him.

"I'm here to help," she said.

He drank in the sight of her. Her blue tank top matched her eyes. Her dark blue shorts showed off shapely legs he'd touched, kissed. A lump filled his throat. This might be his last day to be near her. "You're not supposed to lift heavy things."

"I can push a trolley." She grabbed the front to help guide it over the flagstone path. "And I can spread tablecloths."

"Just…don't strain," he said.

She let him pull the tables off and set them around the fire pit. Then she laid and clipped tablecloths to the tables.

"The last time we did this—" he slid a table into place "—you hated it."

"I don't anymore. I actually feel like I belong." She shook her head and her black curls danced. She pointed at her cheek. "Do you think this is part of my seven years of bad luck after breaking those mirrors?"

"I don't believe you'll have seven years of bad luck." He was close enough to brush away a strand of hair caught on her eyelashes. "I want your life to be happy. Filled with joy."

She froze, staring into his eyes. "Kaden, don't…"

"Oh, good." Bess set an orchid on a table. "I want to add more color out here."

Courtney turned away from him.

"You want me to move pots?" Kaden smiled at Bess. With the Fitzgerald women around, he didn't need a gym membership.

"Would you?" Bess's eyes twinkled. "Since the weather's cooperated and we'll be outside, I'd like to show off my flowers."

"Sure." He loved helping out the Fitzgeralds. They were doing so much for his granddad.

He rolled the cart back to the storage area and brought out a trolley of chairs, then another with more tables.

When Abby stopped by, he asked, "Is that enough?"

"Perfect." Abby patted his shoulder.

Bess showed him which pots to grab from her greenhouse and where to place them. Dolley showed up with her camera. He kept his back to her as she shot pictures.

"Come on, Kaden," Dolley cajoled. "This is for the website. Your face on the page will draw in more ladies."

"I can't have my face plastered on your website." He shook his head. "I'm with the FBI."

Courtney's head snapped up from where she was wiping down chairs. Her jaw tightened. Damn. Another reminder he'd screwed up.

"I'm sorry. I wasn't thinking." Dolley squeezed his arm. "You're such a part of Fitzgerald House. I won't take your picture again."

"No problem." He checked the time. "Another agent will be here around noon."

Courtney's face paled. "Your replacement?"

He nodded, unable to tear his gaze away from her deep blue eyes.

"Good." She turned away and added another stab wound to his heart.

Abby touched his arm. "I know you were under-cover, but I'll miss having you around."

He'd miss being here, too. "I need to pick up my grandfather."

"Nigel won't admit it, but moving him into Carleton House will wear him out." Abby handed him a key card. "Lunch will be delivered to his room so he can rest."

"Thanks." He wanted Courtney to come with him, wanted to spend his last hours with her. But she was finished with him.

To Abby he said, "Thank you for the way you've taken him into your family."

"You're family, too." Abby hugged him. "You'll always be welcome here."

Family. He tripped a little on the flagstone paths heading to his car. He assumed when he lost Grand-dad, he'd be alone. The Bureau was a brutal career. Now here were these big-hearted Fitzgeralds welcoming him into the fold. Their B and B was a refuge.

As he drove to the rehab center, he didn't have to think about the route. His SUV could almost be on autopilot from all the trips he'd made in the last eight weeks.

Granddad held court in the sunroom, already dressed in pressed khakis and a button-down shirt. His walker sat next to his chair and the group of friends he'd accumulated surrounded him.

"There's my grandson." Nigel waved him over. "Come meet everyone."

After introductions, his grandfather said his goodbyes. "Let's pick up the rest of my stuff."

In his room, boxes filled a cart. "I guess you're ready to leave."

"Have been since the day you moved me in here." Granddad pointed at two of the boxes. "We can leave those at the nurses' station. I've labeled the plants and goodies and they'll distribute them."

"Will do." Kaden pushed the cart slowly down the hallway. Granddad couldn't move very fast in his walker.

Nigel sighed. "I'd rather go straight home."

"I know." Kaden set the boxes on the nurses' station. "We'll get you there. My replacement arrives today. I need to brief him on what's going on. Then I can take you home."

"What?"

"Roger finally freed up my replacement."

"But you can't abandon Issy. Forget what I've said about going home. You're needed at the B and B," Granddad protested as he eased into the SUV. "The Fitzgeralds can fuss over me for a week or two. You need to protect that little girl."

"But I didn't protect her."

"Is that why you're all het up about being replaced, because you didn't think you did your job?" Granddad snorted. "From what I heard, if you hadn't interrupted, Courtney could have been hurt worse and Issy might be gone."

Kaden drove out of the parking lot. Courtney was better off without him. "But Courtney's injuries are my fault."

"Bullshit."

Kaden jerked. His granddad did not curse.

"I know you." Granddad pointed a finger at him. "You think bad things are always your fault."

Everything inside him was as raw as an open wound. "When I care about someone, they get hurt."

"Not true. You care about me. You should be the one watching out for Issy and Courtney." He poked Kaden's arm. "I saw how you looked at Courtney. I used to look at your grandmother just like that. You care. And Issy? You would never let anyone hurt her. Hurt any of them. Do you really think some agent who hasn't been with Issy or Courtney for the last two months will do the job I know you can do?"

Oh, hell. His granddad was exposing his every fear. "I failed."

"No. You were there for them. How will you feel if they need you again and you're *not* there?"

Granddad's words ripped holes in his chest. "Terrible."

"You want to leave their safety to someone who thinks they're just a job?"

"No." Boyd was a good agent, but he didn't love Courtney. He didn't care about Issy.

"Then you'd better figure out how to fix this." His granddad shut his eyes and was asleep by the time they'd driven another block.

He pulled in next to Carleton House and watched Nigel sleep, love pumping through him in sync with his heartbeat. Was his grandfather right? Were Courtney and Issy safer with his protection?

But what if he stayed and put them in greater danger?

Boyd didn't know Courtney had the heart of a warrior. He wouldn't understand how far she would go to protect Issy and Josh.

He had to stay and had to protect them. He had to put Bole away.

Then he could leave Courtney to live her life in peace.

"Do you want these here, Miss Courtney?" Josh tugged a storage tub of art supplies into the playground area.

"Perfect."

"What are we doing with this stuff?" Josh waved a hand over the supplies on the play area picnic table.

"I thought kids could make crowns today."

"Princess crowns?" Disgust filled Josh's voice. "That's for girls."

"Crowns are for princes, too." She tried to think

of a cartoon character who wore some sort of crown and came up blank.

"Can I make a helmet? Like Thor?" Josh asked.

"Absolutely."

Josh looked around. "Do you need anything else?"

"I think we're good for now."

"Great. My dad made a big Jenga set." Josh waved his hands around. "I told him I'd stack the blocks."

"Go." Courtney set out the blank cardboard crowns she'd found. Then the glue, glitter and paint. She wasn't sure how many kids would attend the party, or if the activity was age-appropriate for all of them, but she'd wanted the day care to be part of the Fitzgerald House celebration.

As much as she hated to admit it, she'd found her purpose in Savannah. Found her calling. Her father might not think running a day care was worthwhile, but when Josh and Issy hugged her, when they learned something new, or even when they did something sweet for each other, her life had meaning.

"I like seeing you smile." Kaden's deep voice had her looking up and taking a foolish step toward him.

Darn her stupid body for wanting to touch him. "I didn't know I was smiling."

"You were." His smile disappeared. "I'd like to introduce Agent Reynolds."

She hadn't noticed the man standing next to Kaden. *The replacement*. Kaden was really leaving. This was what she wanted…right? "Hi. I'm Courtney. Nice to meet you."

"I'm Boyd." The agent shook her hand and kept holding it. "I'm sorry you were hurt."

She pulled her hand back at the same time as Kaden bumped Reynolds's shoulder. Had Kaden told the agent he shouldn't mention the injury? Did they think she was weak? "I needed to keep Issy safe."

Boyd stared at her. "Kaden was just going to show me the day care's security. Would you like to finish the tour?"

"I've got this handled," Kaden growled. "Follow me."

"Good, I found you, Courtney." Nathan stuck his head through the courtyard gate. Issy was perched on his shoulders. "Any chance you can watch Issy? Daniel and I are picking up the beer kegs and Cheryl is putting the finishing touches on the cake."

"Absolutely."

"Thanks." Nathan set Issy on her feet. "We shouldn't be gone long."

"Don't worry about the time." She held out her hand and Issy smiled at her. "What about Josh?"

"He's helping Bess set up the games."

"Issy, will you move the beanbag chairs into the

classrooms from the activity room? I thought we would have tours today."

"Yes, Miss Courtney." Issy slipped past Kaden and Agent Reynolds, and headed inside the day care.

"Is the security system off?" Kaden's voice was sharp.

"For the party." She grabbed the door handle, but he stopped her.

"Reset it." His voice was so deep and serious, a shiver slid down her back. "Now."

"I want the staff and their family to tour the center." Courtney set her fists on her hips.

"At least have it on while you're alone," Kaden insisted.

"Fine."

"Don't be so intense, Farrell," Boyd teased.

"Wait. What do you know?" She shifted so she could see Issy through the windows. "Has Heather been spotted?"

"Not Bole." Kaden reached for her, but she ducked away. "I'm worried."

He was doing it again. Keeping things from her. "Why?"

"One of the cars parked in the square this morning was registered to a Salvez."

"Why didn't you tell me?" Boyd stepped closer to Kaden. "Is it Hector?"

"A Michael Salvez. Roger's checking to see if they're related."

Courtney pressed her hand to her chest. Issy was safe, dragging beanbag chairs into each of the rooms. She wouldn't let her out of her sight. "Have you told everyone?"

Kaden shook his head. "I don't know yet whether anyone should be concerned."

"But you've warned Nathan and Cheryl and the Fitzgeralds?"

"I'm waiting on confirmation whether this Salvez is connected to Hector Salvez."

She poked him in his chest. "Tell everyone, or I will."

"I will." He rubbed where she'd jabbed him.

"Do it." She fled into the center. Punching in the code, she reset the security system.

If she hadn't asked, would Kaden have told her anything?

He was making the same error again. He didn't learn from his mistakes. She couldn't trust him. He didn't know how to be part of a team. It was good he was leaving.

And once he was gone, she would concentrate on her day care.

And maybe her heart would heal.

KADEN CLENCHED HIS hands into fists so he didn't grab his grandfather's elbow as they moved down the ramp and into the courtyard. At least their slow pace allowed him to scan the crowd.

Issy played a beanbag-toss game with Nathan.

Cheryl and Josh stood next to the drink station. He checked off all the Fitzgerald sisters.

Boyd was walking the perimeter and checking for the Land Rover Kaden had spotted this morning.

Where was Courtney? His heart picked up extra beats. Back at the day care? He wanted his eyes on her. Once he got his grandfather settled, he would pin down her location.

Staff and guests filled the open spaces and spilled over the walkways. No Bole or Salvez among them.

His facial recognition software had buzzed with false alerts for the last half hour. He was tempted to turn off the damn thing, but the last time he'd ignored an alert, Courtney had been injured.

"How're you doing?" he asked his granddad as they hit the walkway.

"Great." But Granddad leaned hard on his walker.

Bess met them near the fire pit and gave his grandfather a hug. "Nigel, I'm so glad to see you up and about. We've set up a place of honor for you."

She parted the crowd and made space for Nigel's walker. Staff and guests called his name.

It was obvious Granddad was loved and respected. Kaden couldn't have been prouder.

Bess led him to a chair set next to a low wall. "We thought this spot would protect you from people tripping over your leg and hip."

It would. Chairs fanned out so people could visit.

"Perfect." Nigel sank into the chair with a smile as Liam approached. "Thank you."

"What can I get you to drink?" Kaden asked.

"I'm on it." Liam went and quickly returned with a tumbler of amber liquid. "Jameson neat, right?"

"You've got a great memory." His grandfather took the glass. "Thank you."

Liam tapped his glass with Granddad's. *"Sláinte."* "Cheers."

"Not too many of those," Kaden warned him. "We don't want you breaking your other hip."

Granddad grinned. The staff descended to welcome him home.

Kaden slipped back, letting the ladies give hugs and the men shake his hand. Every now and then, Granddad would look at Kaden and smile or touch his heart.

If this had been an FBI gathering and he'd been injured, would people flock to greet him? He didn't think so. What did that say about his life?

He was doing important work by getting drugs and drug dealers off the streets. But he hadn't made connections with his teammates. Being in the Bureau was highly competitive, everyone climbing to the top, trying to get the tastiest assignments.

"You're scowling." Courtney stopped next to him. "What's wrong?"

He'd been checking the crowd, but she'd come

up behind him. How could he keep anyone safe if he couldn't stay aware of who was around him? "Nothing."

"Kaden, not everything is a state secret." She crossed her arms, her body language icy. "It's good to see Nigel."

"It is." He huffed out a sigh. "Does he look tired to you?"

"Maybe." Courtney stared a bit longer. "But I see a man who is happy and well-loved. I also see a man who cares so much about his grandson that he keeps checking to make sure you're still here."

How could he have ever thought Courtney was shallow? He'd been the one who was shallow and thought all she cared about was how she looked. She'd proved him wrong. "You're amazing...and right."

Granddad waved and touched his chest.

"Why is he doing that?" Her arms dropped like she planned to run to his grandfather's aid. "Is he having chest pains?"

"No." Love for Granddad and Courtney flooded his body. "It's our signal. When we're in public, it's his way of reminding me that he loves me."

"Oh. Oh." Her blue eyes shimmered. "That's... beautiful."

His chest tightened at the sight of her tears. "I don't want you to cry."

She pulled her sunglasses down from her head and covered her eyes. "Don't worry about it."

Granddad waved them over and Courtney couldn't leave Kaden's side fast enough. Marion and Amy stood and gave them their seats.

"How are you doing, Mr. Ganders?" Courtney asked.

"Nigel." He took a sip of the glass in his hand. "And I'm plenty relieved to be out from under the watchful eyes of the nurses."

Her dark eyebrows arched over her glasses. "Are you sure you're supposed to be drinking?"

Granddad winked. "I'd rather talk about you. First you're opening a day care right here on the property and then you're a hero for keeping my Issy and Josh safe."

She blushed. "Anyone would have done that."

"Maybe. But it was you, Courtney Smythe." Granddad took her hand and kissed her fingers. "I can't wait to hear children's voices in the courtyard. If I were a little more nimble, I would have asked Kaden to show me the new space."

"You would have critiqued the quality of my work," Kaden joked.

"I would have helped put the place together." Granddad nodded at Courtney. "Tell me your plans."

She scooted her chair closer.

Kaden's phone buzzed in the pocket of his shorts. He tensed and Courtney frowned at him.

Roger. Finally. "I need to take this call."

His superior didn't say hello. "The SUV is registered to Hector's second cousin. He's in the family business."

"Hell." Kaden held his breath, searching and finding Issy with her family by the fire pit and Courtney sitting next to his granddad. His exhale didn't release the tension stiffening his back. He moved away from the crowd hovering around the food and looked for a quiet spot.

"Is the Land Rover still there?" Roger asked.

"Boyd is checking." Kaden connected Boyd to their call.

"I've searched the streets surrounding the B and B and the parking lots," Boyd said. "Not here."

"Stay sharp," Roger said. "It's too much of a coincidence that the car was parked near the B and B. This is our chance. I feel it."

Kaden wanted to shut down the party, herd everyone into Fitzgerald House and lock them in the ballroom.

He told Boyd to meet him next to the fountain, dialed Nathan and gave him the same instruction.

Moving next to Courtney, he whispered, "The Michael who owns the Land Rover is related to Hector."

Her face went pale. "Thanks for letting me know."

He hurried to the fountain where Boyd already waited. Nathan arrived with Daniel, Gray and Liam.

"What's going on?" Nathan asked.

The men stood in a semicircle around him as he introduced Boyd. "He's my replacement."

"But Issy is used to you," Nathan said. "Knows you."

"We'll transition and expose her to Boyd." The idea of Boyd playing Quarto with Courtney, Issy and Josh made his gut ache.

"Is that all you needed?" Nathan asked.

"No." Before he could explain, the alert buzzed. Kaden checked. Courtney and Issy were moving around the patio.

"There was a car parked in front of the B and B this morning. It's registered to Heather's partner's cousin." Kaden looked at the men.

"Is Heather here?" Nathan pushed back his cap.

"I've just patrolled the parking lots and streets. No sign of the Land Rover, Bole or Salvez." Boyd held up a hand. "But the streets are packed. It doesn't mean anyone who left this morning would get a parking spot near the B and B."

"I'd like to shut this party down," Kaden said.

"So would I." Gray sighed. "But Abby and her sisters would have my head. This is the staff party."

"Can you ask her?" Kaden checked for alerts. Nothing.

"I'll ask," Gray said. "But unless you spot Issy's mom on the property, I'm guessing she won't kick everyone out."

"Maybe the kid's safer with all these people around," Boyd said.

"Could be." Kaden hated Boyd calling Issy "the kid." He held up his phone. "Here's what Bole and Salvez look like."

"Send me the pictures," Liam said.

He sent them to everyone.

"Boyd, keep patrolling the streets," Kaden instructed.

Boyd raised an eyebrow. "For some reason I thought you were *my* backup."

Granddad's words echoed in his head. *Do you really think some agent who hasn't been with Issy or Courtney for the last two months will do the job I know you can do?*

"Not until I leave. Right now, I'm in charge."

Boyd opened his mouth, but Kaden shot him the same look he used to intimidate interrogation suspects.

"Fine," Boyd said. "You know the territory."

"Good. I'll check the parking lots." Kaden couldn't stand around and eat as if everything was normal. "Everyone keep your eyes open. If you spot them, call me. Don't engage."

For once Kaden wished the alert would buzz.

COURTNEY ASKED NIGEL, "Can I get you anything else?"

"I could use one of Abby's brandy pecan bars." Nigel winked.

"My brother's favorite." Courtney pushed out of the chair and headed over to the food tables. Abby and Bess manned the incredible spread. "Nigel would like a pecan bar, but when I'm done, do you need any help?" Courtney asked as she moved through the line.

"I think we've got it covered, but thanks. You've done so much already." Abby whispered, "The people who toured the day care are excited. I think there'll be a few more registrations."

"Martha was giving one more tour." Each day she liked her assistant more and more.

"The school buses will have to make a stop at the day care soon." Abby handed her a plate with the pecan bars.

"I called the school district last Friday." Courtney couldn't hold in her smile. "The woman in charge will call me back on Tuesday."

"You're way ahead of me." Abby took her hand. "I'm so glad you're my sister-in-law."

"Me, too," Courtney choked out. For the first time ever, she belonged.

"Hungry people behind you," Marion called from the line. "Stop the gabbing and start the grabbing."

People laughed. But it wasn't *at* her. It was *with* her.

"You okay?" Bess asked.

"I'm better than okay," Courtney said. Inside, she was as warm as a fire during a blizzard. If her relationship with Kaden had been real, everything would be perfect.

She sat on the patio floor and watched Nigel devour two bars. Cheryl came over with Issy and Josh. "Nathan's missing. Do you mind if Issy and Josh sit with you? I have to bring over the cake."

"Not at all." Courtney held out her arms and Issy sat on her lap, Josh at her feet.

Nigel patted his leg. "Issy, I don't think I've had a hug from you."

The little girl scooted off Courtney's lap and let Nigel lift her up.

"I wonder where Kaden is," Courtney said. She hadn't seen him for a while, not that she was keeping track. But he hadn't eaten. And she wanted an update on the Land Rover.

"Probably with the other men." Nigel waved his hand. "A group of them headed to Fitzgerald House. Could be they're smoking cigars."

"Yuck," Issy said.

"They smell good," Josh protested.

"Hopefully they'll keep the stink away from the food," Courtney said. If that's what they were really doing.

"Can we toast marshmallows?" Issy whispered.

"Yeah!" Josh agreed.

She took the kids over to the fire pit.

After making s'mores, Issy asked, "Play Jenga?"

"Sure." Courtney cleaned off the toasting forks

and placed them back where others could use them.
"Josh, are you coming?"

"I'm going to make more s'mores," he said.

"I'll keep my eye on him," Dolley volunteered.

"Thanks." She and Issy headed to the patio outside the Carleton House library, where the giant
game was set up.

They played as a team against Daria, Courtney's
newest student, and her mother, Maggie.

Daria tugged on Courtney's shorts. "I like my
new school, Miss Courtney."

"It was fun having you there Thursday and Friday." And on Monday there would be another new
student. She was ready, she hoped.

"Let's try this one," Courtney said, testing a
block.

Issy, her tongue caught between her teeth, pushed
out the piece while Courtney held her up. It wasn't
the safest, but it allowed Issy to be part of the game.

"You put it on top." Issy handed her the block.

"I don't know. It's pretty wobbly." She set the
piece in the only available spot. The blocks swayed
and finally tumbled, the wood clattering to the
stone.

"Noooo," Courtney said. "I'm sorry, partner."

"It's okay." Issy patted her hand.

As they picked up the blocks and reset them, Issy
tugged on her hand. "I have to pee."

"Go ahead," Maggie said. "We've got this."

She and Issy skipped to the day care, those bathrooms being the closest. They smiled at everyone they met. "Are you having fun?"

Issy grinned. "Mmm-hmm."

Courtney tried to encourage Issy to talk. "What was the best thing about the party?"

Issy sighed, her shoulders going up and down in an exaggerated motion. "Happy."

On the surface the answer didn't make sense. But everywhere Courtney had turned during the afternoon and evening, people smiled or laughed. Their happiness was contagious. And it wasn't just the party. It was every day. The only thing that had ever made her happy in Boston was reading to the kids. Being in Savannah, doing what she was doing, made her happy all day long.

Courtney knelt so she and Issy were face-to-face. "You're so right. There's a ton of happiness. Right here." She brushed a kiss on the darling girl's head. "And being with you makes me very happy."

Issy flung her arms around Courtney's neck. "Happy."

But there was a cloud on her happiness horizon. Kaden. Getting over him would take time. Once she recovered from loving Kaden, she would seek out her own happiness.

Courtney swung Issy's hand and they headed down the path. "We'd better get you to the bathroom so we can get back to the fun."

The gate was open when they got to the day care. She didn't need to use her security card on the door; it was unarmed. Shoot. Martha hadn't reset the security system after the kids left. Kaden would yell if he knew.

The lights were off in the hallway, but they were on a sensor. She flipped on the switch and said, "Go ahead."

Issy skipped down the hallway. Courtney was relieved that Issy had shaken off her fears from Heather's attack.

At the security panel, Courtney entered her code and set the alarm. Then she picked up registration sheets that had fallen off the front desk.

Issy screamed. The sound echoed through the center.

"Issy!" Courtney pushed on the door to the main area, and stopped dead. *Damn.*

Digging her security card out of her pocket, she slapped it against the reader. "Issy?"

She rushed through the activity room and into the bathroom. Empty. Her breath heaved. "Issy, answer me!"

She ran through the open door of the closest classroom and froze.

A man held Issy under his arm. His hand smothered her mouth. He had dark hair, dark clothes and a dark frown.

"We should have grabbed her and run," the man complained to someone behind Courtney. He had a Mexican accent. Salvez?

"Please don't hurt her," Courtney begged, moving closer.

The man stared behind her. "I told you this was a bad idea."

"I don't care. Bella's mine."

Courtney turned her head. *No.*

Heather paced, her movements agitated and sharp. Her hair was a scraggly mess and her face had the emaciated look of a drug user.

"Please, Heather." Icy chills ran down Courtney's spine. "Don't hurt your daughter."

Heather stormed over and shoved Courtney. "I can do what I want. She's mine."

"You're her mother. Don't you want what's best for her?" She had to get Issy away from these two.

"Looks like I got the best of you at our last meeting." Heather poked a finger at Courtney's scar. Searing pain raced across Courtney's cheek. "Keep your mouth shut."

Tears streamed down Issy's face. She stared at Courtney, her chin trembling.

Courtney's heart pounded in her ears as loud as the kids banging on the new drums. "Issy's scared. She can't breathe. Please put her down."

"We gotta go." Salvez hoisted Issy higher on his hip and moved toward the door. "Let's get out of here."

Kaden. Courtney needed Kaden. She slipped her

hand in her pocket and touched her phone. She pretended to stumble as the man and Issy approached.

"Hector, what about this bitch?" Heather jabbed a thumb Courtney's way.

"I'm not killing again for you." Salvez shook Issy. "You're her mother. We can take the kid. No problem."

Killing? Courtney's hand clenched around her phone.

"But I don't like her." Heather pushed Courtney's shoulder.

The push gave Courtney an excuse to fall. She slipped her phone out and cowered on the floor, letting her hair curtain her actions. "Don't hurt me again."

Heather laughed. "I'll hurt you if I want."

She needed Kaden. She huddled over the phone until she got to the right screen.

Heather used her foot to push Courtney. She curled into a ball, hiding her phone. She hadn't been able to complete the call.

"Move it," the man called.

"Don't ruin Issy's life." Tucking the phone in her pocket, she scrambled to her feet and grabbed his arm. They couldn't take Issy.

Salvez spun, his hand in a fist.

Courtney ducked. He caught her in the shoulder. The shock threw her head back. She rolled with the punch, dropping to the floor. Kaden's training kicked in. She pulled her foot back and smashed her heel into his groin.

"Fuck!" Salvez crumpled, dropping Issy.

Courtney tugged the phone out and speed-dialed Kaden's. "Issy, run!"

Issy screamed.

"Stop screaming!" Heather rushed over, swearing. She shook Issy. "I'm your mother. You're coming with me."

Courtney jammed her foot into the back of Heather's knee, making her fall.

"Run!" Courtney stumbled to her feet. She dropped the phone in the pocket of her shorts and ran after Issy.

Salvez caught Courtney's arm, swinging her like a doll into the activity room door. Her body hit the release bar and the door swung open. Her teeth snapped together. Pain lanced up her back and she collapsed.

"Stop! Stop!" Heather screeched. "Bella. Stop right now!"

Issy whimpered and crawled to Courtney. Heather towering over both of them.

Oh, God. She has a gun.

KADEN PROWLED THE Carleton House parking lot again. Since his sweep ten minutes ago, none of the cars had moved. Where were Bole and Salvez?

An alert buzzed. Josh had moved back to the fire pit. The facial recognition software was almost useless in a crowd. It buzzed every time Courtney, Issy or Josh moved around. He couldn't open his phone fast enough to keep up with the alerts.

He checked in with Boyd. "Anything?"

"Not on the street."

He called Nathan and got the same answer.

As he headed back to the Fitzgerald House parking lot, he scrolled through the alerts he hadn't had a chance to delete. Courtney, Issy, Courtney, Courtney, Josh, Josh, Bole, Salvez, Courtney, Issy, Josh.

He froze. Scrolled back. Bole, Salvez—FH P Lot.

He'd been in the Fitzgerald House parking lot five minutes ago. He checked the camera. No sign of them.

His hand shook as he dialed Boyd. "Bole was in the Fitzgerald House parking lot. Are you close?"

"I'll head right there."

He repeated the same message to Nathan. Then he sprinted around the buildings.

Nathan and Gray waited. Boyd joined them. Daniel and Liam ran over from Fitzgerald House.

"Anyone spot them?" Kaden gasped.

"No."

"Not me."

"Nothing."

"Boyd?" he asked.

"Land Rover was there. No sign of Bole or Salvez."

Courtney's ringtone played.

Kaden answered, "Courtney?"

There was no reply. Static filled his ear. Had she butt-dialed him? "Courtney?"

He caught a few muffled words. *Stop. Isabella.* The men were talking. He held up his hand. "Quiet!"

"Please Heather…gun away…no one here…us." He strained to hear. "No one's…day care."

A gun? In the day care?

Heather. He took off.

When footsteps pounded next to him, he was halfway to the center. Boyd jerked his arm. "What the hell are you doing?"

Kaden slammed to a stop. He couldn't charge in. Heather had already been in one gun battle. This time Courtney, Issy or Fitzgerald House guests could be caught in the crossfire.

Nathan, Daniel, Gray and Liam ran up, too.

He took a cleansing breath. "Courtney's phone is on. She's being held at gunpoint in the day care. Issy's with her."

"Issy!" Nathan gasped. Then ran.

Kaden caught him and pulled him to a stop. "We have to be smart. We have to make a plan."

He had to think. Regroup. Use logic instead of the love bursting inside, insisting he rescue Courtney. Panic wouldn't help.

Boyd should take the lead. *How will you feel if they need you again and you're not there?*

He would not leave the safety of the woman he loved in someone else's hands. This was his mission. He had to trust his training. He could do this.

He checked his service revolver. Boyd did the same. Two guns against the unknown.

"What do you want us to do?" Nathan inched toward the carriage house.

"You, Liam and I will head into the restaurant and approach from the rear. Boyd, Gray and Daniel, we'll need a distraction."

"No civilians." Boyd shook his head.

"That's my daughter." Nathan glared. "I know the building better than anyone."

"Three people have already died around this woman," Boyd said.

"That's not going to happen here." Kaden took a deep breath.

"Where do you want the distraction?" Daniel asked.

"The playground. A fight. A loud discussion." They could figure it out.

"Got it." Gray nodded.

Kaden stared at Boyd.

The agent gave a sharp nod. "We'll relay where they're positioned in the center."

"Liam. Call Gray or Daniel when we're a go."

Liam nodded.

They approached the restaurant from the back. Nathan unlocked the door, ushering them inside. Kaden's breath rasped. Their footsteps echoed in the empty building.

"Heel, toe," Kaden whispered, hoping they understood how to quiet their steps.

Nathan and Liam nodded.

He hesitated at the metal door that led into a hallway between the day care and restaurant. He pointed at the security panel. "System's armed."

"I've got my access card," Nathan said quietly.

"The day care hallway is on the other side of this door, right?" He had to confirm, even though the center's floor plan ran through his head.

Nathan nodded.

"Can you open this without making a sound?" Kaden asked Nathan.

Nathan nodded again.

"I'm armed." Kaden's whisper sounded as loud as a nail gun. "I go in alone."

Liam's phone must have vibrated. "Yes?" He nodded. "Thanks."

"Where are they?" Kaden asked.

"East classroom," Liam whispered. "Heading to the activity room."

Kaden had to hurry. They were moving closer to where he would enter. He inhaled and exhaled. *Calm. Cold. Get in. Assess. Extract.*

Nathan waved his card over the security panel and input his code. He eased the door open. The metallic click of the lock sounded like gunfire.

Kaden inhaled and exhaled, forcing his racing heart to slow.

Locate Courtney and Issy.

ID and neutralize target.

Simple. "When I want you to call Gray and Daniel, I'll hold up my fist."

Liam tapped his nose.

Kaden exhaled once more and nodded to Nathan. He'd give his left nut for a fiber optic camera right now.

Nathan opened the door wider.

Crouching, Kaden peered through the crack. Empty. Better yet. The hallway was dark. Staying low, he slipped inside. He slid along the wall to the handwashing station.

"You're scaring Issy." Courtney's voice carried down the corridor.

Kaden froze.

"My daughter's not scared of me." Heather. A manic quality laced her voice. "And don't call her Issy. It's Bella. My sweet Bella. Come here, baby."

Heather paced the main activity room. Her shadow jittered and bounced across the entrance to the hall.

"No, Mommy," Issy sobbed.

"Now, Bella!"

Issy whimpered and he heard the shuffling of feet.

"She needs to use the bathroom," Courtney said.

Kaden crawled, using the handwashing station as a shield. He peered around the corner into the activity room. Was it only the two women and Issy?

"Let's get out of here," a male voice said.

Damn. Salvez, too.

"We have to do something with the bitch." Heather passed by the hall, Issy's hand in hers.

"I told you." Salvez again. "I'm not shooting her."

Thank God. Kaden shrank into the shadows. If Heather turned around, she'd spot him.

Issy looked right at him and Kaden put a finger to his lips.

The girl blinked. Did that mean she understood?

Heather had Issy, but where was Courtney? Salvez? This had lose-lose all over it.

"Unless you want an accident, I should take Issy to the bathroom." Courtney's voice was strong.

Kaden's heart pounded at her bravery. He slipped into the inset door of the boys' bathroom. Could it be this easy? Could he get Courtney and Issy out through the restaurant and then take on Heather and Salvez? Hoping Nathan or Liam could see him, he held up his fist.

"She's my daughter," Heather said. "I'll take her to the bathroom. Then we'll deal with you."

Damn. He exhaled, straining to hear footsteps on the cushioned sports floor. Door hinges creaked. Heather and Issy were in the girls' bathroom. Should he surprise Bole? Would she hurt her own child? He waited, ready to grab Heather as they moved back into the hall.

"We got problems out here," the man yelled.

Boyd, Gray and Daniel. He could hear their raised voices as they created the diversion. Time to rescue Courtney and Issy.

"Hurry up!" Heather ran out of the bathroom, tugging Issy behind her. "What's happening?"

Issy tried to stop and pull up her shorts and tripped.

Salvez answered, "Three guys arguing."

"Are they coming in?" Heather's voice squeaked.

Kaden peered around the corner. Salvez was in the activity room, standing sideways next to the classroom door. He stared from the doorway out the window.

"Get over here and help my daughter," Heather snarled.

Courtney came around the corner. She spotted Kaden and staggered but didn't fall.

He held his finger to his lips.

"Let's pull up your shorts, sweetheart," Courtney choked out.

He pointed at the door behind him. *Walk over here.*

Courtney jerked her head in a nod.

"Where do you think you're going?" Heather snapped.

"I didn't… Did Issy, I mean Bella, have time to go to the bathroom?" Courtney tucked Issy behind her as she faced Heather.

"She took care of business." Light flashed off the chrome finish of Heather's gun and danced along the walls. "Just get her clothes on and wash those hands. I don't need any germs."

Courtney turned and looked at him, but didn't move any deeper into the hallway.

He moved his hand in a come-here motion.

Courtney knelt and whispered something in Issy's ear. After a quick glance behind her, she said, "I'll turn on the water for you."

Issy stayed on her hands and knees.

"Make sure you get lots of bubbles." Courtney bent over the washing station. Issy crawled around it. "Let's sing the ABC song."

Courtney sang. Loud. And stared into his eyes. He touched his heart and she stumbled over the words.

Issy crawled close enough for him to scoop her up and whip her out of sight. He hustled to the door and tapped.

Nathan cracked it open and Kaden handed Issy into his arms. Nathan's face was a landscape of relief as he clutched his daughter to his chest.

"One more time, Issy. Let's wash those germs down the drain." Courtney kept singing.

He couldn't love her more. Now he needed to get her out of here.

"Stop!" Heather screamed. "Make her stop, Hector."

No. Kaden had to get to Courtney, but Salvez moved across the main room, heading for the hallway. He ducked next to the boys' bathroom again. The inset door was barely deep enough to hide him.

"What the...?" Salvez swore. The water stopped. There was a slap. "Where is she, bitch?"

Rage burned through him like a gas can igniting.

Hector had hit Courtney. No one hurt the woman he loved. He wanted to burst through into the hall, gun blazing.

But if he did, Courtney might get hurt.

"Bella?" Heather called. Her footsteps grew closer.

This was his chance. Heather pushed open the girls' bathroom. She was inside for a moment.

"Bella. Not funny." Heather moved toward where he was plastered against the boys' bathroom door. "We have to go."

She stomped around the corner. Her eyes went wide.

Kaden grabbed Heather. With one hand, he muffled her mouth. With the other, he squeezed her wrist and the gun clattered to the floor.

Salvez called, "Heather?"

Bole kicked him. He pulled her tight to his body. She smelled like vinegar and ammonia. Hell, she was a meth user. She squirmed, but he squeezed harder.

If Salvez would just walk back, he could apprehend both him and Heather without injury.

"Let go," Courtney cried. "Stop!"

A chill raced down his back. He wanted to look. Wanted to know what Salvez was doing to Courtney.

Heather squirmed like a snake. His arms tightened around her body.

"Heather!" Salvez barked out.

She tried to bite him, and he clamped his fingers tighter.

Heather twisted and kicked. Her heels smashed his shins, then the wall and floor. He hefted her up so she didn't reveal their location.

"Let go," Courtney complained.

"Shut up."

Footsteps echoed on the hallway floor. The girls' bathroom door squeaked.

Would Salvez have Courtney in a hold or be pulling her by the arm? How could he minimize the possibility of Courtney being hurt? He clutched his weapon. He needed one clean shot and this could all be over.

The girls' bathroom door squeaked again. Zero hour.

He leveled the gun over Heather's shoulder, shielding his body with hers.

Salvez wasn't subtle or quiet. He barreled around the corner.

"FBI. Freeze," Kaden shouted.

Salvez stopped, but didn't freeze. His elbow was curled around Courtney's neck, his gun pointed at Kaden. "Let Heather go."

Kaden kept his eyes trained on Salvez.

Courtney's hands were between her neck and Salvez's arm. Good girl. Her eyes darted around the hallway.

"Issy's safe." Kaden let go of Heather's mouth.

"Bella! I want my Bella." Heather tried to twist

out of Kaden's arms, but she didn't have Courtney's training.

Kaden squeezed harder.

"Let her go." Salvez rubbed the barrel of his gun on Courtney's cheek.

Kaden's rage built like a geyser, making his hand shake. "Release her, Salvez."

Courtney stared at him. She gave a small jerk with her head.

His heart stopped. Then pounded triple time, trying to batter its way out of his chest. She was going to do something dangerous.

The world went into slow motion. Courtney collapsed in Salvez's arm, dragging him down. Then she sprang up. Her head smashed Salvez's nose. Blood erupted.

Boom! Salvez's gunshot echoed in the small space. Kaden's ears rang. Courtney screamed.

Salvez lost his grip. Courtney slammed her elbow into his chest and spun away from the man, but tripped and fell.

Warm sticky wetness dripped on his arm. Heather's body sagged. He dropped her and dove for Salvez. They smacked against the floor.

Kaden clutched Salvez's hand, fighting to control his gun. They rolled, smashing into the wall. He swung the butt of his gun, trying to connect with Salvez's face.

Salvez blocked the hit, jarring Kaden's gun out of his hand. Salvez still had his gun.

Disarm. Kaden lunged and grabbed Salvez's wrist with both hands. He had to win this battle. The gun boomed again, but the shot fired into the ceiling.

Courtney scrambled on the floor and came up with Kaden's gun. "Stop!" She leveled the gun right at Salvez's head. "Now!"

"FBI." Boyd's voice rang out from the classroom. Too far away.

Salvez tried to wrench his hand free from Kaden's grip. Kaden squeezed harder.

Another blast. This time next to Salvez's legs. Courtney screamed. "I said stop!"

Salvez stopped. Kaden ripped the gun out of his hand and clambered back, pushing off the wall to his feet.

"Die, bitch." Heather lay on the floor in a pool of blood. She aimed at Courtney, her hand shaking.

"No!" Kaden dove to protect her. Twisting, he fired.

Heather jerked and her gun went off.

There was a smack and a sting on his thigh.

"Kaden!" Courtney's mouth dropped open.

He tried to stand, but fire shot through his leg. He crawled next to Courtney. "Are you all right?"

"Yes." Tears filled her voice.

"Don't cry."

Boyd skidded to a halt. "Clear?"

"Clear." Kaden's head spun. "Forester. Call 911. We need an ambulance."

"On their way," came the cry through the door.

Doors slammed. Footsteps pounded through the classrooms. Boyd touched Courtney's arm. "I'll take that."

"Good idea." Courtney's voice shook, but she didn't let go of the gun.

Boyd peeled her fingers off the grip. "I've got them covered."

His vision flickered. His gun slipped from his fingers.

"You're bleeding. Bad." Courtney scooted to Kaden's side and slapped a hand on his thigh.

Pain shot through him like a bolt of lightning. He cursed.

"Lie down. Someone get a chair," she yelled.

"Bole. Salvez." His words tangled as he tried to talk.

"Stay. Still." Her voice cut through all the noise.

People filled the hall. Someone slapped paper towels in her hands and she pressed them hard on his leg.

He groaned.

"Get his leg up. There's so much blood. Did she hit an artery?"

Was this floating feeling him dying?

"You saved me." Her face was ghostly white against the black of her hair. Her blue eyes were sharp spots of color. "I'm not letting you die."

He couldn't think. Couldn't keep his eyes open.

"Liam. Help me!" she cried.

Where had Liam come from? "Someone…"

Pain clamped down on his leg.

"Compression. Wound above his heart," Courtney recited. "What else can we do?"

"Pray, lass," Liam said.

"Blankets," she shouted. "We need to keep him warm. In the classroom."

His vision was tunneling. *Not good.* He reached for Courtney, trying to talk. Nothing came out. He forced his hand to his heart.

"Kaden," she whispered. "Hang on. Please hang on."

Courtney's voice was better than a blanket. The melody of her voice washed over him.

"Stay awake." She brushed a kiss on his forehead. Tears splashed his face.

He tried to open his eyes, for her. And failed.

Sirens wailed. Footsteps jarred the floor.

"In here," Liam called.

"You'll be all right." Courtney stroked his hair. "Hang on."

"Ma'am, you need to move."

"Can't I stay with him?"

Something tightened around his leg and flames lanced through his body. Blackness washed over him and took him away from the pain and fire. Away from Courtney.

CHAPTER TWELVE

COURTNEY PACED THE small waiting room.

Gray touched her arm. "You should go back to the ER. Or at least sit down."

Sit? "Kaden took a bullet for me." A bullet that had nicked his artery.

Her brother's lips formed a straight line. "It was his job."

Was. Oh, God. He couldn't die. She rubbed her forehead. When he hadn't been able to speak, he'd touched his heart. Did he love her? Or was the message for his grandfather?

She stared at the waiting room door, wishing the surgeon would give them another update.

Gray came back with a nurse in tow.

"Ma'am," the nurse said. "Your face should be checked."

Courtney touched her cheek and found dried blood.

"Come on, brat." Gray helped her back to the ER.

"Gray, please go back and wait to see how Kaden's doing."

"I'm worried about you." Deep lines etched her brother's mouth, but Gray did as she asked.

The ER staff cleaned and added two more stitches to her cheek, compliments of the hit from Salvez.

Her face didn't matter. Kaden did. He'd leaped

in front of her as Heather fired. What if he didn't make it?

Tears streaked her face as she washed his blood from her hands. *Please don't let him die for me.*

She should have trusted Kaden. Should have trusted that he was doing everything he could to keep Issy safe. Her pride had gotten in the way.

What if she never got the chance to tell him she'd forgiven him? That she trusted him.

Back in the waiting room, people filled the space. FBI. Police. Her brother had disappeared.

"I should have been notified Farrell was undercover." A woman poked the chest of the man who'd introduced himself as Roger—Kaden's superior. "One phone call."

"This is my case, Margaret. We've been working it for months." Roger brushed the woman's finger away.

"It's procedure to let me know. And professional courtesy. Of course, you wouldn't recognize courtesy if it bit you in the ass." Margaret poked him one more time. "You're too wrapped up in your career. This is my territory. You'll follow my rules."

Courtney couldn't take it. With her hands on her hips, she shouted, "Stop it! What's wrong with you two? There's a man injured. He's not a pawn in your…power games."

Margaret rubbed her head and sighed. "I'm sorry."

Gray walked in with a tray from the cafeteria.

He stared at the three of them facing off. "What's going on?"

"I've just been reminded what's important." Margaret turned to Courtney. "Thank you. You're right. What you witnessed was…personal."

Roger glared at Margaret. But he apologized to Courtney.

A surgeon pushed through the door, pushing off his cap. His eyes widened when everyone stood.

Courtney pressed her hand to her heart.

Roger stepped up. "Do you have news on Agent Farrell?"

"We've repaired the damage to his artery. It was superficial, but still life-threatening."

People clapped. She collapsed onto the sofa.

Gray pulled her into a hug. "I'll call Nigel."

"Yes." The Fitzgeralds were holding vigil with him at Fitzgerald House.

The doctor held up a hand. "The EMT said there was a woman on the scene that probably saved his life." Everyone looked at her.

Courtney buried her head into Gray's shoulder.

"Go ahead and cry, brat." He stroked her shoulders. "You've earned it."

Her shoulders shook. She wasn't worth dying for. Kaden was. She still loved him.

SOMEONE TOUCHED HER SHOULDER, waking Courtney.

Roger stood over her. "Kaden's awake. He'd like to see you."

"Here you go, sis." Gray squeezed her shoulder and handed her a cup of tea. "Go find out how he is."

She raced down the hall. Two cops guarded a room. *A little late for that.* "Is this where Kaden Farrell is?"

They nodded.

"I'm Courtney Smythe." She swallowed. "He asked for me."

One man held the door. She moved inside, afraid of what would happen next. Kaden had stopped Heather. He didn't need to stay in Savannah anymore. Was this goodbye?

He was asleep. Blood streaked his arm and there were scratches on his pale face. His leg was in a cast, propped above the covers.

She covered her mouth with her hand. Why hadn't they cleaned him up?

What if this was her fault? Maybe she shouldn't have kicked Salvez. Maybe she shouldn't have tried to escape his hold. Maybe she should have waited for Kaden and Boyd to rescue her and Issy. If she'd waited, maybe Kaden wouldn't be lying in a hospital.

As quietly as possible, she slipped into the chair next to the bed. It was her fault he was injured. She had to apologize.

KADEN'S HAND BRUSHED something soft. He buried his fingers into silk. When he took a deep breath, the sharp bite of bleach made his nostrils flare in disgust. He tried to stretch, but his leg wouldn't move.

Even his eyes, crusty and heavy, remained shut. He concentrated, forcing them open.

Hospital bed. Damn. He'd been shot. Kaden frowned. A doctor had said the only reason he was alive was the quick thinking of a woman at the scene. Courtney. She'd saved him.

And she was here. Her arms cradled her head as she slept on his bed.

Hope flickered in his chest.

Maybe he wasn't destined to lose everyone he loved. Maybe he and Courtney had a chance to make a life together.

"Kaden?" Courtney's voice cracked.

"Hi." His voice wasn't much better. His throat was as dry as a sandstorm.

"How are you feeling?" She sat and pushed her hair back over her shoulder.

"Like I was run over by a cement truck."

She pulled a cup with a straw off the rolling table and held it to his mouth. He sucked greedily, watching her face, but she wouldn't look at him.

He pushed away the cup and caught her arm. "Are you all right?"

"Fine," she choked out.

"Courtney." He could see she wasn't. "Did your cut reopen?"

"Salvez…hit me."

"I'm sorry." He wanted her to look him in the eye. Wanted to know what she was thinking.

"You shouldn't be sorry. *I'm* sorry. It's my fault you were hurt. My fault." Tears streaked her face, coursing along old tear tracks. "I shouldn't have tried to escape. I should have left the heroics to you and Boyd."

"What?" He caught her hand, tugging her closer. "You were so brave. Don't cry. Not over me."

"But…" She finally looked at him.

"You did what I'd taught you to do." He rubbed a thumb over her knuckles.

"Heather was going to shoot me." Tears streamed down her face. "You jumped in front of a bullet. For me. You could have died. My life's not that important."

"It is to me." He'd saved the woman he loved.

Her blue eyes flooded over. "But…"

"No. No *buts.*" He tugged again and she sat on the edge of the bed. He was close enough to touch her face and wipe away the tears. "You saved me, too. The doctor said I might not have made it without your quick thinking."

"Don't say that," she sobbed.

He tugged her hand and she curled into his shoulder.

"I can't imagine the world without you," she blubbered. "I'm so sorry I didn't trust you. I'm so sorry."

He stroked her hair, letting her soak the ugly-ass hospital gown.

Courtney was in his arms. He didn't know how long it would last, so he held on. "You are the most incredible woman I've ever known."

She gulped and stared up at him. "Me?"

"You helped get Issy away. Saved me."

"You saved Issy."

"We worked together." And he'd been able to keep Courtney and Issy safe.

It was like he'd pushed away the burdens weighing down his soul. The darkness had given way to the light Courtney brought to his life.

"We were a team," Courtney whispered, wonder in her voice.

Team. What did she mean? He was afraid to ask and have her kick him to the curb again.

"What happed to Bole and Salvez?" he asked.

Courtney closed her eyes. "Heather was in surgery the last I heard. But that was a while ago."

"Salvez?"

She shrugged. "I don't know. I only cared about you."

He brushed her tears away, when he wanted to kiss her. "I wish I hadn't screwed up and lost your trust. I wish we could go back to the start. I wish you could forgive me."

Courtney drew patterns on his hospital gown. "I do forgive you. I do trust you."

"You do?"

She nodded. "After you were shot, you...touched

your chest. Was I supposed to give that message to your grandfather?"

"Damn. My granddad." A shock ran through him. "Does he know what happened? Is he here?"

"He knows, but he's not at the hospital." She laid her hand on his arm. "Gray and the Fitzgeralds are keeping him posted."

"Good. Good."

"So the signal *was* for your grandfather," she whispered, pulling away from him. She withdrew, taking away her warmth.

The hope that had been a mere flicker ignited like gasoline thrown on a bonfire. "Did you think it was for you?"

She brushed her hair back. "Other people will want to talk to you."

"Courtney, don't you dare leave." Not now that the pieces of his life were finally falling into place.

"I should..." Tears filled her eyes as she pushed off the bed.

"It was for you. That signal." He gently grasped her arm and inhaled. Time to take the biggest risk of his life. "I love you."

She blinked. Her body shook. "You what?"

"I love you." It was easier the second time. He tugged her close and his IV draped across her head. "I've never said that to any other woman."

"I love you." She swallowed, batting the tubing away. "And I've never said that to any other man."

He tried to shift but a sandbag pinned his leg. "I want to kiss you, but I can't move."

She wiggled until their faces were side-by-side on his pillow. "How's this?"

He didn't answer. He sank into the welcome of her mouth and was home.

When they finally broke apart, he gasped, "How long am I here for?"

"For as long as you need to be." She kissed his nose. "I should let Gray know you're awake again so he can tell the Fitzgeralds and your grandfather."

"Wait." He cupped her face. "Have you... changed your mind about staying in Savannah?"

Her smile lit up the room. "This is exactly where I belong."

Lightness shot through his body. "Is there a place in your heart for me?"

Her breath stuttered out. "My heart's been waiting for you all my life."

EPILOGUE

KADEN SWUNG OVER on his crutches and tore down the yellow police tape. It didn't belong in Courtney's happy place.

The day care center hadn't reopened since the confrontation with Bole and Salvez. Courtney had used Carleton and Fitzgerald House rooms instead. Finally, Kaden had the clearance to let Courtney back into the place.

"What are you doing up?" Courtney stormed across the play area. "You and your grandfather are supposed to be napping."

"My phone was ringing off the hook. I had to leave so Granddad could rest." He bent and kissed her nose. "Roger called with the all-clear."

"Oh." She scanned his body. Boy, he wished it was for reasons other than her worrying about his health. "You could have called me. The kids have all been picked up."

"Did you lose any students?"

"I gained students. One mother said she trusted me with her child's life." She touched his chin. "I know whom I trust with my life. And heart. You."

Joy burst through him at her words. "You're the bravest and strongest woman I know. You're my warrior."

She grinned. "I'll never get tired of hearing you say that."

"Then I'll have to keep telling you." All his life if he had his way.

"Marion's team is ready to clean. I don't know if they can get out the blood that's been spilled." She set her hand on his back. "Your blood."

"Heather's, too." He kissed her cheek. "Nathan can replace tiles."

"I know." Courtney massaged his shoulder where his muscles ached from using the darn crutches. "Is it wrong if I don't feel sad that she died?"

"She was a terrible mother."

"But she was Issy's mother."

"And Issy is better off with Nathan and Cheryl. And you." Kaden leaned against a table. He set the crutches aside and pulled her into his arms. Right where she belonged. "She has two parents who will get her through this latest trauma. She's a survivor."

Courtney burrowed into his chest. "Was one of your phone calls your boss asking when you would head back to Atlanta?"

He rested his cheek on her hair, letting her deep, sexy scent wash over him, cleanse him. "I've… It was from Margaret. She heads up the Savannah FBI office."

"I met her when she was arguing with your boss."

"That's her ex."

She pulled away and looked up at him. "Now their animosity makes sense."

He laughed. "It's going to be worse. She wants me to transfer to Savannah and work for her."

Courtney's arms tightened around him. "You'd be working from here?"

He nodded. "I want to be where you are. Live where you and Granddad live."

"So you told her…?"

"Yes."

A tear slipped down her cheek. He brushed it away. "Are you crying because you don't want me living so close?"

Her blue eyes swam. "It's because I yelled at your new boss. If she takes out her frustration on you, she'll have to deal with my wrath. She may be tall, but I can take her."

"My defender." He tugged her into a kiss. As he poured his love into it, desire heated both their bodies.

When they finally broke the kiss to breathe, he said, "Nathan called today. He has a house for us to look at."

She shook her head. "A house?"

"A house. Walking distance to Fitzgerald House and the day care and your family." The words rushed out. "It needs a lot of work, but the Foresters have always wanted to get their hands on this one. It's not going to be anything like where you grew up, but

Nathan says it will be incredible once they've reno-vated the place."

"You want us to live together?"

He touched the ridge that had sprouted between her eyebrows. "I was thinking about us living together—forever."

"Forever." The ridge disappeared. She stood on her toes and kissed him. "If you think that qualifies as a proposal, think again. I expect a ring, fanfare and a romantic candlelight dinner."

"You'll get it." He hitched her body closer. "I want to spend the rest of my life making you happy."

She laughed. "I think I'll hold you to that promise."

"It's a deal." And they sealed it with a kiss.

* * * * *

Read more in the FITZGERALD HOUSE *miniseries to learn how the Fitzgerald sisters and Cheryl find their happy endings!*

SOUTHERN COMFORTS
A SAVANNAH CHRISTMAS WISH
THROUGH A MAGNOLIA FILTER
THE OTHER TWIN

All available now from
Harlequin Superromance.

Get 2 Free Books,

Plus 2 Free Gifts—

just for trying the Reader Service!

Get 2 Free Books,
Plus 2 Free Gifts—

just for trying the
Reader Service!

HPI7R2

Get 2 Free Books,
Plus 2 Free Gifts—
just for trying the Reader Service!

◆ HARLEQUIN®
HEARTWARMING™

Get 2 Free Books,
Plus 2 Free Gifts—
just for trying the Reader Service!

HII7R